Legacy of Darkness

SISTERHOOD OF LIGHT

2

ARTHUR BARILLAS

Legacy of Darkness

SISTERHOOD OF LIGHT

2

ARTHUR BARILLAS

ISBN Paperback book 978-1-77400-050-2
ISBN Electronic book 978-1-77400-049-6

To God above all else and his only son Jesus Christ.

To his Blessed Mother, the Virgin Mary.

To my loving wife Cristina that has guided and supported me in my craziness.

To my daughter Grace Nicole. May this book show you that

nothing is impossible if you believe in God, family, and yourself.

To my son Gerardo. Always fight for your dreams

To my editor Sandra and my publisher Gwen who provided help and guidance on this vision.

"Without the burden of afflictions, it is impossible to reach the height of grace. The gift of grace increases as the struggle increases."

-St. Rose of Lima

PROLOGUE

Saint Helena, California; September 01, 10:50 P.M.

TIME WAS OF THE essence as Nicole Rogers ran through the vineyards. To the ordinary eye, the young redhead was just a blur while she moved through the night. Her loose hair streamed behind her as she made her way through rows of grapevines. Her army boots pounded the soil and grass while darting from one side to another, jumping over a wooden fence. Her heart rate did not seem to increase with the laser-focused demon hunter sprinting at full speed, jumping and flipping over a large, gray boulder. Nikki parkoured her way through a few large crates, dodging and hopping over them as she reached a tall white wall. Without breaking stride, the girl let her legs do the work with her black army boots using the concrete wall as a platform. The redhead stood on the ledge, admiring one of the six dark cemeteries that surrounded the cursed town of St. Helena. She jumped in and landed softly on hallowed ground. Nikki continued her sprint toward the graveyard's center jumping and dodging several headstones and vaults. She reached a large chest tomb and touched it with her right hand. "Time!" she exclaimed.

The teenaged girl looked up and saw her blonde-haired Guardian, Elizabeth Somiere O'Brien, sitting cross-legged on top of the tomb with a stopwatch in her hand. "You're thirty seconds behind Grace's time," the older woman said with a smile as she stood up on top of the concrete sarcophagus. Nearing her forties, the former demon hunter and now Guardian of demon hunters did not look a day over thirty. She neatly tied her blonde hair in a ponytail and put the stopwatch in the pocket of her red jacket. "It's still an impressive run," Elizabeth said, looking down on Nikki, who had a disappointed look written on her face.

"Dammit!" Nikki exclaimed, somewhat frustrated as her sister demon hunter Grace Wu giggled a bit at her side. "What are you laughing at?" the redhead asked her dark-haired sister, knowing full well she deserved the teasing. Both she and Grace had formed an unlikely bond since their last adventure. Even though they always tried to get on each other's nerves, the sisterly love never disappeared. But now, it was time for Nikki to get a bit fazed.

"Nothing," Grace said with a sly smile. "You just seem so out of breath from that little run."

"Just wait until I know the area," Nikki said, tying her red hair into a neat ponytail. The teenaged girl adjusted her denim jacket and dusted off her dark blue jeans as she looked at her other sister, demon hunter Isabella O'Brien. The brown-haired girl had her sight focused in the opposite direction. Her pet wolf, Aidan, sat next to her, waiting for a command. "Feel something, O'Brien?" Nikki asked her friend as she adjusted her black-framed eyeglasses. "Or is my short marathon time not interesting enough for you?"

Izzy looked back at her sister and smiled. "You missed a double jump on one of the boulders," the teenaged girl said. "That's why you messed up your time."

Nikki looked at Elizabeth, who only shrugged as she made her way down from the chest tomb. "Do you feel anything?" the older woman asked her teenaged protégés.

"Darkness," Izzy replied, rubbing her arms softly. Her black leather jacket didn't seem to protect her from the shivers she felt. "The entire town emanates this profound sense of doom and fear, as if hell is going to swallow it up." The green-eyed girl knelt next to her pet wolf and rubbed his side. The animal remained focused, staring at the horizon, ready to attack. "Aidan feels it as well."

"Demons and vampires are everywhere," Nikki said, walking over toward Izzy. "I felt some of them watching me as I made my run."

"The monsters are aware of us," Grace said, joining both her sisters. The girl tucked some strands of raven hair from her face behind her ears. The teen crouched down and touched the green grass. "It feels as if they recoil from our very essence. I feel their fear and rage as well." The black-eyed demon hunter stood up and admired her team. She smiled to herself, feeling a sense of pride and belonging to this particular group of women.

"Very good," Elizabeth said, looking at the trio. "But it is still too general. You need to focus your energy and pinpoint their location, even blindfolded. Where is this dark energy stronger? Can you locate its very source?" Elizabeth asked the demon hunters.

Both Grace and Nikki pointed eastward toward the hillside woods beyond the vineyards. The infamous cave where two demon hunters had perished a few weeks prior was there. "There is more than that," Izzy said. Elizabeth, Grace, and Nikki looked at the brown-haired girl. "Darkness knows this town is vulnerable. It feeds from hopelessness and despair."

"Demons feed on fear," Grace said, remembering literature passed down from her previous Guardian. "They get you first with fear for your life and the life of everything you hold dear."

Elizabeth frowned. Ever since the death of the two demon hunters that guarded the local hell spot, news and rumors about the town circulated. New demons, vampires, and other creatures of the night had flooded the region. "Well," Nikki said, pulling out a stake from her jean jacket. The blue-eyed demon hunter started walking in the direction Izzy referenced with her gaze. "Let's make our presence known."

Izzy nodded, whistling at Aidan for him to take the lead as all of them started walking toward the center of town. The demon hunters jumped over the graveyard's metal fence and made their way up the streets, followed by their Guardian. The teenaged girls looked left and right at the small businesses and shops, all closed at the late hour. "I have to say it," Grace said to Izzy. "Your mom has a great sense of style."

Izzy smiled, looking back at her mom and admiring her. The blonde woman looked elegant in her red leather jacket, white blouse, dress pants, and black boots. Even in the darkness, Izzy felt secure with her mom around. "She does, doesn't she?" Izzy said. "You don't look bad yourself," admiring Grace's blue trench coat. It covered her black blouse, jeans, and white Adidas.

"I try," Grace said as she looked at Nikki. "One of us needs to stand out as bait for the undead."

"Uh-huh," Nikki said. "The old trope of luring a demon, so they prey on an innocent girl. I wish these vampires lived in the twenty-first century."

"Good luck with that," Izzy said as they all continued walking forward on the main street.

Elizabeth felt a vibration on her phone. Pulling it out, she frowned at the new text she received. "What is it, Mom?" Izzy asked without even looking at her. "Is it bad news?"

"How did you know I just received a text?" Elizabeth asked as the older woman put the phone away and continued walking behind her girls. "Let alone what I felt?"

Izzy shrugged. "I just felt it," she said. "Like a change in the air around us."

Elizabeth nodded and looked at both Grace and Nikki, who were waiting for her to give them the bad news. "A demon hunter and two guardians have disappeared from Nevada," Elizabeth said. "No clues as to what happened."

"What is it with kidnapping demon hunters?" Nikki asked. "Can't they think of a new plan?"

"It's a power thing," Grace said. "I guess it makes them feel in control. We're close to Nevada. Are we going to look into this?"

Elizabeth shook her head. "Other Guardians are on it," the blonde woman said. "We have our orders. St.

Helena needs our complete focus."

The four warriors continued walking until they reached the high school where the three teens would attend that year. Aidan strolled around a bit before rounding back and sitting next to Izzy. The girl crouched down, patting her wolf on the side as she took in her surroundings' negative vibrations.

"Is this the source of darkness?" Grace asked as she looked at the brown and gray building. "If it is, I wouldn't be surprised. The place gives me the heebie-jeebies."

"Scared of the demons inside?" Nikki asked.

"Not the demons," Grace said, shuddering a bit. "High School."

All three teenagers looked at each other and then at Elizabeth pleadingly. "You're all going to school," the older woman said, causing the teens to groan in protest. "This is not up for a debate."

"Says the demon hunter who burned down her high school in her senior year," Izzy said, pushing her mom's buttons. The other two demon hunters giggled.

"I didn't burn it down," Elizabeth scoffed. "The demons did that. I was just there to throw them in the fire."

The teenaged girls started laughing, breaking the somber mood. They all stopped, suddenly feeling a disturbance in the air. They turned around and saw three police officers and a bald man in a gray suit walking toward them. Izzy signaled Aidan to run off just as the men approached.

"What are you doing out?" the bald man asked as he neared the foursome. He looked terrified, even though the bags under his eyes indicated a high level of exhaustion.

“Hello,” Elizabeth said. “I am Elizabeth Somiere O’Brien. My family is new in town, and we were...”

“Sorry to interrupt, ma’am,” one of the police officers said as he extended his hand to guide the blonde woman away from the school. “There’s a curfew.”

“A curfew?” Izzy asked, looking at her sister demon hunters.

“Yes,” the second officer said, looking around nervously. “No one is allowed outdoors after dark. For your protection.”

“There are some gangs that are tormenting the town,” the first police officer said. “People have been disappearing.”

“A gang?” Grace asked, somewhat incredulously. “Let me guess. Some of these gang members have painted skin. They’re wearing masks and don’t seem human.”

“Some have red eyes,” Nikki said, looking around. “And they only appear in the dark. In the daytime, the police can’t find them anywhere.”

The man in the suit and the police officers looked at each other. They couldn’t hide their amazement at how much information the teenaged girls possessed. They seemed to want to say something when a growl from a distance interrupted them. The girls looked behind them and saw ten humanoid demons and vampires walking up the street toward the school. Elizabeth was about to give out an order when she saw the man in the suit start to run away.

The three police officers stayed and put themselves in front of the girls to protect them. “Stay back!” the officer said. “Get out of here!”

Elizabeth frowned, looking at the imminent danger

as the demons strolled toward them. The features of the first six resembled the vampire breed. They had bulging red eyes and long fangs, with extended claws. Their facial features seemed distorted, eager to feed on the living. The remaining four monsters seemed to be slave demons. They had brown, scaly skin with long black fangs that matched their dark, dead eyes. They seemed to stagger in contrast to the vampires, who walked like any normal human being would. "You girls got this?" Elizabeth asked her demon hunters. The trio just smiled at her while the policemen looked confused. "I'll take care of the man in the suit," Elizabeth said. "I fear he's running toward his death." Saying this, the blonde woman started running after the older man.

"Run!" one of the police officers ordered the teenagers. "This is no place for kids!"

The other two police officers ran toward the pack of demons. "Freeze!" one of the officers yelled at the group of monsters as he drew out his sidearm.

"Wait!" Izzy exclaimed, fearing the worst, but it was too late. The vampires and slave demons started running toward the police officers.

Izzy, Grace, and Nikki sprang into action. The police officers started firing rounds at the monsters, but the demons just took the bullets in stride. The tallest vampires ran toward the first police officer, grabbing and lifting him over his head. He threw the human to the side as if he were a sack of potatoes. The man fell on the ground, smashing his head on the pavement, going unconscious instantly.

"Hey!" Nikki exclaimed at the horde. "Why don't you pick on someone your size?"

The vampires and demons looked up and threw the police they'd picked up off to the side, knocking them out as well. Izzy could see the officers were still breathing but had been knocked out. *They'll wake up with a nasty headache,* Izzy thought to herself, as the demon horde regrouped and strolled toward the girls, who stood their ground.

"So, I take the tall vampire in the middle?" Izzy asked, referencing the six-foot-four vampire with long black hair who seemed to lead the pack.

"Yes!" Grace and Nikki said at the same time as the pack reached them.

"What do we have here?" the long-haired vampire said, smiling at the girls. "Little girls are barking orders to the undead."

Izzy was about to say something when Nikki spoke. "Oooh, we're so scared," the redhead teased with a mocking tone.

"That was supposed to be my line," Izzy said awkwardly, feeling she had nothing else to say.

Grace giggled as she noticed the pack of demons moving to surround them. "Ten against three hardly seems fair."

"What?" the main vampire said. "You mean you want to put up a fight before we bathe in your blood?"

"Wouldn't be fun if we didn't," Izzy said as she fired a punch at the vampire's face.

The vampire instinctively caught the young girl's fist, surprised at the attack. He growled as he realized the truth. "Demon hunters," he said, starting to crush Izzy's fist.

"You're strong," Izzy said, wincing a bit as the beast squeezed her hand. She delivered a front kick right into the vampire's midsection, pushing the monster away. "We're stronger," Izzy concluded as the girl jumped and did a double-kick, knocking the vampires to the side. As she landed, she crouched and delivered an uppercut right below the chin to the staggering tall vampire. "Now, Aidan!"

Izzy's wolf appeared from the shadows and attacked the horde, tearing a slave demon apart with his fangs.

Grace and Nikki attacked from the side, moving like lightning and making short work of the pack, their wooden stakes cutting through demon flesh like butter. The demons fell lifelessly to the ground as vampires started combusting, filling the air with dust and ash. Only the main vampire remained as he tried to crawl away. Izzy smiled at his cowardice slowly walking to the vampire's side. "Going somewhere?" she asked the defeated creature. "Aidan—do that new trick you showed me last time."

The wolf growled and bit down hard on the vampire's arm, tearing it off of its torso. The vampire screeched in agony as blood spurted out from its severed limb. The vampire tried to stand up, but clumsily fell over.

"I kind of feel bad for him," Grace said, noting Aidan's carnage as she snapped a slave demon's neck.

Nikki ran from the ashes of a dusted vampire and jump-kicked the lead demon in his upper back, bringing him down. The vampire screeched in fear as Nikki flipped him over and started beating his face with her fists. Izzy and Grace grimaced as Nikki pummeled away. "I think you defeated him," Grace said to her sister, seeing Aidan backing away from the redhead's fury.

But Nikki wasn't stopping. Izzy reached out touched Nikki's shoulder, only for the redhead to try to punch the brown-haired girl, managing to contain herself just in time. "Hey," Izzy said. "Are you okay?"

"Sorry," Nikki said sheepishly, realizing she'd lost control . "Adrenaline got to me." The red-headed girl looked at her fists, covered in blood. She could feel her heart beating faster. She tried to breathe and calm down, but somehow she couldn't. The young girl started hyperventilating as a sense of claustrophobia was entering her mind. Flashes of the ground burying her flooded her thoughts; the memory of a cave collapsing while she was trying to get out overwhelmed her mind. Nikki fell to her knees with sweat dripping from her head.

"She's losing it," Grace said, standing in front of Nikki. "Look at me," the dark-eyed demon hunter instructed her counterpart, "Breathe." Izzy frowned as she staked the last vampire, turning him to dust. She reached out toward Nikki, letting her know she was there for her.

Nikki was on all fours now as she tried to regulate her breathing. She closed her eyes and opened them, trying to shake off the sense of doom. "What a sucky feeling," Nikki managed to say, taking big gulps of air.

"It's okay," Izzy said. "We'll help you deal with it."

"Talk to me, girls," Elizabeth's voice sounded over their earpieces. "Was the situation handled?"

"Streets are clear," Izzy replied through her communicator. "Police officers tried to get involved. We'll help them to their feet and meet up with you."

"Okay," Elizabeth said. "Head back to the Inn. We have things to discuss."

"Please don't tell your mom about this!" Nikki pleaded with Izzy. "I can deal with it!"

Izzy thought for a moment and looked at Grace. Grace shook her head, not agreeing. "We need to keep her in the loop," the dark-haired demon hunter said. "She's our guardian."

Izzy looked at both of her sisters. All three of them had internal struggles that needed to be dealt with individually, and perhaps as a team as well. The question was when the right time would be to do so. The brown-haired girl looked at Aidan, who returned the stare through those grayish-blue eyes. "We're on our way," Izzy said to her mom through her communicator.

CHAPTER I

Saint Helena Harvest Inn, California; September 01, 11:30 p.m.

THE THREE DEMON HUNTERS entered Elizabeth's hotel room, taking a moment to admire the simplicity and beauty of the space given to them by the Inn. The room color was a soft green that went great with the walls and the floor's wooden finishes. The neatly made queen bed had two wooden chest drawers to the side. To the rear, a wooden table with three comfortable chairs was covered with all types of food and treats. Mounted on the wall was a large screen where Elizabeth had projected a town map using a white tablet. "How did it go?" she asked while looking at the small screen in her hand.

"They came, and we conquered," Izzy replied, looking at Grace and Nikki. "The police officers are doing okay, although they didn't seem to buy our excuse on how they had scared the gang away."

"Okay," Elizabeth said with a frown on her face. She shook away the feeling and pointed at the food on the table. “I ordered some room service for us while we discuss the town’s situation.”

“Is it bad?” Nikki asked, opening one of the aluminum food trays. She grabbed a few fries and started digging in, feeling a bit better after her ordeal. But the dark images still plagued her mind.

“The man in the suit was the school principal,” Elizabeth said.

“The one who ran like a coward?” Grace asked frowning at the food spread ordered by her Guardian. The food seemed to be lackluster, compared to her dining tastes.

“That’s not fair,” Elizabeth said, trying to explain to her teenaged warriors the town’s predicament. Again, the deaths of the demon hunters who guarded the small community had to be brought forth in a conversation. “After the death of Anna and Teresa, deaths and disappearances have increased exponentially,” Elizabeth said. “According to the principal, it’s a known secret that the damnation of this town is beyond redemption. No one talks about it, but most know something goes bump in the night. The principal specified that things had gotten worse ever since the Smiths moved out of town. People are living in fear, especially at night. Most try to convince themselves that the legends of darkness are just that. Legend. But it’s becoming more difficult for them to swallow that lie. Something supernatural plagues this town, and people are beginning to realize that.”

“The Smiths moved?” Izzy asked as Grace threw her a green apple from the fruit tray. She thanked her sister with one look and took a crisp bite of the fruit.

"They are not staying in a town where their two oldest daughters died," Elizabeth said. "That's when the curfew started. As soon as the sun sets, businesses close, and no one is out again until daybreak. The current mayor and the chief of police claim they're working on the problem, but there is no success yet."

"What's the plan?" Nikki asked, with her mouth filled with food.

Elizabeth smiled, seeing Nikki eat the hamburger like there was no tomorrow. "Well, I have a meeting with the school principal tomorrow," Elizabeth said. "Have to start explaining why sixteen-year-old girls were so knowledgeable on the gang activity." The girls giggled, but Elizabeth was not having any of it. "We've got to be careful with this," Elizabeth said in a grave tone. "A demon hunter's identity is vital. The more civilians know about us, the more they're put in danger. That goes for us as well. A civilian can become an enemy with a single desire. Even when a human gets turned into a vampire, the demon conserves the memories. We can't just blurt out what we are." The girls remained silent after the little scolding. "After my meeting," Elizabeth continued. "We work on lifting the curfew put over the town."

"I assume you've got more details than that," Grace said.

"Demons and vampires have flooded the region," Elizabeth said, pointing at the map. "Our field tech, Andy, managed to map out the underground cave system that connects all six cemeteries in town, with the help of the twins. That same system also leads to the Hell Spot portal." As Elizabeth spoke, she pressed a button on her remote. The screen changed, and it showed red lines that branched out into town.

"It's as if the dark energy uses the caves underground as its circulatory system," Grace said, looking at the pattern. "That's why the air is so heavy everywhere. That is why when we touch the ground, we can feel these monsters."

"With the heart being the Main Gate," Izzy said with a shudder as she pointed to the spot where her predecessors had died.

"Sean inspected the main cave line that leads into town and connects with the Hell Spot Gate," Elizabeth said. "It's clean—or as clean as it can ever be. But that cave system could harbor countless creatures."

"Where do we start?" Nikki asked.

Elizabeth smiled. "We have a few days before school starts," the Guardian said. "By day, we clear the caves. Make our presence known. By night, we make sure the demons and vampires are too scared to come out."

"What about our secret identity?" Grace asked. "I guess going out with a name tag that says we're demon hunters is out of the question."

Elizabeth nodded at the question. "You all conserve your names," the older woman said. "Grace and Nikki are staying with us while you go to school here. Sean and I are your legal guardians, so when you get in trouble in school, we get called in."

"We're foster sisters?" Nikki asked, giving Grace a mischievous look. Grace just scoffed at her and the idea.

"Something like that," Elizabeth said.

"Are we going to stay in this Inn?" Izzy asked. "Or are we getting our own place?"

"Your father has been working on it for the past couple of weeks," Elizabeth said. "I've seen some pictures. I think you're going to love it. We move into the house tomorrow afternoon."

"Separate bathrooms, please," Grace said.

"Why am I not surprised?" Nikki laughed out loud.

"We'll see tomorrow," Elizabeth said with a knowing smile. She looked at her tablet and then at Izzy. "One last thing, Izzy." Izzy looked up. "You need to establish contact with the local priest. Provisions are running short."

"Is he aware of what we do?" Izzy asked.

"Not sure," Elizabeth said. "Why don't you find out tomorrow?"

"I want to be there," Nikki said. "I want to see how Izzy breaks the ice with a Catholic priest about demons and vampires."

Grace giggled a bit at the idea. "You have another task tomorrow," Elizabeth said.

"What?" Grace asked.

"You get to mingle with the locals," Elizabeth said. "Get to know the people in town. You and Nikki." Both girls started to protest, but Elizabeth just shut them down. "If we don't have anything else, you can go."

"Good," Nikki said as she and Izzy started to leave.

"There's one other thing," Grace said. Nikki and Izzy froze as they looked at their sister. Nikki turned pale and pleaded with her eyes. "I need to tell you something that happened in Ireland," Grace said. Elizabeth looked at Izzy and Nikki and finally at Grace. "I shared the story of how my parents died with Izzy and Nikki," Grace continued.

Elizabeth nodded and gave Grace her full attention. The senior Guardians knew Grace's parents had been targets for any demon or vampire because of the couple's historical research. An ancient vampire did the deed leaving a twelve-year-old girl alone with her parents' bodies at her feet. "Go on," Elizabeth said in a soft and caring voice, giving her demon hunter some emotional room for her to open up.

Grace was a little hesitant before speaking. She looked at Nikki, trying to find the words. "The same vampire that killed my parents was in Ireland," the demon hunter said as she sat on Elizabeth's bed. Both Izzy and Nikki looked at each other as they approached their sister. "When we entered the underground town of York," Grace continued as she looked at Nikki, bringing back the memory of their final battle. "Nikki and I separated so I could take out the sorceress who blocked the sun. That's when he appeared. He was in the underground cave right before it collapsed. I tried to fight him, but he was too powerful."

"Do you know his name?" Izzy asked carefully. "You never mentioned him."

"His name is Neil," Grace said. "From the little information I've gathered on him, he is more than two-thousand years old."

Nikki's mouth dropped. She had read about ancient vampires, but she couldn't fathom their advanced age. "The older the vampire is, the stronger they are," Nikki said.

"Did he hurt you?" Elizabeth asked.

Grace shook her head. "He just spoke to me. He said I still reeked of fear." Elizabeth sat down next to Grace and put her arms around her shoulder. "Neil haunts my nightmares," Grace said. "Every night, he's there. I try to fight him, but he's untouchable."

"Have you told anyone else?" Izzy asked.

"Just my old Guardian in Hawaii," Grace responded, looking at the floor. "I shared some information with the new Guardian, John Simmons. I asked him if he could find more information from my father's diaries. Something to give me an edge over this beast."

Elizabeth looked at Nikki and Izzy. "If John did find something," Elizabeth started. "What would you have done?" Grace remained silent at the question. "We are Delta Squad in St. Helena," Elizabeth said. "We're strong as long as we cover each other and trust each other. Individual strengths become our strengths. The same thing happens with our weaknesses and our fears. We're here for each other."

Grace nodded and looked at Nikki and Izzy. "I had bottled everything up," Grace said to her sisters. "I've learned to control the fear and rage. But the nightmares are back, and I'm still trying to get a grip on that."

Nikki looked into Grace's eyes. She remembered how vulnerable she had become the day she shared her story. It was the beginning of the strong bond that held the three demon hunters together. Nikki took a deep breath and looked at her Guardian. "I'm claustrophobic," Nikki managed to say. "I've been claustrophobic all my life. But my demon hunter strength has helped me keep that fear controlled." Elizabeth looked at the red-headed demon hunter. The information was new to her. Nikki's files failed to mention this side of the teenaged warrior. "When we temporarily lost our powers, things became a little bit more difficult."

"How so?" Elizabeth asked.

As the question left the woman's lips, images flooded back into Nikki's mind. She could feel the walls close in on her. Nikki started breathing faster with sweat dripping from the side of her forehead. She could feel her heart start beating faster and her knees buckling under her weight as her face turned pale. She could hear and feel the cave coming down. The smell of rocks and dirt hurt her nostrils.

Elizabeth acted quickly, grabbing hold of Nikki and sitting her down on the bed. The older woman could feel the girl's sweaty palms as she laid her down. "Put a pillow under her head!" Elizabeth ordered her daughter.

Izzy obeyed, looking distraught as her sister fell back into a panic attack. The brown-haired girl placed a pillow under her friend's head and took her hand. "We're here, Nikki," Izzy said. "You're here with us in the Inn."

Nikki held Izzy's hand and squeezed hard as the memory of her being dragged out from the cave filled her mind. She tried to hold on to that thought as she put her hand on her heart, trying to calm down. It took a couple of more minutes before Nikki started breathing normally again.

"Did this happen while you were out there with the vampires?" Elizabeth asked Grace and Izzy.

Both demon hunters nodded as Elizabeth's face drew a concerned look. "For what you three have gone through, I was expecting this to happen." Nikki seemed to recover, but had tears in her eyes. She hated feeling this way. “It’s okay,” Elizabeth told Nikki, looking into her blue eyes. “We’ll deal with it.” She turned toward Grace and Izzy. “We will help each other through this.”

“What about you, Izzy?” Grace asked. “How are you dealing?”

“I’m dealing,” Izzy said. Elizabeth, Grace, and Nikki looked at her with doubt in their eyes. “Really,” Izzy said. “I’m doing okay.”

“Because getting stabbed through the chest with a mystical sword is something you do every Wednesday,” Nikki said, trying to crack a joke to cut the tension in the room while wiping her eyes.

“Look,” Izzy tried to explain herself. “I know I’ve gone through some traumatic stuff these past weeks. But seriously, I deal with this stuff better on my own. I have my music and all my artistic projects. I always vent through that. You know this, Mom.”

“That’s true,” Elizabeth said as she rose and stood in front of her daughter. “But you don’t have to deal with this alone. You have your sisters now. You have me. You’ve always had me.”

“I know,” Izzy said, looking at the floor, feeling a little guilty. She was never good at opening up and sharing with others. “Please give me time. You know me better than anyone.”

Elizabeth took a deep breath. “Okay,” she said, turning her attention to the other two demon hunters. “Grace, Nikki, can you leave me alone a few minutes with my daughter? She will join you shortly.”

Izzy looked apologetically at Grace and Nikki as both girls walked out of Elizabeth’s room.

Izzy turned toward her mom and stared into her deep green eyes. It was like looking inside a mirror.

"I wanted to tell you that I understand," Elizabeth said to her daughter. "I respect your decision to shield your feelings. You open up when you're ready."

Izzy nodded, knowing full well there was a 'but' in her mom's speech. She wasn't disappointed.

"We're in the field now," Elizabeth continued. "Trust is a big issue, and being open not only to me as your Guardian, but to your sister demon hunters, is crucial in building trust."

"I know," Izzy said, looking at the floor.

Elizabeth walked over to her daughter, hugging her. "I know you do."

Izzy savored the moment of being in her mom's embrace. She noted that Grace and Nikki were not as blessed to have their moms with them, due to unforeseen circumstances.

Elizabeth let go of Izzy and turned back to the monitor. "When we scout the cemeteries these coming days, I would like to spend some alone time with Grace and Nikki," the blonde Guardian said.

Izzy nodded, knowing full well why her mom cleared that with her first. Elizabeth knew how Izzy worked in the field. She needed to know how Grace and Nikki did their job just as well. "Cool," Izzy replied. "Goodnight, Mom."

"Sleep well," Elizabeth said.

Things are going to get interesting, Izzy thought to herself as she exited the room.

CHAPTER II

Abandoned Wine Cellar, Saint Helena Outskirts. September 02, 1:30 a.m.

THE DAMP AIR OF the abandoned wine cellar burned Josh's nostrils. The thumping of his heart pounded in his ears as the hideous creatures dragged his tied-up body through the dark tunnels filled with wooden cases and empty wine bottles. The word 'terrified' was no longer something the twenty-year-old could experience—the emotion he felt in those precise moments was far worse. One minute he was heading home from work, the next, he felt rough hands dragging him underground. Now bound and gagged, the fiends hauled his body through the darkness. It wasn't until candlelight reached his sight that his fear sprung up. He looked around, desperate to scream, only for the gag in his mouth to silence his voice. Human-like figures with disfigured faces surrounded him; drool dripped from their fangs. Their red eyes seemed to be piercing through his soul. Josh tried to scream again when he heard a deep voice from behind the mob of demons.

"Step aside and let me see," the young man heard. The crowd of monsters parted, revealing a tall man dressed neatly in a three-piece gray suit. His features were ordinary, with piercing blue eyes and fair skin. His short light brown hair was neatly combed to the side.

Josh screamed for help through his rag-stuffed mouth, only for the blue-eyed human to approach. "Are you scared?" the man asked Josh as he crouched before him and removed the gag from his mouth.

"Please help me!" Josh pleaded looking from side to side at the demons that held him tight.

The man stood up and signaled the demons around him. The monsters growled in approval as they sank their fangs into Josh's limbs; he screamed in agony with his flesh being torn apart like butter. The vampires silenced his voice feasting on the human's blood and bones.

"What was wrong with him, Cassius?" a female voice asked softly.

The blue-eyed man turned toward a gorgeous six-foot-one blonde woman lying on the ground next to a few empty wine barrels. A dark silk cloth wrapped her naked body as she stretched in the confined space. The man strolled toward her, waving his vampires away. "He was not worthy," Cassius said. "There was nothing for you to break or corrupt. His spirit was already broken."

The woman looked at him in disgust. "Get that hideous mug off your face," the blonde woman ordered.

"Vampires are not human. I don't understand why you continue to lie to yourself, appearing as such."

Cassius smiled as his face distorted to reveal his demon form. His blue eyes turned bloodshot red with his sharp fangs growing and his facial features distorted. "Better, my lady?"

The blonde turned around and scoffed. "I hate this human form," the woman said. "I am more than this. I need to be free." Cassius walked toward her, but he felt an invisible barrier stop him. He tried to press on, but the unseen wall did not let him reach her. "You can't break it," the woman said. "Only I can."

"You can't blame me for trying, UrthaMal," Cassius said.

UrthaMal stood up, dressed in a long white gown. "I feel something," the tall woman said. "It seems the light of hope has been re-ignited."

Cassius was about to say something when a six-foot-ten dark-skinned vampire entered the room. The newcomer looked at Cassius with a grim expression. "Demon hunters have arrived in town," the man said.

Cassius looked at UrthaMal and then at the newcomer. The vampire was good at hiding his real emotions. "How do you know this?"

"Lou's boys got killed a few hours ago," the tall vampire said. "There were three of them."

"Do you know where they are?" Cassius asked as he looked at the wine cellar ceiling.

"Are you concerned, Cassius?" UrthaMal asked. "Once I am free, three human girls will be no match for me."

"Not concerned," the vampire responded. "Just cautious. With the events that transpired in Ireland, I wish to tread carefully. I want to keep your existence a secret. Being trapped down here in this useless human form, the Guardians and their demon hunters will find a way to destroy you. I can't allow that. I won't allow that. With the death of my ward and several others, I'm to lead my clan now. And I will lead it to a glorious tomorrow."

"Am I your secret weapon?" UrthaMal asked calmly. "If so, do as I say to set me free, and I will elevate you above all other vampire clans. I make this vow to you."

Cassius looked at the woman before him for a few seconds as several thoughts crossed his mind. When news reached him that his ward Lucinda had perished, he felt vulnerable, as did the rest of his vampire clan. The vampires located on the Pacific coast looked to him for guidance as second-in-command. It was now his call to lead his vampires and the small army of demons at his disposal. Cassius looked at the tall, dark-skinned vampire who gave him the news. "Draco, find everything that you can about these demon hunters. I don't want any surprises."

"Do you want me to call for assistance from my order?" the tall demon asked. "It will be no extra cost if these girls are who I think they are."

Cassius thought for a moment. "Make it so," the vampire said. "If they manage to kill them, your order will get a bonus."

Draco stepped outside, leaving Cassius and UrthaMal alone. "You are focusing resources on the demon hunters while not tending to my needs," the woman said, acting hurt. "You have me! Unleash me!"

"I will," Cassius said. "The resources I spend on

the demon hunters will not interfere with what we're doing. With the Order of Karratt dealing with the top world, you have my undivided attention. I have even sought out advice to help us in our quest. She arrives tomorrow."

"You continue to rely on others when I possess all the knowledge you need," UrthaMal said.

"You seek to corrupt. How can you corrupt a town that reeks of fear?" Cassius asked.

UrthaMal closed her eyes, feeling the soil between her toes. The forbidden desires of the townspeople seeped into her. She could almost breathe in what the humans of the top side wished for in their secret desires. She tried to focus on the most illicit pleasures—a clear image of two men formed in her mind, bringing a devious smile. "You haven't fully grasped what I can do and what my purpose is," the woman said. "Don't worry. I will guide you. We will begin slowly, my friend. Just feed me, and I will elevate your vampire clan above everything else in the world."

Main Street, Saint Helena, California; September 02, 8:30 a.m.

Elizabeth drove her black SUV through St. Helena's main street, seeing a few businesses opening their shops. People walked the sidewalks as if they didn't have a care in the world. Elizabeth looked in her rearview mirror and saw her three demon hunters riding in silence. The trio had developed a strong bond in the past weeks, but somehow Elizabeth felt a crack in their fellowship. The blonde Guardian guided her vehicle along the street and parked across the St. Helena Catholic Church. She turned around only to see Izzy step out of the car with a large duffle bag. "Keep us posted," Elizabeth said to her daughter. Izzy nodded and looked back at Grace and Nikki, who didn't return the stare. Izzy just frowned but remained silent. Elizabeth noticed the icy situation and drove off, leaving Izzy alone on the sidewalk across from the chapel.

The young brunette slipped on her earbuds, and music started blasting from her cell phone, trying to drive the negative thoughts away. The night before ended not in Elizabeth's room, but her own. Both Grace and Nikki recriminated her for not opening up to them. Izzy had tried to explain, but somehow with each personal turmoil came an emotional wall. Soon it was Nikki accusing Grace of spilling everything in front of Elizabeth. After the night ended, all three demon hunters were not on speaking terms.

Izzy looked at the building in front of her. It was a simple structure compared to the gothic cathedrals she had visited in Europe, nothing extraordinary or majestic about it. Izzy sighed, feeling somewhat disappointed. She turned to the side and saw a dark-haired, good-looking boy sitting on a bench, drawing on a large sketchbook. He couldn't have been more than seventeen years old. Izzy approached him without interrupting his activity. The boy either did not notice or care about Izzy looking at his drawing. Then again, his headphones were at maximum volume, blasting metal music. Izzy found the artist's taste in music odd. His attire was that of an ordinary boy—a plain polo shirt with jeans and loafers—far from the metalheads she had met in Amsterdam.

The young girl focused on the drawing he was developing. It seemed that he was canvassing one of the stained windows with the Virgin Mary's image. Izzy was amazed at the amount of detail the young boy put into his drawing. The window was just the base of his picture. The artist brought depth into the drawing that she hadn't seen before. It was, to some extent, more impressive than the original stained window.

"Do you like it?" the boy asked without looking at her as he removed his headphones.

Izzy felt her cheeks warm a bit, feeling embarrassed she got caught looking over the boy's shoulders. She removed her earbuds and looked closely at the drawing. The Lady had tears streaming down her face. "I love it," Izzy said. "The face carries this sorrow I don't see in the window."

The boy nodded sadly, as if he had ventured into an unpleasant memory. "That's the idea," he said, extending his hand. "Stephen Connolly."

"Isabella O'Brien," Izzy said, shaking the boy's hand. Stephen smiled as he stood up, revealing his five-foot-ten height. His brown eyes hid a sad past that the teenaged girl could detect. She was about to say something when a police cruiser pulled up in front of the parish. Two police officers got out and entered the chapel. "What's going on?" Izzy asked.

"You'll see," Stephen said with a grim look on his face.

The chapel doors opened, and the two officers came out with an old priest in handcuffs. The older man looked worn out, as if his life was extinguishing from within. A younger priest followed behind him—

both holy men dressed in black slacks and black shirts with a white clerical collar. "You only came to condemn me," the older priest said bitterly to the younger. "You will rot in hell for this, Raphael."

"You're a disgrace to our order, Fleischmann," Father Raphael said. "You have shamed our faith and cloth. I'll pray for your conversion. As of now, it's up to the authorities to determine your fate."

"That's enough," the police officer said as he forced the older priest into the back seat of the squad car. "You, sir, are going to have a blast." The officer later got close and whispered into the older man's ear; no one could hear his whisper but Izzy. "I'm going to make you pay," the officer said to the old man. The officer then turned toward the younger priest. "Thank you for your cooperation, Father Raphael," the officer said. "You will need to present yourself at the station to write up your testimony this afternoon."

"I'll be there," Father Raphael said as the police officers drove off. The priest looked distraught. He closed his eyes for a moment; when he opened them, he realized Izzy and Stephen were staring at him. He signaled for them to approach. As the teens walked up to the chapel, Father Raphael started going in. "Sorry for the spectacle," he said to the teens. "I could've handled that private matter a lot better."

As Izzy entered, she looked at her surroundings. The simple exterior of the chapel replicated itself inside—simple finishes with artwork to match. The religious imagery was humble compared to anything similar in Europe. The turmoil in her heart found peace inside, though, especially seeing the Blessed Sacrament hidden within the church tabernacle in the back. The hallowed shrine was painted gold, with a large cross carved in the middle and two angels kneeling to the side in a reverent position.

"How may I help you?" Father Raphael asked Izzy, bringing her back to the real world. She saw Stephen walk up to the front of the tabernacle and kneel. Besides him, the priest, and herself, there seemed to be no one else in the church.

"I'm new in town," Izzy stammered. "I always try to find the closest catholic chapel. Keeps me grounded."

"You're a practicing Catholic," Father Raphael said, extending his hand. "My name is Raphael Arrigo. I am the new pastor for this parish."

"Izzy O'Brien," Izzy said, shaking his hand. "The old administration just left in a squad car, I noticed."

Father Raphael frowned. Izzy could see a deep sadness reflected in the young priest's face. For the first time, she noticed a gentle kindness in his eyes. She had seen that look before, on others trying to do good in a rotten world. "Yes," Father Raphael managed to say. "Whatever past issues you hear, they're part of the old administration. I'm here to start fresh. I assume you are, too."

"You could say that," Izzy said while looking at the pamphlets placed on a table. She grabbed one and looked for the mass and confession times. "Only one mass a week?" she asked, showing the pamphlet to the priest.

Father Raphael took it and frowned a bit as he read through the schedule. "I have to clarify all this," he said. "I'll update the information on the website. Is there anything else you need from me?"

Izzy looked at him. She knew the man was busy, but she didn't want to go back to her mom and sisters empty-handed. "I have some things that need to be blessed," she said. "Can you help me out with that?" The young girl knelt and opened her duffle bag, revealing stakes, knives, arrowheads, crosses, and small vials of holy water.

The priest looked puzzled, glancing first at the girl and then at the contents of the bag. "That's some strange collection of things you need blessed," the priest said, crossing his arms and examining the girl for the first time. "Why do you need this?"

"Oh," Izzy said. "I love to keep blessed items in my room. Keep bad spirits away and all those things."

Father Raphael smiled as he knelt and picked up a crucifix. "False witness in the house of God," he said. "Bad form for a practicing Catholic."

Izzy blushed and looked down. "I usually ask for this outside the temples," the teen said.

Father Raphael looked at the beautiful crucifix in his hand. "Do you know why demons fear what is holy?" he asked as he examined the artifact in his hand.

"Because it represents everything that they despise," Izzy softly said.

Father Raphael smiled and looked at the rest of the contents of the bag. "The genesis of these evil beings stems from selfishness–an unhealthy desire to put their own needs before anything else in the world." The priest stood up and looked directly into Izzy's green eyes. "Demon hunters are the opposite of that. They risk their lives for mortal men to sleep well at night. What is right and pure is always putting personal well-being second to tend to the needs of those who are weak and powerless to the darkness." Izzy remained silent as the priest looked back at where Stephen silently prayed. "I thought you were a myth. It wasn't until I arrived in this town that I concluded what goes bump in the night is more than abstract."

"You've heard of us?" Izzy asked, keeping her voice low.

"Certain circles handle this knowledge," the priest said as he turned back toward the brown-haired girl. "Some are granted the gift to carry out the battle spiritually. Others do it physically."

"At first, I thought like that," Izzy said, opening up a bit. "Now, I think it's a curse that I wish would end."

Father Raphael nodded as he knelt again, setting the crucifix down. "It sounds as if you mourn," Father Raphael said. "Yet you shut people out while you deal with all that is inside—an excessive burden to fight the darkness from these creatures while you have this internal turmoil. I sense fear in you."

"I've managed," Izzy said, closing back up and refocusing on her task. "Can you help us by blessing our gear?"

Father Raphael nodded. "*Adjutórium nostrum in nomine Dómini,*" the priest whispered in Latin.

"*Qui fecit cœlum et terram,*" Izzy replied.

Father Raphael smiled as he looked up at the teenaged girl. "*Dóminus vobíscum,*" the priest said.

"*Et cum spíritu tuo,*" Izzy responded without missing a beat.

Father Raphael smiled, continuing his Latin rite as Izzy looked away. "*Orémus. Rogamus te, Dómine sancte,*

Pater omnípotens, æterne Deus: ut dignéris bene-dicére hoc signum Crucis, ut sit remedium salutare generi humano; sit soliditas fidei, profectus bonorum operum, redémptio animarum; sit solamen et protéctio, ac tutela contra sæva jacula inimicórum. Per Christum Dóminum nostrum," the priest whispered as the demon hunter tried to focus on Stephen, still praying at the tabernacle. She wondered what drove him to this place. His art reflected a pain that needed relief. Izzy felt she lost track of time while she contemplated the beautiful golden box. She took a deep breath and felt the air fill with peace as if she were in a small rose garden. The priest's whispered Latin prayer brought a sense of comfort and ease to her heart.

As soon as the sensation started, it stopped. Izzy looked at the priest, who was closing her bag. "Done," he said as he looked up at the girl. "Please visit the parish website for other information. If you need spiritual guidance, you can dial the parish number."

Izzy picked up her bag and nodded. "Thank you, Father Raphael," she said walking away.

"Don't be a stranger, Izzy," the priest said. "We're on the same side."

Main Street, Saint Helena, California; September 02, 8:40 a.m.

Grace and Nikki got out of the SUV and looked at Elizabeth. "I'm setting up another cover a few blocks down," the Guardian said. "Then, I meet with the Principal and the head of the school board. If you need anything, please give me a call."

"Where do we meet up?" Grace asked, looking around as individual businesses started to open up. "Or do we just call you?"

"Call me," Elizabeth said. "I will come for you and take you to our new home." Finishing the sentence, the blonde woman drove off.

Grace looked at Nikki, who just ignored her. "It's easier if we do this as a united front."

"You forced my hand yesterday," Nikki complained. "I've been dealing with this all my life. I don't need you or anybody to help me with it."

"Maybe," Grace said. "But, you've never had other girls at your side when this happens." Nikki remained silent. "Listen," Grace continued. "I get it. We've dealt with stuff on our own before. God knows I have. But things have changed. When we're out at night, and something like yesterday happens, things can go south really fast. And I know that's the last thing you want."

Nikki looked at Grace. "I hate that you saw me like that," the redhead said.

Grace hugged Nikki. "It's okay," the dark-eyed demon hunter said. "I hate you, too."

"What are we going to do about Izzy?" Nikki asked as both girls walked toward the local coffee shop. "She's bottling things up good."

As they entered the shop, they noticed that no one was in sight except for a man in his late forties cleaning the counter. The girls silently greeted the man and headed toward the end of the shop.

"She's keeping things from her mom," Grace said. "Yesterday, we put her on the spot. Remember when she told you about her origin? She has mom issues."

"What I would give to have those issues," Nikki said, reflecting a bit on her past and the loss of her biological mother. "I don't know. She lost a close friend a few weeks ago. She was like a sister to her. She saw her die. Then she had to fight this master vampire. Not to mention the dimensional trip she took."

"I know it's a lot," Grace said as the door opened. The demon hunters looked up and saw a teen boy and girl walk in. The boy had dark hair and seemed to be five-foot-two in height. The girl appeared to be the same height as the boy, with medium-length black hair and dark-brown skin. Both teens seemed to be the same age and looked a bit worried. They walked up to the opposite end of the coffee shop. "We said things yesterday," Grace continued. "We have to clear the air, us three. Out there, we depend on each other—no one else."

Nikki nodded as the door opened again. This time a group of teenaged boys and girls entered the shop. The boys wore varsity colors representing the school's symbols. They had to be from the football team. The girls around them seemed to be their respective girlfriends. Something tugged inside Nikki as she saw the new group walk directly toward the first couple of teens that had entered. She had seen this before at other schools. The redhead noticed the coffee shop owner tense up and continue cleaning while the varsity teens laughed.

Grace noticed her sister's behavior as she now focused on the varsity team. "Want to make a splash?" Grace asked Nikki as she stood up. "Want me to show you how we break into the social scene?"

"Thought you'd never ask," Nikki said, following Grace's initiative. Both girls started walking up to the teens. As they approached, they noticed the varsity team was teasing the couple mercilessly.

"What's the matter, Bryan?" the older and taller football player asked. "No set of weirdo twins to help you out?"

"Cut it out, Clay," the girl next to Bryan said. "That's not funny."

"Stay out of it, Jaime," Clay said. "You two better start to realize before school starts who runs the place. And it's not a set of dead twins."

The way he was expressing himself made Grace's blood boil. But she kept her cool as she looked back at Nikki, who nodded. "I'm sorry," Grace interrupted the verbal abuse. "We're new here and wanted to introduce ourselves."

Clay and his cronies looked up and saw Grace and Nikki standing there. The way Clay looked at the girls gave off a sense of disgust. "Well, well," Clay said as he stepped outside his group and towered over Grace. The older teen looked down at the dark-haired demon hunter. "You found your guide, doll. Clay Jensen, star quarterback, and completely at your service."

"Wow," Grace said. "That's quite something. What do you think, Nikki?"

"I think you know what I'm thinking," the redhead said as she stepped to the side and measured the situation.

"Come on, doll," Clay said, putting his hand on Grace's shoulder. "I'm a nice guy once you get to know me."

Nikki winced at Clay's move. "Bad idea," she murmured under her breath.

Grace grabbed the quarterback's hand and twisted the wrist ever so slightly. "Arghhh," Clay exclaimed as he fell on his knees.

"Hope this isn't your throwing hand," Grace said with a slight smirk. "Would hate to break it before football season starts."

The other players were about to jump into action, only for Nikki to step in front of them. "All these strong men ready to hurt a young girl?" she asked with fake shock in her voice. "Does the entire football team of St. Helena behave like this?"

Grace turned around and faced the harassed teens while still holding onto Clay's hand. The football player just moaned helplessly as the teen girl manipulated his arm. "Now," Grace said as she applied a little more pressure, making Clay yelp. "This is where you apologize."

"I am sorry," Clay gasped in agony.

"Couldn't hear that," Grace said as she leaned closer while twisting the arm a bit more.

"I am sorry," Clay whimpered, with a tear coming from his right eye.

"Mean it!" Grace ordered as she twisted the jock's arm one more time.

"I am so sorry!" Clay screamed.

Grace released him, and the quarterback crumbled to the floor as she turned her attention to the other teens. "I will probably see you in school next week," Grace started. "Just wanted to clear up that I take great offense to bullying and harassing. See you then."

The varsity team started helping their fallen quarterback up and walked him out of the coffee shop. "Well," Nikki started as she looked at the young couple. "My sister showed them."

"How did you do that?" Bryan asked Grace. Nikki

noticed a particularly adoring glaze in the young man's eyes as he stared at Grace. Nikki could not hide her smile, even though the comment felt out of place.

"Jiu-Jitsu class," Grace said. "Been training almost ten years now."

"Wow," Bryan said, ultimately letting the emotions get the better of him. "I've never seen a girl that was able to do that."

"You dork," Jaime said, shaking her head at her friend's childish behavior. "You'd be surprised what girls are capable these days."

"I know," Bryan said to her friend. "I just never seen it in real life."

Jaime just rolled her eyes and looked at Nikki and Grace. "What he meant to say is, thank you," Jaime said.

"No problem," Nikki said as she waved her hand. "I'm Nicole Rogers, and this is Grace Wu. We're new in town."

"I'm Jaime Wright," the dark-haired girl said, waving back. "This overgrown child is Bryan Donahue."

"Hi," Bryan said, standing up, trying to greet Grace. In doing so, he spilled his drink over the table.

Nikki giggled a bit while Grace looked oddly at the awkwardness of the boy. Jaime, on the other hand, looked embarrassed. "You're making me look bad," Jaime said as she helped the boy clean the table. After the cleanup, the boy sat back down, looking embarrassed. Grace smiled politely at both teens. "Want to join us?" Jaime asked.

"Sure," Nikki said, sitting down across from them while Grace sat next to her. "Have you guys lived here in St. Helena all your life?"

"Yes," Bryan said. "Ummmm. Well, Jaime and I have been friends forever. We've both grown up in this town all our life. What about you?"

"Well," Nikki said as she looked at Grace, who was studying the young teens. Somehow Grace couldn't relax. "We're foster sisters, and we've just arrived from Ireland."

"That's so cool," Bryan said. "We're planning to go to Europe as our graduation gift. So we've got time to save money."

"If we make it to graduation," Jaime muttered.

Grace couldn't make out whether she was serious or joking. "What do you mean? The social pressures are too much at school?"

"What?" Jaime asked, somewhat confused. Then she understood. "Oh, you mean those guys. That's nothing, and fairly recent, to be honest. The school spirit has always been very welcoming. Everyone just gets along. The varsity team wasn't like that at all. They've changed over the summer."

"How so?" Nikki asked. "They seemed to be mean-spirited."

"It's not just them," Bryan said. "This entire town is just not the same. Not since..." his voice trailed off.

"Okay," Nikki said, trying a different approach. "We went out last night."

The moment the words left her lips, the teens tensed up. "You shouldn't be out at night," Bryan blurted out.

"There is a curfew," Jaime said, with a bit of panic in her voice. "Bad things happen at night."

"We heard," Grace said. "The police pulled us out of the streets."

"Yeah," Jaime said. "This gang just showed up one day, and they don't stop terrorizing the town."

"It's not a gang," Bryan mumbled under his breath.

"What do you mean?" Nikki asked.

Bryan looked at Jaime, who only shook her head. "No one wants to admit it," Bryan said. "It's something else. Something dark. It all started after Anna and Theresa left us."

Grace and Nikki looked at each other. "Anna and Teresa?" Nikki asked innocently.

"Friends of hours," Jaime said, wiping her eyes. "Recently deceased."

"Sorry to hear that," Grace said as the video footage of the twin demon hunters crossed her mind. Their death indeed still held a grip over the town's spirit.

"Yeah," Jaime said, with a bit of bitterness in her voice. "Everyone is sorry."

That was a definite conversation killer. There was an awkward silence that loomed over the entire coffee shop. "I am sure these girls were cool," Nikki said.

"They were awesome," Bryan said. His voice cracked a bit as he spoke. "They were the soul of this town, always helping and looking out for those who needed it most."

"They were brilliant," Jaime said. "Remember how they tutored math with you. They were going to start Notre Dame this fall. The town is just not the same without them. And everyone's odd behavior is proving all that."

"I am sorry to hear that," Grace said. "Hopefully, we'll fit in this town."

"Yeah," Nikki said. "We have to start school next

week. It would be great to see some familiar faces." As the redhead said this, she noticed a tall man staring at them from an alleyway across the street. He was around six-foot-one, with dark skin, sharp blue eyes, and a military crew haircut. A long black trench coat covered his muscular frame. Powerful energy emanated from his body, giving the young demon hunter enough information that the stranger was not human. As soon as she noticed his presence, the man disappeared into the alley.

"We can show you around," Bryan said, looking at Grace. "I mean... if you don't have anybody."

Nikki smiled, turning her attention to the teen couple. She was about to say something when a splitting headache pierced her forehead. The redhead winced in pain, as if blinding light was hitting her in the eyes. A deep and tearing pain tore through her stomach as well.

"Hey," Jaime said, somewhat concerned. "Are you girls okay?"

Nikki looked at Jaime and then at Grace, who was also cringing in pain. Grace grabbed hold of her temple and tried to focus. She saw a white SUV with tinted windows roll up the street. The dark-eyed demon hunter's instincts pulled toward it like a magnet. "Must be the jet lag," Grace managed to say.

"Why don't we exchange digits?" Nikki asked, pulling out her cell phone. "We can DM and get together these next few days before school starts."

Bryan pulled out his phone in a flash as he started dictating numbers. "Share my number," Grace said as the pain lessened. "I think I need some air. It was nice meeting you." The young demon hunter stepped out onto the street and looked at the back of the white SUV. The license plate had mud all over it, making it unreadable as the heavy vehicle drove away.

What the hell was that? Grace thought to herself as Nikki joined her with a confused look on her face.

Main Street, Saint Helena, California; September 02, 8:50 a.m.

Izzy stared at her phone as she strolled down the sidewalk. She scrolled over the recent news concerning the local parish, as well as the disappearances in town. The girl frowned in disgust as her mind processed what was happening in Saint Helena. It seemed the previous local priest had been the subject of an ongoing investigation concerning sexual abuse. According to the article, they said there was a crucial witness in the situation, and that the archdiocese was cooperating in every way.

Izzy just shook her head in disapproval as she read the story that followed. Three teens were still missing from the past week. Police suspected a link between the missing teens and the late-night gang activity, but there were no arrests and no new leads.

The final story that the local papers were running was that of Anna and Teresa's death. The town mourned the loss of the teenaged girls still. It seemed that the wound was fresh in the town's consciousness. The opinion piece was very scathing toward the twin's family. They left town and provided no answers to questions concerning the girls' death. Even though the police had investigated, there seemed to be no wrongdoing—just an accident. But the town suspected something else.

Izzy looked up from her phone only to see a white SUV come down the road. As the vehicle approached, the young demon hunter felt a piercing headache that made her flinch. Sharp pain in her gut followed just when the SUV passed her. She tried to refocus her attention, but the car just sped away. The pain lessened as the vehicle got further away. Izzy blinked and shook her head—it felt as though she'd been hit with a sledgehammer to her brain. She looked at the car, but it had turned a corner. She turned around only to see Grace and Nikki run up to her. "Did you feel that?" Grace asked.

"The nail piercing my skull?" Izzy said. "Yeah, I felt it. What the hell was that?"

"I have no idea," Nikki said. "First time I've felt something that intense."

"Could it be a new type of demon?" Izzy asked. Nikki and Grace both shrugged, not knowing what to say. "Let's regroup with Mom," the young brown-haired girl said. "She may know something we don't."

CHAPTER III

Spring Street, Saint Helena, California; September 02, 9:15 a.m.

SABINE UNCAPPED A BOTTLE of pills and placed two capsules on her palm. She put the medicine in her mouth and drank from an expensive bottle of water. The woman could feel the pain in her head start to subside a few minutes later as she stared at the businesses they were passing by.

"Are you okay, Lady Sabine?" the seventy-year-old dark-skinned driver asked, looking at the digital screen that projected the image of his passenger in the back. His deep voice brought the woman back to reality.

"Everything is fine, Ian," Sabine said to the driver in her British accent. "Mind the road."

"You haven't spoken for several weeks now," Ian said as he looked at the young woman. "And I see that you now carry a bottle of pills."

"In the last fifty years that I've let you work for me, how many times have I kept things from you?"

"A handful of times," Ian said, with a sly smile, knowing full well his employer.

"Just add this to that handful," Sabine said, looking at the window. "You answer to me. I don't answer to you."

"Beg your pardon, ma'am," Ian said, tipping his dark driving cap. "Just bringing to your attention that your mood has changed dramatically."

Sabine sighed as she adjusted her white dress suit; her white stiletto heels tapped the floor of the car. She looked at her driver and pondered at his humanity. She had made her peace regarding why she kept the man around—he had a keen intellect, as well as this hidden insightfulness for a mortal man. He had seen right through her human façade. His curiosity still got to her, though. It wasn't easy letting somebody in, especially for someone who had walked the earth as long as she had. The woman looked outside the window as Ian drove on. "Demon hunters," she murmured under her breath.

Ian looked up at the screen again, focusing on the woman. "Oh," he said, apparently not at all fazed. "How many? Did you see them?"

"Three of them," Sabine said. "I caught a glimpse of them. They're little girls."

"Well," Ian said. "It is part of the requirement. You're not surprised, are you? Demon hunters near this hell spot are like bees to honey."

"They're a tiresome nuisance," Sabine said. "There is no distinction in their ways. They always attack first and question later."

"They're programmed to do that," Ian said as he turned the car at the next right. "Or so I've been told."

When he said the last part, he looked at the screen again and smiled at his boss. The woman did not seem a year over twenty, but she was ancient behind her human mask. Her silky black hair streamed down the side of her pale white face. Her light green eyes almost looked like two emeralds that reflected the light. The man felt sorry for anyone that crossed her path. Ian turned the car on the next left and headed straight toward the far side of town. He looked at the demon and saw his employer in deep thought. He wanted to say something, but he swallowed his ideas.

"Say what you're thinking, Ian," Sabine said. "You know your thoughts are transparent to me."

"I don't want to intrude, ma'am," Ian said.

"Say it," Sabine ordered. "Bring it out into the open."

Ian looked at the road, and then at the screen. Her green eyes stared directly into his soul. He knew she would not kill him, but he hated adding to her foul mood. "You have a vow," Ian muttered.

Sabine smiled at the words. "I have a vow," she repeated, as if the words meant nothing. "This is why I pay your salary—to point out the obvious." Ian shut his mouth. He knew Sabine could peer into his thoughts, so there was no point in conversing with her. Still, he looked at the screen one more time. Sabine was smiling at him. "I like the sound of your voice," she said. "It keeps me sane."

"Glad I can serve, ma'am," the man said as he made the final turn. The car entered the most remote area of St. Helena, where several abandoned vineyards stood on each side of the road. The vehicle reached a dark warehouse at the far end; its structure was gray and deteriorated. Ian parked the car at the front and stepped out. The seventy-year-old driver let a smile crawl across his lips as he slid on a pair of sunglasses while walking toward the vehicle's trunk. He opened it and pulled out a large black umbrella. The man looked at the blue sky, where there was no cloud in sight. He opened the umbrella and walked toward the SUV's back door, opening it in the process. The man lifted the umbrella, making sure the sun's deadly rays did not pierce Sabine's skin.

The elegant woman motioned Ian to walk with her toward the front door of the warehouse. She knocked on the door, and a pale, red-eyed male vampire opened the door. "Sabine to see Cassius," the woman said. The vampire looked at her curiously, then at the man who accompanied her. The sound of his accelerated heartbeat was not strange to the vampire. The demon stepped out of the way so that Sabine and Ian could enter.

Sabine looked at her surroundings as Ian closed his umbrella. The entrance of the warehouse appeared worn down; broken and empty wooden barrels were scattered around. The place looked dirty and neglected, perfect for a vampire nest and a demon-hunter magnet. Sabine sighed as she stared at the five red-eyed vampires who guarded that first room. She could feel Ian's heart rate increase as his fear was getting the best of him.

"You bring a human to our home," a sizeable and muscular vampire said as he towered over Sabine. The vampire stood at a comfortable six-foot-two, compared to Sabine's five-foot-six, even with four-inch stiletto heels. "Kind of a miserable offering for Cassius, bringing this old man."

Sabine smiled approaching the tall vampire. Her face morphed to her demonic alter ego. Her green eyes turned bloodshot red, and her fangs grew while she looked at the fiend. "Touch him and die," she said calmly.

The taller vampire laughed, not believing this petite vampire was threatening him. He reached out to her as if trying to pat her shoulder. Sabine growled, grabbing his arm and striking hard against the demon's elbow with the free fist. A loud crack echoed in the room, making every other vampire jump with the taller demon's scream. Sabine pulled a dagger from her sleeve and shoved it into the demon's eye. Smoke poured out as the monster screamed in agony. Sabine grabbed the vampire by the scruff of the neck and by his waist, spinning and launching him through the wooden front door. The vampire's body crashed through, landing on the ground outside. He cried in pain as the rays of light pierced his skin, setting the demon ablaze.

"Moroi Schulmeister!" Cassius's voice called out. Sabine looked toward the leader of the vampire clan who approached her. The other vampires looked startled and knelt before her as the name echoed in the room.

Ian looked surprised, while Sabine looked bored at the clan's behavior. "Stand up, you idiots," the vampire said as her face morphed back to her beautiful features.

"I apologize for my vampire's behavior," Cassius said bowing before her. "I hid your identity from them so that your enemies would not be aware of your arrival."

"You don't trust your clan," Sabine said as the vampires stood up and looked at her in awe.

"Not because they could deliberately betray us," Cassius said looking at his minions. "Lucinda was not keen in her selection process. We do not have the sharpest minds. She cared more about quantity than quality."

"You're the new boss now," Sabine said. "I assume you are changing that."

"Trying to lay low," Cassius said, looking at Ian. "Before we go on, do you have special instructions for us so that we can make your companion's stay more comfortable?"

Sabine smiled and looked at Ian. "I am here to listen to what you have to say," Sabine said. "Ian and I will not be staying with you. Just don't feed off him."

Cassius nodded and looked at his clan. "Seal the door," he ordered. "Make sure Schulmeister's companion is comfortable."

Sabine reassured Ian with a smile and walked with Cassius further inside the warehouse. As both vampires walked, their steps echoed in the dark confines of the building. "Your clan hides well in the shadows," the woman said as her vampire eyes saw red dots in the darkness.

"They try," Cassius said. "Some are cautious, with the new powers that emanated from Ireland. Others have been careless and naive. I lost several vampires yesterday to the new demon hunters."

"You have three of them now patrolling your town," Sabine said as Cassius opened a door that led to a darkened stairwell.

"Is the information confirmed?" Cassius asked as they walked down.

"Yes," Sabine said. "I assume you have a plan for this."

Cassius nodded as he opened the door to the cellar. Both vampires entered and saw the six-foot-ten, dark-skinned vampire standing next to a tall, blonde-haired woman. "Schulmeister," Cassius said. "Meet Draco. He is the new head of the Karratt Order."

Sabine measured the tall vampire. "I am sorry for your loss," Sabine said, referencing the death of his order's leader.

"Schulmeister," Draco said, bowing down. "If I'd known you were coming, my day agents would have guaranteed your safety."

"No one knows I exist," Sabine said as she looked at the blonde woman. "And I want to keep it that way. So if you put your agents to *watch* my back, I will personally dispatch them."

Draco growled, but nodded as Sabine turned her attention back to Cassius. "What have you heard from Ireland? Was it a complete loss?

Cassius nodded, looking ashamed. "I'm afraid so. Almost all the European clans were decimated. The respective wards of western and eastern Europe didn't make it."

"I heard," Sabine said, admiring the tall blonde woman. "News from Sigfried? I heard the Karratt Order got him out."

"The demon hunters split his back in two," Cassius replied. "Even with his newly enhanced vampire powers, he doesn't seem to heal. He's laying low."

"I see," Sabine said, taking a step forward toward

the blonde woman.

"Schulmeister," the clan leader said. "Meet UrthaMal. Dark princess of the underworld."

It was now Sabine's turn to bow before the blonde beauty. "At your service," the female vampire said. "Your acts are legendary across the void and in this plane."

UrthaMal looked closely at the female vampire. Unlike the other vampires, this one hid her vampire form. "You come with this human facade before me."

"And yet you know I am not human," Sabine said, not bothering to morph back to her demon side. "Nor I need to prove myself to you."

UrthaMal growled at Sabine, smashing the invisible wall, making Cassius and Draco tense up. But Sabine remained serene at UrthaMal's outburst. "It seems you need me more of me than I of you," the female vampire said as she paced in front of the transparent prison. "You almost escaped hell, but when the hell spot closed, this trap triggered itself. Now you are stuck between the hell world and the real world." Sabine touched the invisible wall while Cassius and Draco watched. The female vampire strained herself as she pushed with one hand. Her strength seemed to be penetrating the transparent wall. UrthaMal looked amazed as purple light emerged from Sabine's pale hand as she broke through. The blonde woman looked at Sabine's manicured fingers. She touched and smelled the freshly applied nail polish with one hand, while she felt the invisible wall with another. Sabine removed her hand from the prison and smiled at the bewildered Cassius and Draco.

"You're a strong being," UrthaMal said. "More so than a normal vampire. But you can't set me free."

"I can't," Sabine said. "But you know this already. What do you need?"

"I need to feed," UrthaMal said, pouting a bit. "But Cassius refuses to feed me."

Sabine looked at Cassius intriguingly. "My lady," Cassius. "I don't want to feed you scraps."

"You've never been on the hull of a ship, have you, Cassius?" Sabine asked. "When you're starving, even the blood of vermin is appetizing. Feed her anything, and she will be strong enough to get out. Am I wrong to assume this is what you want?

"No, Moroi Schulmeister," Cassius said.

"Do you know what UrthaMal does?" Sabine asked both Cassius and Drago. "She turns pleasure into nightmares." Both vampires looked confused, causing Sabine to roll her eyes. "I forget my audience is not on the same level as me."

Draco growled, getting angrier at Sabine's air of superiority. Sabine just smiled, while Cassius had a genuine search for knowledge and wisdom. "This hell-demon controls temptation," Sabine continued saying. "She lures the will of human beings to fall prey to their deepest desires. And when they fall into slavery to their pleasures, UrthaMal leads them to damnation."

"Can she lead the demon hunters to their doom?" Draco asked.

"No," Sabine said. "Demon hunters are not wired like humans. The darkness inside them makes them immune to UrthaMal."

"Immune, yes," UrthaMal. "But you are wrong.

The legacy of darkness within the demon hunters is no more. Two days after I was released, the nature of things went back to what it should be."

It was now Sabine's turn to be surprised. "What do you mean?" the female vampire asked.

"You seem to be in the dark about this," UrthaMal responded. "The legacy of darkness has ended for them. They are now under a legacy of light. They have liberated Apocalyps."

Sabine frowned and looked away, while Cassius looked confused. "Apocalyps?" the male vampire asked.

"Few carry the burden of that knowledge," Sabine said, composing herself. "Those facts don't change the current reality. Demon hunters are still dangerous, and will stop any plan you have before you carry it out."

"Your friend is right," UrthaMal said to Cassius. "Feed me, and I will rid you of the demon hunters that torment you so."

Sabine looked at Cassius and Draco. "There you go," the elder vampire said. "She has her demands. Get her some flesh so she can corrupt it."

"I have someone," Cassius said as he looked at Draco. "Get them here as soon as tonight. Get everything ready for them."

Draco nodded and walked out, leaving Sabine somewhat intrigued. She looked at Cassius and peered into his thoughts, seeing well beyond his intentions. The images of two men and a news article popped into her head. She said nothing and looked at UrthaMal again. "Always seeking knowledge?" the blonde woman asked Sabine.

"Always willing to learn," Sabine said. "Knowledge is the only valuable treasure this realm can offer."

"Because you've not seen other realms," UrthaMal said bitterly. She longed to be free of the dimensional shackles that kept her prisoner.

"While you're in this realm, you are vulnerable," Sabine said. "Not mortal like a human, but not invulnerable like the monsters from below. No matter what form you take, in this world, you can be destroyed."

"Just like you," UrthaMal hissed. "The pleasures of immortality come with a hefty price. We're all destined for damnation. Why not change the rules? This world is supposed to be ours. It was never meant to belong to the pestilence of the human race. They waste their potential on trivial and vain things. That is my purpose—to guide humans to their doom through that which they cannot control—to open the door to their unhealthy desires."

Cassius stood next to Sabine. "Teach us," Sabine said as she looked at Cassius. "Tell us more, and you will be free."

Guardians' Home, Saint Helena, California: September 03, 11:15 a.m.

Elizabeth drove her vehicle up the road, pondering for a moment what the girls had told her. She looked at Izzy, who was in the passenger seat this time. "You felt this when the white SUV passed by as well?" the blonde guardian asked.

Izzy nodded. "It was just as the car passed by my side. I have never felt that with a demon in my life."

"Me neither," Grace said from the back seat.

"Nor me," Nikki added.

"What about this blue-eyed demon you saw?" Elizabeth asked Nikki, looking at the redhead through the rearview mirror.

"The dark energy was there," Nikki said as she looked out the window. "His dreamy physique couldn't hide the darkness."

Elizabeth looked at Izzy with a curious smile, then at Grace, and finally at Nikki, who hadn't realized what she'd just said. "Dreamy physique," Grace echoed. "That is the first time I've heard that description used for a demon."

Izzy giggled as she looked at Nikki, who blushed as she realized what she'd just said. "Was he a California hottie?" Izzy asked. "Or was he from out of town?"

"He was evil," Nikki said, trying to convince everyone in the car as she tried to hide behind her glasses. "He was interesting-looking."

"A demon in human form, but not a vampire," Elizabeth pondered. "Sounds like a daywalker." The blonde woman looked at Nikki and smiled. "Should I call your dad and ask if you can date older men?" the Guardian asked.

Grace and Izzy burst out laughing as Nikki was getting angry about the teasing. "Is it my fault that he looked like a Calvin Klein model?" Nikki asked. "Maybe that is his power. Besides, both of you girls were oblivious to his presence."

"I will be on the lookout now," Izzy said. "I'll be sure to ask for his phone number for you."

Grace laughed as Nikki just sulked in the back, taking the verbal abuse. "It's okay, Nikki," Elizabeth said. "You'll forget about the Calvin Klein demon once we get to the safehouse."

Nikki looked outside the window and smiled as the SUV entered a semi-paved road with vineyards on both sides. As they rounded the last curve, the demon hunters looked amazed at the luxurious house they were approaching. Sean waited outside with a broad grin on his face as the girls got out of the car and looked at the two-floor gray-roofed structure. The outer walls were pastel-colored, with European finishes; the second floor had a large balcony that connected three bedrooms. Green vines surrounded the columns that contained the second-floor gallery. "Welcome to our safehouse," Sean beamed.

"I had a different idea of what a safe house was," Grace said as she looked at her surroundings. The house was much smaller than her home in Hawaii, but the luxury she had grown up in was evident.

"Your rooms are upstairs," Elizabeth said. "They are all the same size, so I don't want any fighting."

The girls didn't need to be told twice before they ran in. The house was just as gorgeous on the inside, with a polished wooden staircase that curved as it reached the second floor. The girls got to the second-floor hall, revealing three closed doors with their suitcases and gear placed on the floor in front of the rooms. Izzy looked at Grace and Nikki. They returned her stare as they mentally tried to figure out who got which room. Grace took the first step to the middle door. "Dibs," the dark-eyed demon hunter said as she grabbed the doorknob. Izzy and Grace almost tripped over each other as they both tried to go for the room on the right. The girls crashed into each other, falling to the floor. Grace burst out laughing as Nikki and Izzy scrambled to get up and be the first to reach the doorknob.

Izzy got up and was about to touch the doorknob

when she heard her violin case fall to the side. Izzy gasped and forgot about the room as she went for her prized possession. "Mine!" Nikki exclaimed victoriously as she turned the knob.

"Fine," Izzy said, admitting defeat. She headed to the door to the left and looked at her sisters. They all smiled at each other as they opened their respective doors at the same time. They gasped in awe, seeing the delicate touches each room had—simple but elegant, with a single bed, vanity table with mirror, spacious bathroom, and closet.

"I'm happy with my room," Nikki said as she stepped back into the hall with a broad smile. "It's bigger than the one I had at the Air Base."

Grace joined her sister and nodded in agreement. "I can do with this room," she said as Izzy joined them. "The closet can only take a quarter of my wardrobe, but it will do."

"Nothing surprises me from you anymore," Izzy said, smiling.

"Girls," Sean called from below. "Unpack later. We need to talk."

The girls looked at each other as they marched downstairs to the house's backside, where Sean and Elizabeth waited in the kitchen. The girls' amazement seemed to show no end. The kitchen had a beautiful backdrop of the house's outdoor pool, followed by what seemed acres of vineyards. "Sorry to interrupt, girls," Sean said, holding a remote and pointing behind them. The girls looked up and saw a large screen that turned on as they approached. A loud ringing brought the girls' attention to the kitchen's speakers. The picture of a pale-looking Guardian, John Simmons, popped up.

"Good morning, Delta Squad," John said over his reading glasses. The young twenty-year-old guardian seemed more cheerful than usual, but he looked like he hadn't slept for days.

"How goes it, John?" Sean asked. "What is the word from Ireland and the world?"

"All things are quiet here," John said. The young man took a sip from his large mug.

"You look like you could use a nap," Grace said. "How long since you've slept?"

"This is my natural state," John said as he typed a few things on his keyboard. "I function better like this. My brain is always on fire, anyway."

"Any news from the main hell spots?" Elizabeth asked.

"What do you want to know?" John said. "Want to talk about the mad warlock in Europe? That is an interesting story. We can also talk about the zombie uprising in Cameroon. Then there is this fire-resistant demon that popped up in Eastern Russia." The Delta squad all looked at each other, looks of concern in their eyes. "Relax," John said, breaking the tension. "The demon hunters are doing fine. Clara and Alex traveled to Africa to provide extra support. Other than that, everything is as expected."

Izzy, Grace, and Nikki sat at the counter on high barstools while they watched John, who pulled out the map that Elizabeth had shared with them the day before. "Recommendations on what we discussed concerning this curfew?" Elizabeth asked.

"Sean and I came up with an idea," John said as he acknowledged the older man. Sean nodded as he paced at the back of the kitchen. "It seems that the tunnels have a methane leak. With Sean in a specific location to light up that leak, the demon hunters would have to make sure that they have pushed as many demons and vampires as possible inside the cave system."

"Any specific access points we should drive them to?" Izzy asked.

"There are two we can work with," John said, pointing them out on the map. "With Elizabeth on the field, I was considering two teams. Push from North and South."

"Can't have my man and my girls have all the fun," Elizabeth said. "Sounds like a plan."

"That is my only input on your curfew problem," John said. "On other notes, we have a demon hunter missing from Nevada." Delta squad hushed at the news they were hearing. "With all the commotion from the past few weeks, this news is a couple of weeks old. Two Guardians in the area have gone missing. Lewis and Williams are working on that."

"Anything else?" Elizabeth asked.

"One last thing," John said as he removed his glasses and rubbed his eyes. The younger guardian needed some rest; he seemed about to collapse. "It seems a new demon has popped in Mexico. Nothing young Anna can't handle, but the demon hunters in the area don't seem to respect the girl. Her young age is becoming an issue to the more experienced demon hunters in the region."

"That sounds like something Joy should handle," Elizabeth said.

"I know," John said. "Just wanted to throw that out there."

"Who's Anna's Guardian?" Izzy asked. "I forgot to ask her during the gathering."

"She has two Guardians," John replied. "The Rodriguez twins Luis and Victoria. They're Anna's older siblings. Both mechanical and electrical engineers."

"They're the ones responsible for most of the upgrades of our weapons and gear," Elizabeth pointed out to her demon hunters. "Great assets to have. They sent us a care package, didn't they?"

John nodded as he grabbed a piece of paper. "Correct. New gear for your new assignment in St. Helena. Made in Mexico. Top of the line."

"Okay," Sean said. "John. When was the last time you took a few days off?" John looked surprised at the question. He needed to think for a few seconds. Before John could respond, Sean spoke again. "Pack a bag," the older man said. "Williams and Lewis have approved some time off. You have a free pass to come to California." The demon hunters and Elizabeth looked at Sean inquisitively. "You can take some time off and help set up a bit of tech down here."

"So, this is a work vacation?" John asked.

"You take a plane ride," Sean said as he shrugged his shoulders. "We have a pool, and a guest house on the other side of the vineyard. You can decompress."

John looked somewhat hesitant at the offer when a door behind him opened, and Senior Guardian Jasmine Taylor entered the room. She smiled at the camera, waving. "Hello, Delta Squad," she cheerfully said in her Birmingham accent. The older guardian turned toward John and handed him some papers. "Your flight leaves in three hours," the dark-skinned woman said. "You're relieved. Take a break."

John gulped as he stood up. "We'll be waiting for you, John." Sean said. "Thanks, Jasmine. If we have any issues, we'll call." The guardian turned off the screen and looked at the women before him.

"Bringing him here?" Elizabeth asked. "Is that the right call, bringing a junior guardian to one of the most dangerous places on earth?"

"He needs the fieldwork," Sean said. "Besides, we need a tech down here, and Andy is in no condition to be helpful."

Elizabeth frowned. She wasn't sure about her husband's call, but she let it slide. She didn't want to discuss it in front of the girls. "What's the plan for tonight?" the blonde demon hunter asked.

"What we discussed with John," Sean said, turning the screen back on to show the map of St. Helena. "Two teams driving the undead from the North and South. Once in position, I light them up. Best estimate, we take care of sixty percent of the demons with that."

"Okay," Elizabeth said as she looked at her girls. "Izzy and Nikki will take the south side, while Grace and I go from the north." Izzy and Elizabeth shared a look as she nodded at her mom's choice designation. Izzy had gone on countless demon-hunting incursions with her mother. Nikki and Grace would be suitable to share time in the field with a seasoned demon hunter. "We prep up at seven tonight," the senior demon hunter said. "Explore the house, find weapons, and will see you then."

"No dinner?" Nikki asked, looking worried. "I can't hunt on an empty stomach."

CHAPTER IV

Saint Helena North Side, California; September 02, 9:45 p.m.

ELIZABETH MANEUVERED HER SUV up the dark streets of St. Helena, letting her demon hunter instincts guide the way. She felt eyes upon them the entire time, watching from the darkness. Despite not seeing her enemies, their essence was not strange to her. Like second nature now, the demon hunter could feel them all around, observing from afar but not intervening.

The blonde demon hunter turned toward her side and saw Grace focused on the road ahead. "I admire you in more ways than you can imagine," Elizabeth said.

Grace turned toward her Guardian with a puzzled look.

Elizabeth smiled sadly. "Ancient vampires leave no one alive," the older woman said. "Yet, you've been in the presence of Neil more than one time, and you still lived to tell the tale."

Grace shook her head. "A sadistic bastard," the

teenaged demon hunter hissed. “He knows my fear of him paralyzes me. I am just a toy to him that brings amusement. I can see it in his eyes.”

“Vampires and demons love to do that,” Elizabeth said as she turned her vehicle at the next corner. “They hate that we don’t fear them. So they find creative ways to inject dread into our souls, and throw us off our game to finish us quickly.”

“That’s just it,” Grace complained. “Neil has had so many chances to kill me, and he doesn’t. He just relishes me being afraid.”

“I know the feeling,” Elizabeth murmured.

Grace looked at her guardian with a questioning look. “You?” Grace asked. “Afraid? The great Elizabeth Somiere?”

The Guardian smiled and looked at the teenaged girl. “I’ve had my share of demons. You know my story. You know about Ankrnot.”

Grace looked at the road and thought for a moment, remembering the passages of Elizabeth’s journal—required reading for every demon hunter. “Ankrnot the vicious,” Grace said. “Ankrnot the cruel. Ankrnot the despised. Ankrnot the most unholy.”

“The one and only,” Elizabeth said under her breath.

“The journals said you killed him,” Grace said plainly.

“That’s what Williams wrote in the journal,” Elizabeth said. “You know better than that. I’m sure your parents told you the truth about my battles against Ankrnot.”

“He tortured you,” Grace said. “He killed two of your best friends. One was a demon hunter. He almost tortured Williams to death before you saved him.”

"My toughest rival," Elizabeth said, turning the SUV at the next left. "No demon has ever made me feel more afraid than that monster."

"How did you deal with the fear?" the young demon hunter asked.

"I relied on my friends," Elizabeth said. "They provided the courage I needed to face him head-on. With their help, we managed to banish him."

"What would he do if he came back?" Grace asked.

"He would continue his obsession with me," Elizabeth said. "He would focus on destroying the ones I love. Sean and Izzy. You and Nikki. But he won't come back."

"How do you know?"

"Because I trust Sean," Elizabeth deadpanned. "He won't let that monster out. Not while he still draws breath."

Grace nodded as Elizabeth parked her vehicle to the side of the road. "Do you feel that?" the older woman asked as the dark essence around them intensified.

Grace nodded. She felt the heaviness of the air around her. A shiver ran down her spine as her instincts called her to the side. "There is something strong behind that building," the young girl said, pointing to a closed wine shop.

"Very good," Elizabeth said. "Is there anything else?" Grace looked at her guardian, somewhat confused. "It's okay," Elizabeth said. "Close your eyes."

Grace nodded as she closed her eyes. She concentrated and felt the heavy air turn into dark and uncomfortable energy closing in on them from all sides. "They're surrounding us," Grace said as she opened her eyes. Her tone was calm, controlled, and collected. She could feel more than a dozen demons fast approaching their location.

"You must learn to hone that instinct," Elizabeth said as she got out of the SUV and walked toward the back door. She opened it just as Grace joined her. The older demon hunter opened a secret door inside the car, and it revealed several medieval weapons. "There are going to be few civilians out there," Elizabeth said. "Free choice today." Grace smiled as she pulled the small automatic crossbow. It came with three clips. She tucked the clips inside her pants pockets as Elizabeth pulled out a short sword and two stakes. "Always take a stake," Elizabeth said, handing the weapon to her younger counterpart. "They come in handy."

Grace twirled the weapon in her hand as two red boxes, side by side on the SUV trunk wall, caught her eye. They were both stamped with a white cross. They were both closed with a silver metal lock. She was about to ask about them when a growl from behind caught her attention.

Both demon hunters turned around and saw five vampires drooling and ready to tear them apart. "Fresh meat," one growled.

"Can you give us a second?" Elizabeth said calmly at the confused group of vampires. The older woman turned toward the teenager. "We start here and move our way down the street."

"Got it," Grace said as she prepped her crossbow. Elizabeth and Grace each stepped to opposite sides of their vehicle. The vampires launched themselves at them—three went for the younger prey, while the strongest ones attacked the blonde guardian.

Grace smiled as she felt the power inside her surge, dodging to one side as one vampire tried to grab her. She extended her foot and tripped him, making him fall flat on his face on the concrete sidewalk. The second one came forward. The teenaged demon hunter threw the crossbow at him, which he caught instinctively. He was so surprised at her actions, he didn't see the girl thrust her stake into his chest. The vampire screamed as his body turned to ash while Grace grabbed the crossbow from his crumbling hands. The third vampire growled at her in anger as his comrade fell. The monster ran toward her while Grace bolted in the opposite direction and saw the first vampire get up. The demon hunter jumped and flipped over his shoulders. The demon was disoriented, not knowing where the girl was, when he felt a stiff kick to his chest. The monster fell back and crashed against his advancing partner, both collapsing on the ground. Grace front-cartwheeled toward them and staked both vampires quickly, leaving only a cloud of dust behind.

Elizabeth fought both vampires, who attacked at her sides. She blocked and moved to strike both with hard and precise punches on the face and chest. The vampires grabbed her arms; Elizabeth smiled at their weak attempt to restrain her. She grabbed the vampires' wrists and brought her arms together, causing the demons to crash into each other. The demons grunted in discomfort as Elizabeth moved forward, twisting their arms in the process. The Guardian's strength, combined with the vampires' lack of balance, was all it took for both monsters to flip over and fall on their backs. Elizabeth staked them both before the idea of getting up ever reached their brains.

"It's a start," Grace said as she looked into the shadows, joining Elizabeth's side. She could feel eyes from the darkness staring at her soul. "Where to?" the young girl asked her Guardian. Elizabeth stood up and tied her hair in a ponytail. She was about to open her mouth when she felt the demons scurry to one side. "They're moving west," Grace stated. A chilling scream echoed in the night.

Both demon hunters bolted in the direction of the scream. It was human, and the creatures of the night were now focusing on that. Both Grace and Elizabeth ran down a side street. They could hear the monsters running at their side now, still invisible to them. "Somebody! Please help us!" a young female voice screamed. The sense of urgency made Grace's heart beat faster. They turned a right, and they saw an old, solitary building that was apparently ready to be torn down. Grace gasped as she saw three greenish demons pop up from the rooftops and jump down to the street. More than a dozen vampires were running inside the warehouse. "Help us!" a voice echoed inside the building.

"Go to the warehouse," Elizabeth ordered as she pulled her short sword. "I will join you after I take these goblins out."

Grace nodded and sprinted toward the warehouse. The demons tried to reach for her, but Elizabeth screamed at them, slashing her sword down. Blood spurted as a goblin felt the cold steel pierce its flesh.

Grace left her Guardian as she entered the warehouse. The place was shrouded in darkness that her demon-hunter vision ignored. She could see a staircase leading to the second floor. Steps echoed from above. "Help us!" a girl screamed. "They're going to break down the door!"

"No one can hear you!" a vampire screamed back as Grace heard the breaking and creaking of old wood.

The demon hunter started running up the stairs, only to be greeted by more than a dozen vampires crowding the second floor's main hall. Grace could see they were breaking down the door from the last room of the story. "Having problems with the door?" Grace asked as she pulled her crossbow.

The vampires turned toward her just as she pulled the trigger. Wooden arrows started shooting in rapid succession, striking the vampires in their chests and faces. The monsters screamed in agony, while others turned to dust as the wood pierced their hearts. Ash and dust started clouding the hall as Grace dropped the empty clip and reloaded it with another. She slid the bolt cartridge in just as two vampires emerged from the scattered ashes, their fangs and claws ready to tear her apart. She moved to one side of the hall as one stumbled past her. The other one reached for her arm and growled in her face, ready to bite it off. Grace smashed her crossbow against his chest, pushing him away. While he was stunned, Grace fired; the arrow pierced the vampire right below the mouth, making him scream in pain as he let go. Grace fired down toward the vampire that was on the floor. The arrow found its mark, turning the vampire into dust.

Another vampire appeared, firing a roundhouse kick aimed at the young girl's head; Grace blocked and smashed her crossbow across the vampire's face. She kicked his chest and pushed forward, shooting more arrows at the horde that still remained; more vampires turned to dust. Grace removed the empty clip as the cloud settled, only to see three remaining vampires growling at her. Grace smiled as she aimed her weapon at them. The girl suddenly felt a pair of brute hands grab her by the neck and waist. She panicked for a brief second as she was hurled through a wooden door, her crossbow slipping from her hands. Her body landed hard on the wooden floor. She winced in pain as she sat up, only to see two kicks coming toward her face. The young warrior raised her arms to block as the legs collided with them. Grace winced again at the impact. She rolled back and stood up, only to see five vampires inside the room with her.

"Okay," the girl said. "Will it be one at a time, or all at once?" The vampires growled and rushed her; their attacks were quick and precise. The number of them, with their enhanced strength, took a toll on Grace, but she refused to go down. A demon fired a hard haymaker at her face, which she blocked successfully. She grabbed the arm and flung the vampire against two of his comrades. Grace spun in the air as the three vampires fell, extending her legs, delivering a spin kick to the two remaining brutes. With her momentum, she cartwheeled back to where she had dropped her crossbow. The teenaged girl picked it up and turned around just as a vampire reached her. She fired a couple of arrows, turning him to dust. She stood up, only for one of the vampires to kick the weapon from her hands. Grace grabbed the vampire and flung him out the window two stories down.

The young demon hunter turned toward the remaining vampires, who had regrouped. *This fight is taking too long,* Grace thought to herself. *I have to end this.* The girl pulled out the stake given to her by Elizabeth and charged at the trio of demons. She acted quickly, feeling a power surge in her as she moved like lightning around the three vampires. She could almost see their movements in slow motion, passing right through them just as they all burst into ashes.

Grace looked astonished at what she had just done—she had never moved that fast in her life. "It's coming through the window!" the demon hunter heard the girl scream. The terror in her voice snapped Grace back into action. She got back into the hall and ran toward the door, ramming it with her body. Her strength did the trick, breaking right through it. As she got inside the room, she saw two teens cowering in the corner while a single vampire had climbed through the window. Grace threw her stake at it, recognizing the demon as the one she had thrown out of the building. The stake impaled the vampire's chest, turning the beast into ash.

Grace calmed her heart and looked at the teens. Her mouth dropped, seeing it was Bryan and Jaime from earlier in the day. The teens looked at her, amazed at what she'd just done. "I knew it," Bryan whispered.

Grace's face was pale. She was about to say something when Elizabeth ran up the stairs. "I'm here," the Guardian said as she looked at Grace and then at the teens. From the look on Grace's face, she knew something was up.

Both teenagers stood up and looked at Grace, and then at Elizabeth, looking somewhat sheepish. "Good evening," Jaime said, trying to act casual.

"What are you doing out here?" Elizabeth asked. "This is no place or time for children to be outside."

"We're usually careful when we go out at night," Bryan said. "This is the first time this happened."

Grace looked at Elizabeth. She could feel more vampires on the way, but she couldn't say anything. Elizabeth, on the other hand, seemed more concerned with something else. "What do you mean the first time?" the guardian asked. "You've been out before?"

Bryan and Jaime looked at each other. "With Anna and Teresa," Jaime said. "This is the first time we went out on our own."

"Told you it was a bad idea," Bryan murmured under his breath.

"You knew Teresa and Anna?" Elizabeth asked.

"We were friends," Bryan said. "We also knew about their demon-hunting business."

Grace looked at them, surprised. "They told you about that?" the demon hunter asked.

"We caught them in the act," Jaime said. "Like we caught you right now."

"Are your foster sisters also demon hunters?" Bryan asked.

Elizabeth was about to explode as her mind tried to process her thoughts. She looked at Grace, who just had an urgent look on her face. "What is it?"

"We've got to get them out of here," Grace stated. "Now!"

Elizabeth nodded at her demon hunter. "We're taking you home now," Elizabeth declared. "Let's go!"

Jaime and Bryan nodded as they walked out of the room and toward the staircase, followed by Grace and

Elizabeth. "Are you the ones who were going to relieve Anna and Teresa?" Bryan asked.

Grace hesitated a bit before answering as she looked at Elizabeth. Elizabeth just shrugged. "Yes," the demon hunter said. "What else did they say?"

"Nothing, really," Jaime said as they stepped out of the warehouse. "They just said that when they went to college, others would come to protect the town. They would help out."

"They shouldn't have done that," Elizabeth said as they hurried back to their SUV. The Guardian could feel eyes all over them, but they seemed to have stopped in their tracks. "The fact that you know this puts your lives in greater danger," the Guardian continued. "In these cases, the less you know, the better."

As they reached the vehicle, Bryan turned around and handed a box to Grace. "This is for you," he said. Grace looked surprised at the small wooden chest the boy gave to her. She gave the boy and Elizabeth a puzzled look. "This is the reason why we were in that building. Teresa told us that if something bad happened, we should give the box to the relieving team that would arrive in town. It has information on the town that you urgently need."

"Did you have this?" Elizabeth asked. "Or was it hidden inside that warehouse?"

"They hid it in the warehouse," Jaime said as she sat in the back seat.

"You should have waited," Elizabeth said as she started the engine, and everyone buckled up. "You could have gone in the daytime—or better yet, you could have waited for us."

"Daytime darkness is far worse than nighttime," Bryan murmured. "There's other stuff in the day."

Elizabeth was about to ask what he meant, but then shook her head. She turned toward Grace. "Call the girls," she ordered. "Let them know we're delaying the plan by fifteen minutes."

CHAPTER V

Saint Helena South Side, California;
September 02, 10:00 p.m.

NIKKI FROWNED AS SHE looked at her empty A&W paper bag. Three burgers later, and she was still hungry. She looked at Izzy, who had watched her, amazed at what she had just eaten. "I'm still hungry," Nikki said with a frown on her face.

"Well, everything else is closed," Izzy said as Aidan and both demon hunters strolled the deserted streets up north. Nikki crumpled the bag into a tiny paper ball and kicked it to a garbage can twenty-five feet away. The paper bag went through without hitting the rim.

Izzy ignored her friend's antics and focused on the surrounding environment, sensing a faint dark presence a fair distance from them. Her wolf strode beside her, awaiting orders. The demon hunter had noticed that her pet's angst had diminished considerably in the past few days. It was clear that Aidan had grown accustomed to the new California ecosystem in the short time they had been there.

"How did you meet your friend?" Nikki asked, nodding at Aidan as she adjusted her eyeglasses. "I don't think you ever mentioned that encounter."

"It's a long story," Izzy replied.

"As long as he's walking alongside us and not attacking me, I'm cool with him," Nikki said. "But he's part of the team. Maybe getting to know about him would make me less nervous."

"Still not used to him, huh?" Izzy said. "I met Aidan three years ago in Austria. Elsa's parents had discovered this high-end dark Wicca coven plaguing the people of a northern town with curses. They used a pack of wolves, along with human sacrifices, to fuel their dark magic."

"Used them how?" Nikki asked, almost fearing the response.

"They mixed the blood of homeless people and wolves to create a dark spell," Izzy said. "It's all very technical. We freed the humans, but did not get there in time to save the pack of wolves. With the spell shattered, the witches and warlocks were powerless. That's where I found Aidan—among the dead wolves was this lonely cub. I grabbed him and cleaned him up before releasing him to the wild. But every year I visited Austria, he was always waiting for me near Elsa's home."

"Why did you name him Aidan?" Nikki asked.

"It was the name of the alley where the Wiccans had their base of operations," Izzy replied. "It seemed appropriate at the time."

"Why didn't he stay with Elsa or her parents?" Nikki asked.

“Not sure,” Izzy said. “When I left Elsa’s home, he walked in the shadows behind me. I boarded a train, and when I got off at the next stop, he was there. My mom knew everything, but my dad is like you—he hates wolves.”

“That is why I get along with your dad,” Nikki said as they continued walking.

A brief silence followed. Nikki noticed something in Izzy’s eyes. She was walking with them, but her mind was somewhere else. “Do you have a lot on your mind, O’Brien?” Nikki asked point-blank, aiming for the elephant in the room.

“Just news about the town,” Izzy said, remembering the articles she had read earlier in the day. They added to the emotional weight she already carried. “Not sure if the predators in the day are worse than the ones that come out at night.”

“What about you?” Nikki asked. “You haven’t been the same since all that happened in Ireland.”

“Well, it’s a lot to take!” Izzy snapped. “You know that when we’re fighting all that stuff, there isn’t time to think—no time to feel. Just move and stay alive. It’s after the water settles that you realize the weight of all that transpired.”

Nikki just nodded at Izzy’s explanation. “I get it,” Nikki said. “Like surviving a plane crash. It’s only after everything you realize the magnitude of what’s happened.”

Izzy sighed and looked at the ground as she walked up the street. The images from all that had happened flashed before her eyes: the master vampires and his minions all desiring the demise of her kin with hatred in their eyes; watching demon hunters fight for their lives, with limited power. They had battled and won, but not without casualties. The image of Elsa's helpless body inside the wooden coffin plagued her mind. She couldn't shake the sense of loss, replaying the scene of the master vampire piercing Elsa's heart and taking her life.

"You couldn't do anything," Nikki said softly. Izzy looked up at her friend, somewhat surprised she knew what she was thinking. "We share dreams, remember?" the redhead continued while she tapped her temple. "That has plagued your head for days now."

Izzy sighed, trying not to cry on the spot. "She was more than a friend," Izzy managed to mumble. "It's like a piece of my heart died that day as well. She was my sister. Now there is only emptiness, and I can't stand it."

"You're one of a kind," Nikki said, smiling a bit, drawing a questioning look from the brown-haired girl. "You led an army of demon hunters against the undead. You fought to the death with a master vampire. You led us to victory. We won when the odds were against us. Yet here you are, mourning the death of your friend."

Izzy drew a sad smile, recognizing the compliment.

"Hey," Nikki continued. "You're Catholic. Isn't death just part of life? It's not the end. Death is only another path, one that we all must take."

"That's 'The Return of the King'," Izzy stated. "But I get what you're saying."

"I think Elsa would be proud of you," Nikki said. "For all that you've done."

Izzy stopped walking and took a deep breath. "I just miss my friend," she simply said, trying not to burst into tears.

Nikki stopped next to her friend and hugged her. "It's okay to mourn," the redhead said. "You don't have to do this alone. Grace and I are right here with you."

Izzy was about to say something when the dark essence from the south brought her back to reality. She wiped her eyes and looked down the street. "Stupid undead," the demon hunter said, pulling out a stake. "Always interrupting."

Aidan growled in the direction the demons were coming from, ready to attack.

"We give them hell," Nikki said as she pulled a short sword and a stake of her own. "We pause and continue later."

Both demon hunters looked down the street, seeing an old white shuttle bus lazily driving up the road. Over two dozen vampires and demons were either inside or surrounding it. They screamed and growled, not noticing the girls in their way. "We're about to engage," Izzy said through her communicator to Elizabeth and Grace.

"Plan of attack?" Nikki asked.

"Start dusting, and hope we lead them to where Dad wants them to be," Izzy said, pulling out a short sword of her own and signaling her wolf to attack.

Both girls started running toward the large pack of demons, with Aidan darting to the side. The vampires noticed the pair of demon hunters running toward them and growled, ready to pounce. Nikki threw her stake at the disfigured, red-eyed bus driver. The wooden stake shattered the windshield, then impaled the vampire's heart. The demon crumbled into ash, causing the vehicle to slow and drift to the side. The bus softly collided with a small tree, coming to a halt.

Izzy took the right side of the bus, swinging her blade at the first vampire, connecting with its neck and decapitating it while staking a female vampire in the chest. Another vampire tried to tackle her, but Izzy just sidestepped and brought the sword down on the back of his neck. All three vampires combusted, generating a cloud of ash.

"Demon hunters," a female vampire growled from the top of the bus. She jumped down onto Izzy, who simply spin-kicked her right out of the air. The vampire fell with a thud while Izzy thrust her stake into the vampire's chest.

"Guess that takes the mystery out of this incursion," Izzy said with a smile, as vampires started to surround her. The demons formed a circle around the sixteen-year-old. "One at a time or all at once, it's all the same to me," the girl said. The demons threw themselves at the girl, who jumped over them while decapitating two in the process. Izzy ran up to the bus and sprinted on its side with her blade extended, while smoke and ash filled the air. Howls of pain echoed in the air as she landed. The girl spun without even looking, kicking a vampire in the face while punching two that came from the front. She swung her blade and decapitated one that emerged from the side. "I thought you guys would be tougher," Izzy said, overly confident, when several more vampires emerged from the darkness, as if on cue. "Me and my big mouth," she said as a new horde approached.

"This is only getting started!" Nikki yelled from the other side of the bus. The redhead slashed across her field of vampires like they were butter. She wasn't aiming for their necks, but letting the holy water-infused blade do its work against the undead. Vampires fell to the ground screaming in agony as the sixteen-year-old slashed across them with her sword.

Aidan joined Nikki in battle, pouncing over to two vampires who were about to attack Nikki from behind. The animal tore into their undead flesh, ripping them up as the demons screeched in pain.

The redhead looked inside the bus and saw even more vampires trying to get out the front door. Nikki pulled out a small glass canister of holy water, opened it, and threw it at the vehicle entrance. The liquid sprayed all over the vampires, burning their undead flesh as they tried to get out.

The demon hunter came down hard on the entrance as she kicked the first vampire in, bringing him down. She swiped the blade sideways, decapitating his head. She looked inside the bus and saw all types of demons and vampires inside, all growling at the girl. "Let's get this show on the road, shall we?" Nikki said as she stormed in, slicing at the vampires and demons inside. She held her breath as blood and ash started to build up on the walls of the vehicle. As the teenaged warrior battled through, she felt as if the walls of the bus were beginning to close in on her. Nikki decapitated the last vampire and turned around, feeling the ash surround her. *This was a bad idea*, Nikki thought as her heart started beating faster. She fell to one knee and put her right hand on her chest, trying to calm down. She closed her eyes and tried to control her breathing, but the ash smelled like dirt and soil, and she couldn't shake the feeling that it was going to bury her alive.

Izzy finished her latest batch and fell on one knee, exhaustion taking over her. She looked up and saw a small pack of demons emerge from the darkness and make a run toward her. The young brown-haired girl ran to the other side of the bus, only to see more vampires come through the shadows. Izzy whistled to Aidan signaling him to escape the battle as she jumped inside the vehicle and closed the door, regretting it the moment she did. She saw Nikki on her knees, having difficulty breathing. Izzy ran up to her and stood her friend up. "Nikki!" Izzy called. "You have to snap out of it!"

Nikki looked at Izzy, hearing her voice echo as if from afar, even though her sister was right in front of her. The horde of vampires and demons had both girls trapped inside the bus while they surrounded the vehicle. Nikki heard someone yell, "Break the bus down!" from the outside. The glass windows started exploding a few seconds later, sending dangerous, sharp projectiles inside. Nikki looked back toward Izzy, who returned her stare in the middle of the commotion. "The roof exit!" Izzy yelled out over the sound of breaking glass.

Nikki nodded. She stood up and willed herself through the panic trying to take over her heart and mind. The demon hunter tried to channel her fear by swiping her sword sideways and taking care of a vampire trying to come in through one of the broken windows. She tried to reach the roof exit, but the bus started swaying from side to side, making the demon hunters lose their balance. "We get it!" Nikki yelled to the outside. "No need to get pushy!"

The bus swayed more aggressively, making both

teenaged girls fall to the side. "Guess they can't listen to reason," Izzy said as she stood up and moved from seat to seat toward the emergency exit on the roof. She launched herself in a handstand and kicked hard with her feet against the emergency door. The hatch burst open, offering a way out.

Nikki was about to use the new escape route when a vampire jumped in through the hatch. The redhead swung her sword and decapitated the beast. She looked up and saw a couple more vampires trying to squeeze themselves inside. The demon hunter was trying to form a plan when Grace's voice came through her earpiece.

"En route. Moving south with Elizabeth," Grace reported through the earpiece. "We've got a lot of demons on us. What's your status?"

"We're pinned down," Nikki said, trying to hide the panic in her voice while she and Izzy stabbed their short swords at the vampires trying to come inside. Vampires and demons started coming through the broken windows, leaving bloody flesh and clothing behind.

Izzy twirled her blade and started cutting at anything that tried to get in. She figured more than thirty demons and vampires were outside, trying to get in. "These have to be all the demons from the south side!" Izzy yelled. "We need to get them to the access point!"

"We need to get out of here alive first! " Nikki exclaimed, letting her demon hunter instinct take over her fear as she struck her blade upward, piercing a demon's skull.

Suddenly the front door of the bus exploded, sending metal and glass all over the driver's seat. A dark-skinned young man in a black trench coat jumped inside the bus. Both demon hunters could feel a mysterious aura surrounding him. He looked at them with piercing blue eyes as he pulled a small silver short sword from behind his back. Both girls noticed that his blue eyes were set ablaze with a soft blue flame. The newcomer didn't acknowledge them; he just slashed with his sword at a demon that tried to enter the bus through the front door. The beast screamed in agony as the blade left a large, searing wound across its chest. The man in black jumped into the driver's seat of the bus and started the engine. "We're going for a ride!" he yelled to the girls as he put the bus in reverse. "Make sure the undead are on our tail!"

The bus roared to life, backing away from the tree and starting to move north up the main street. Demons and vampires still clung to the vehicle, trying to get inside through the broken glass. Izzy was about to jump at the man, but Nikki stopped her. "Do as he says," Nikki ordered her sister. "Get on the roof and take them out as they jump at us. I will handle things here inside."

Izzy looked at Nikki, making sure she was okay after the skirmish. The demon hunter then looked at the dark-skinned man driving the bus. "Hope you know what you're doing," Izzy said. "Guide him to the access point." After saying this, the brown-haired girl jumped on top of a bus seat and climbed her way out the roof hatch.

Nikki twirled her sword, slashing two demons on her left and one at her right while she looked at the bus's rearview mirror. She could see the man appeared to be a young twenty-year-old. But his aura screamed at her—

he was a demon with the body of a human being. "You know where you're going, right?" she called out to him.

"Yes," the driver said as he swerved right. Vampires and demons were running after the bus, while ash came down from the sides. Izzy was apparently doing her job on top of the moving vehicle. "Southside access point to the cave system."

Nikki looked at the back of the bus, seeing a demon jump onto the back door from the street. The beast ripped the door from its hinges, standing on the frame while a horde of vampires and demons ran after them. The redhead ran toward the creature and jumped, kicking him square in the chest. The beast growled in pain, flying back out of the bus and landing hard on the concrete. Nikki stood in the open doorway, watching as vampires and demons appeared from the shadows, targeting the moving vehicle.

"Is he a good guy?" Izzy asked from above, prompting Nikki to look up at her sister.

"Not sure yet," Nikki said. "But he's not trying to kill us. I give him a pass for now."

Izzy jumped, twirling and grabbing the back edge of the vehicle. The brown-haired girl gracefully swung inside the bus via the back door, joining Nikki. "We're on our way," Izzy said to her communicator. "We carry a heavy load."

"How heavy?" the pair heard Elizabeth ask.

"About twenty-thousand pounds," Nikki said as the bus sped up. Vampires and demons were running after the vehicle, trying to catch up to it.

Both demon hunters saw the end of the road, followed by dark woods. "Hold on," the demon behind the wheel said as he accelerated, causing the bus to enter the woods haphazardly. The impact caused the bus to slow down, but not stop, creating an excellent opportunity for the beasts of the night to gain on them.

"Can you make it go any faster?" Izzy asked, seeing the horde inching closer to the bus.

"Let them in!" the demon behind the wheel said.

Nikki's mind clicked at the idea. "He's right!" she said to Izzy. "Let's draw them inside the bus."

Izzy looked confused, trying to read the situation. She then saw the entrance of the cave system a hundred yards away from them. The opening was big enough for the bus to go through. She realized what the demon and Nikki were thinking. "Dad!" Izzy called through her communicator. "Big payload incoming. Are you ready?"

"Ready as I ever will be," Sean replied. "Liz, how is your side?"

"Give me one more minute," Elizabeth said.

"We're going to have to make a run for it," Nikki said as the vampires reached the back door entrance. Demons started climbing up the sides of the bus. Both Izzy and Nikki moved slowly to the front of the bus as demons and vampires started crowding into the unit.

One of the demons launched itself at them. Izzy stepped forward and sliced across its chest, stopping it in its tracks. She then swung horizontally and its head fell off. "Mind your head!" she called out to the rest of the horde.

The horde screeched and moved forward, forcing the demon hunters to run to the front of the bus. Nikki got there first, grabbing the passenger bars from the roof and swinging forward. Her army boots broke the remaining glass of the windshield, followed by the demon hunter landing on the hood of the bus. She moved out of the way as Izzy made her move and exited the bus the same way, just as the vehicle entered the cave. "We're in!" Izzy yelled at the communicator.

"You've got to get out!" Nikki told the driver, who pulled his sword out and stabbed a demon who reached the driver's seat.

"I'm right behind you!" the demon said as he pressed on the accelerator. "You girls have to jump now!"

Nikki doubted her actions for a second, but a tug on her arm from Izzy made her wake up. The redhead followed her sister's lead as they jumped to their respective side of the bus while the vehicle continued to move forward, with most of the horde inside. The demon hunters landed on the ground, pulling out their swords. A few demons and vampires remained with them inside the cave. Nikki was the first to swing across, creating a huge gash on a vampire's chest. Smoke fumed out of the wound as the demon screamed in agony. Izzy followed suit, decapitating a beast on her left side.

"Get out of the tunnels!" Izzy and Nikki heard on their communicators. It was Sean, with a sense of urgency in his voice. "Get out now!"

Both Nikki and Izzy started slashing the demons that still crowded around them. The small horde that remained consisted of several vampires and demons that growled and clawed at the demon hunters, who were now back-to-back with each other. Izzy looked up at the cave and saw the entrance about 30 yards out.

"Want to get out of here?" Izzy asked her sister.

Nikki nodded as she sliced an arm off a demon. "I hope that after the curfew, there is twenty-four-seven diner," the redhead said as she slashed horizontally. A beast took the bait and tried to tackle her. Nikki spun behind Izzy, using her movement as momentum to launch her brown-haired sister at the monster. Izzy sliced the head off with a horizontal slash, when two female vampires tried to kick her face. The young sixteen-year-old backflipped, avoiding the strikes. She then cartwheeled forward, avoiding punches from two male vampires. When she came to her feet, she swung her sword in a full circle above her head, turning the four vampires to dust.

A loud growl came from the depths of the cave. Nikki looked down to where the bus had driven to, and saw a giant silhouette barreling toward them. She looked closer and saw a gray-skinned six-foot-five troll demon growling at them. The hairless, muscular frame looked massive, with ruby-red eyes and sharp fangs. The distraction caused by the bald creature was enough for Nikki to take a blunt kick to her midsection. The redhead grunted in pain as she staggered back, seeing who dared strike her. It was a male vampire who performed a few spin-kicks before standing in a fighting position. "You're going to pay for that," Nikki said, smiling at the challenge.

Izzy looked around and saw that the tall gray demon had reached her. The monster towered over her, signaling for the other demons to stop their attacks on her. The beast lowered himself so he could look directly at the young girl's face. He unleashed a battle cry, revealing his sharp fangs. The demons and vampires cheered as their champion tried to intimidate the young sixteen-year-old. Izzy just smiled and stuck her sword under the giant demon's mouth. The blade pierced right through its flesh, coming out from at the top of the beast's skull. Izzy moved the sword to the side, slicing half the demon's face off. She looked at the horde, which had fallen silent. "Who's next?"

A flash of light, followed by an explosion, caught Izzy's attention as she looked down the cave and saw flames engulfing every inch of space inside of it. The demons screamed and started running for the nearest exit. The brown-haired girl looked at Nikki, who had just dusted a vampire, and signaled them to start running. Both girls started their uphill sprint as the heat was gaining on them. Their speed bested that of the demons, who were beginning to be engulfed by the deadly blaze.

Both demon hunters got to the entrance and parted to each side just as the flames reached the opening. Screams and howls echoed from inside as the fire enveloped whatever creatures, living or dead, were inside. "Report?" Izzy heard her dad over her earpiece. "Is everyone okay?"

Izzy was about to answer when Grace's voice chimed in. "Doing fine on our side," the demon hunter said. "Moving to the south side to join Izzy and Nikki at their cave entrance."

"Izzy and Nikki?" Sean asked.

"We're out," Nikki said, sitting down on the base of a tree trunk. "Waiting for Elizabeth and Grace."

"Copy that," Sean said. "See you later, back home."

Izzy looked at Nikki, who had just closed her eyes.

"That was intense," Nikki said as she let the adrenaline wash over her.

"Do you want to talk about the bus driver?" Izzy asked. "How did you know we could trust him?"

A growl from the entrance of the cave made the demon hunters jump up and take notice. The six-foot-five troll demon emerged with its flesh still burning and the remaining half of his face falling off. "I thought you killed that," Nikki said, pulling her sword. The monster grabbed hold of the flesh falling from his face and ripped it off entirely, revealing a hideous figure behind it.

The beast growled at the perplexed girls as it attacked them. Izzy tried to cartwheel out of its reach, but as her hands touched the ground, the monster grabbed hold of Izzy's ankle. The young girl shrieked as the beast flung her body toward a thick tree trunk. Izzy's back collided squarely against the hard bark, cracking the wood. "Ow," Izzy managed to say, feeling the wind knocked out of her as she slumped down to the ground.

The demon charged at Izzy, only to find Nikki in his way. Nikki sliced her sword across the monster's chest, opening a sizeable diagonal wound. The beast didn't even flinch, firing a hard punch that connected with Nikki's cheek. The redhead's knees buckled a bit because of the blow as her glasses flew off her face. The girl fired a right punch of her own, into the demon's unprotected stomach. It was like hitting stone, but a satisfying painful grunt came out of the beast's mouth. Nikki jumped and tried to uppercut the demon, but the monster blocked her attack, grabbed her wrist, and pulled her up to his full height. "Not good," Nikki murmured as the beast swung her down, slamming her body hard on the ground. A painful grunt escaped her lips.

Izzy ran toward the demon and sliced low at its left ankle with her short sword, bringing the beast down to one knee. Nikki catapulted from the floor, her feet up in the air, using only her hands to push herself off the ground. Her army boots smashed the fiend's ripped face, causing it to stagger toward Izzy, who thrust her blade in the demon's back. The beast growled in agony and rage as it crumpled to its knees. Izzy pulled out the sword and decapitated the monster with one swift motion. "Some demons are just harder to kill," Izzy said.

"You don't say," a female voice said behind them. Izzy turned around, seeing a blonde-haired vampire leading a pack of half a dozen vampires. "You're going to pay for what you did."

Izzy and Nikki braced themselves for another battle when the blue-eyed man popped out of the cave. His half-torn trench coat had burn marks on one side, but aside than that, the demon seemed unscathed. "That was a great maneuver," the man said—he then noticed the commotion of the vampires and demon hunters. "Hope I'm interrupting." The vampires growled as the dark-skinned demon pulled a sword from the back of his coat. As the sword made contact with the air, it lit itself with a soft blue flame all around the blade. The vampires stopped in their tracks, as the being was now armed. The demon took advantage of their inaction, charging them while twirling his sword. The vampires didn't know what hit them before they screamed with their bodies engulfed in blue flames.

Izzy guarded herself, lifting her sword, ready to fight. She had witnessed too much to let her guard down. Nikki, on the other hand, put her hand on her sister's shoulder and addressed the stranger. "You were outside the coffee shop today," Nikki said.

"Yes," the demon said, putting his sword away as the vampires he killed turned to dust. "I'm surprised you didn't run out after me. A demon hunter not killing a daywalker on sight is something rare in this day and age."

"There is something different about you," Nikki said as she felt a different type of aura emanating from the being. He was a demon, and darkness engulfed him, but the sensation was different. The redhead looked at Izzy. "Do you feel that?" she asked her brown-haired sister.

Izzy looked at the demon as she put her sword down. His blue eyes turned to human form and no longer held the blue flames. But the being was not human—his aura vibrated as if he was born from darkness but did not belong to it. "What's your name?" Izzy asked. "Why did you help us?"

"The who and the why," he replied, looking at the horizon. "Your predecessors were just like you. At least Anna was."

"You knew the demon hunters before us?" Nikki asked.

"I did," the demon said. "I am Solas, and I am at your service."

"You were friends with Ana and Teresa?" Izzy asked. "Why didn't you help them in the raid a few weeks back?"

Solas winced at the question. The demon hunters saw a slight look of pain in his eyes. "I wanted to be there," Solas said. "I should have been there. But Teresa wouldn't allow it."

"Why?" Nikki asked. "It seems you don't need permission from anybody to do what you want."

Solas frowned at the girls, making them tense up. "We planned for that incursion well in advance," the demon said. "Anna and Teresa had it all worked out. That is, until news came of an extension of the seal on the west side of town."

"What is that?" Izzy asked.

"The doorway where Ana and Teresa rest has an extension," Solas said. "It's located in an abandoned vineyard on a sublevel of a warehouse. No one knew it was there—not even the Guardians. When Teresa and Anna found out, they realized that if the door opened on the East side, no one would be there to cover the West."

"That's why they sent you there," Izzy realized. "They wanted to cover all the bases." Izzy looked at Nikki, who nodded in agreement. It was a smart play. If they were in the same position, somehow, they would have made the same call.

"Something doesn't add up, though," Nikki said. "The Guardians are in the dark on this. Why? Teresa and Anna would have shared the information with them. Why didn't they?"

Solas thought for a moment on the question before answering. "Teresa had her reasons," the demon said. He was about to say something else when he could feel someone approaching.

Nikki and Izzy looked behind them and saw Grace run up to them with Aidan at her side. "We ran into a situation in the north," the raven-haired demon hunter said. "Elizabeth is waiting for us up the hill. We regroup tonight."

Izzy and Nikki turned back toward where Solas was, but he was gone. "We've got a lot to discuss," Izzy said to her sisters. "But, I think night two was a win for us."

"Okay," Nikki said as the three started walking toward the road where their Guardian waited. "How did it go up north?"

"A lot of death," Grace said. "Did the underwear-model demon ask for your number?" Izzy giggled at the question while Nikki glared at her sister. "Sorry," Grace said. "Was out of hearing range. But I know now what you were referring to."

"Let's discuss this at home," Nikki said as the trio continued their walk. "I have no idea what to think anymore."

CHAPTER VI

Abandoned Wine Cellar, Saint Helena Outskirts; September 03, 3:00 a.m.

SABINE SAT ON THE floor, cross-legged opposite to UrthaMal. Both beings had their eyes closed. The commotion from the surface world did little to interrupt their meditation. "You have a lot of knowledge," UrthaMal said, opening her eyes and looking at the female vampire before her. "But there is a part of your mind that you seal off. Why is that?"

"You can say it's part of my former humanity," Sabine said as she stood up.

Her comment made UrthaMal growl in disgust. "You're a demon," the blonde woman said. "You serve a higher purpose. You are above and beyond what this plane can offer. You and your kind embody the reason we despise vampires. Half-breeds that walk this earth, pretending."

"And yet every time a higher-level demon ends up trapped on this plane, it is the vampire kind that they turn to for guidance," Sabine calmly responded. "Is it because vampires are the few half-breeds that are capable of reasoning?" UrthaMal growled as she stood up and tried to reach toward Sabine. The invisible wall vibrated in response to the higher demon trying to break free. Waves were visible to Sabine's eyes with every attempt. "It must kill you, being in this half-breed form," Sabine continued. "Don't worry. I will keep my promise and help you."

UrthaMal calmed down as Cassius and Draco entered the room. Cassius looked flustered. "The demon hunters and the Guardians crippled us with that attack," Cassius said. "Their actions decimated our numbers."

UrthaMal just smiled and walked further into her cell, while Sabine looked bored. "This is the reason you're a follower and not a leader, Cassius," Sabine said.

"Schulmeister," Cassius said, visibly hurt by her comment. "I'm just looking out for what is best for my clan. How else am I supposed to..."

Sabine slapped the vampire across the face, making Draco wince. "Act like a leader!" the female vampire said. "You answer to the elite of your clan. Foot soldiers are dispensable."

Cassius swallowed his pride. "I'm sorry, Schulmeister," he said. His voice had an apologetic tone in it, but Sabine could see past it. "What would you have me do?"

"I am not here to tell you what to do," Sabine said as she walked toward the entrance. "I'm not your leader, nor was I chosen for that. It falls on you. My role is to provide advice. Nothing more."

"Guide me, then," Cassius said.

"She's not to be trusted," UrthaMal said. "She hides something from you."

Sabine glared at UrthaMal but did not lose her composure. "I was under the impression vampire business was beneath you," Sabine said to the trapped demon. She then focused her attention on Cassius. "Focus on your most reliable and cunning vampires. Our strength is not in our numbers, but in how we outplay the demon hunters. They're mortal, and we have nothing but time. The surface world will eventually be ours. In the meantime, let's focus on our biggest weapon." As Sabine finished speaking, she referenced UrthaMal. "Let's unleash her."

"I am not your pet to be unleashed," UrthaMal growled.

"But you meet our same purpose," Sabine said. She turned toward Draco. "Did your agents find the proper people to feed her?"

"We did," the tall vampire said. "The room next door is set. The internet connection is ready. One observes the other, just as you instructed."

UrthaMal smiled for the first time. "I can feel them," she said with a gleeful grin. "Lust and rage are potent aphrodisiacs."

"See?" Sabine said, smiling. "She's angry because she's hungry. Do you need the victims closer? Or the distance is okay with you?"

"Distance is fine," UrthaMal said as her eyes rolled back in pleasure, feeling the negative energy. "Just give me time. Once rage kills lust, bring rage in here with me."

Draco and Cassius looked confused, while Sabine signaled them to step outside. As soon as the three vampires were out, Sabine walked to the next room, sealed by a black door with a small peephole at the top of it. The female vampire could hear screams of rage from behind the door. "Don't do it, old man!" the vampire heard before she opened the peephole door. "You're dead, I tell you! Dead!" She looked inside and saw a man in a police uniform, chained to a wall. She caught, on the opposite side, an older man with a clerical collar around his neck. One hand was chained to a wall, while the other held a tablet. "I will kill you, old man!" the police officer said. "You'll die by my hand!"

Sabine closed the peephole while the police officer continued to rant at the priest. The female vampire looked at Cassius and Draco. "It's easy to see who is rage and who is lust," she said. "Once UrthaMal feeds off the energy of the priest, release the police officer. UrthaMal will tell you how to proceed after that."

"Will she be free after only those two?" Cassius asked.

"No," Sabine responded, looking beyond them. She could see Ian waiting for her near the stairs that led upward. "But her power will grow. Her range of influence will reach weak-willed humans, making her stronger each day. Soon, she will be strong enough to free herself. What about this firm that assisted you in Ireland? From what I heard, you paid a hefty sum for their services. Where are they?"

Again Cassius looked ashamed, shaking his head. "After the Ireland debacle, they've cut us off."

Sabine shook her head in disgust as she looked at the tall vampires. "The ancient order has disapproved of that organization for centuries. They act as if they're on the same playing field as us. They're not. They're beneath us. But you young vampires have constantly refused to listen to our counsel. Now you pay the price."

"What should we do?" Cassius asked.

"Establish your dominance again," Sabine said. "Wield UrthaMal as your weapon and put order back in this region. Once you accomplish this, the firm will have no choice but crawl back to you in fear."

Cassius smiled at the idea. "It will be done."

"Good," Sabine said, making her way toward Ian, who waited for her.

"Are you leaving our lair?" Cassius asked. "Do you want Draco to put agents on you for your protection? It's not safe with those demon hunters out there."

Sabine smiled without looking back at both vampires. "Do you think I need protection from three little girls?" she asked as she reached Ian. "Follow UrthaMal's instructions. I will come later tonight. I will call you if I want to be updated." Finishing that, she started walking up the stairs with Ian at her heels. "Anything I need to know?" Sabine asked her driver as they walked away from the building's lower levels and moved upstairs.

"Vampires are scared of these demon hunters," Ian said. "They say they're stronger than their predecessors. They seem to have killed one of their demon champions."

"Did they say what demon that was?" Sabine said as they reached the ground floor and made their way toward the exit.

"No," he said. "Only that it took two of them to put him down."

"That's very vague," Sabine said as she and Ian stepped out into the night outside the warehouse. Sabine looked at the sky as she walked toward their vehicle.

Ian hurried his step and opened the back door to let his employer in the car. "What about you?" he asked carefully. "Is this the demon you're searching for?"

Sabine sighed at the question as her driver entered the car and started the engine. "Don't know yet," she said. "I need for her to ascend to be sure."

"Where to?" the driver asked, looking at the image of his employer in the screen.

"Take us to the inn," the female vampire said. "And watch your back. Even though I told Draco no, the Karratt Order agents will be watching us."

"Understood," Ian said as he pulled out of the curve and drove into the night.

Guardians' Home, Saint Helena, California: September 05, 6:00 a.m.

Izzy walked through the dark hallway of the underground tomb. A dozen torches lit the way through the claustrophobic concrete tunnel. The air felt damp, and the smell of mold burned her nostrils. Her heartbeat increased in its rhythm as she reached the core of the tomb, where a single concrete sarcophagus rested and four torches illuminated the area. The clanking of heavy chains against stone caught her attention, where shackled to the right, a dark figure stood prisoner and slumped down. Izzy's eyes adjusted to the darkness, and she saw her father's beaten and broken body. Cuts and bruises adorned his once-chiseled features.

"Dad!" Izzy exclaimed, running toward him, trying to pry the chains off.

"Izzy!" Sean painfully wheezed out as blood poured from his mouth. "This is not your fault! You have to remember that! It's not your fault!"

Izzy felt a pair of hands grab her from behind and fling her toward the stone sarcophagus. "The hell it isn't," a figure in a dark cloak squealed in a high-pitched distorted voice. "You didn't think I'd forget about you?"

"Please," Izzy begged. "What do you want from me?"

"I want to torture you," the figure replied, removing the hood of her cloak, revealing a mirror image of Izzy. The demon hunter looked at her doppelganger, admiring her ghastly and pale features. Her blonde, frizzled hair with pale blue eyes contrasted with Izzy's brown hair and green eyes. "You must suffer as I've suffered."

Izzy looked around. She could see Grace and Nikki behind a locked gate screaming at her, but no noise came from their mouths. Her sisters were trying to reach out to her, but they were unable to. She looked back at her father with fear gripping her soul. Sean screamed in agony as something from inside his body was trying to burst out. The demon hunter then looked behind her, and a dark silhouette with red eyes watched from the door she had entered.

"No one can help you," Izzy's blonde doppelganger said throwing off the lid of the sarcophagus. "Look at what you did!"

Izzy looked inside the casket to see Elsa's pale, dead body. Memories of seeing her friend turn to dust flashed before Izzy's mind. Elsa's eyes opened staring back at the brown-haired demon hunter. "Izzy," Elsa's voice echoed. "Everyone around you dies. Why didn't you save me?" As soon as the word left her lips, Elsa's body started to decompose.

"No!" Izzy screamed trying to reach for her friend, only for a firm grip to stop her. Izzy looked at her blonde counterpart, who had grabbed her arm.

"This is your fault!" the blonde girl said. "You will pay! I'll make you pay!" The blonde girl then threw Izzy against the wall. Izzy screamed in pain, looking up to see her sisters fighting the red-eyed silhouette. "You can't help them," her double said as Grace's body flew across the room, smashing through the concrete wall, leaving only a bloody trail in her wake.

Nikki tried to fight the dark silhouette, but the being was too powerful for the redheaded demon hunter. Nikki's blood splattered across the open coffin as the creature broke the stone, using the young demon hunter's body. Izzy tried to intervene, but her double wrapped her arms around her from behind. Izzy watched in horror while the dark creature beat Nikki down to a pulp. A puddle of blood formed around the redhead's broken body.

"Spilling your blood is a necessity," the silhouette said.

Izzy turned toward her father, whose lifeless body hung from the black chains. His entire chest burst open, with dark blood dripping down into the stone. A black orb of energy floated in front of her.

"No!" Izzy screamed as a tall, dark silhouette formed from the black ball of energy.

The young demon hunter watched in horror as her father's corpse stood up, his eyes ablaze as the silhouette invaded the man's body. The demon gave Izzy a sadistic smile. "Can't wait to meet you, daughter."

Izzy woke up startled. Sweat was dripping from her face as she looked at the clock on her nightstand. It was six-fifteen in the morning. The demon hunter fell back on her bed and looked at the ceiling of her room.

She could feel her heart beat feeling it would burst out. Fear was taking over her every being while she tried to process what she'd just experienced. It wasn't until her mom's voice brought her to the harsh reality.

"Wake up, girls!" Elizabeth called from downstairs. "It's time for school!"

*****

"This is crap!" Nikki said as she stirred the spoon in her cup of coffee. Two hours had passed since Elizabeth had dragged her three demon hunters from the house to the old diner in the middle of town. "We halt a horde of demons and vampires, restoring order to the nightlife to this town, and this is how you repay us."

"No good deed goes unpunished," Elizabeth said, smiling at the redhead who sat across from her in the brown and red booth in the local diner.

"But the punishment does not fit the crime," Nikki protested. "Why do we have to pay this way?"

Izzy remained silent. She had been quiet since she had woken up. Thoughts and emotions bounced off her head, leaving her unable to focus. She just hoped she could hide her feelings from her mom and her sisters. The fear inside her was appalling.

"All demon hunters go through this," Elizabeth said, focusing her attention on Grace and Nikki. "This is not a negotiation."

"I certainly didn't," Grace said softly. Her demeanor was toned down as well, since getting up in the morning. Only Nikki seemed chirpier as her usual self.

"I thought that us being demon hunters spared us from this type of engagement," Nikki said. "At least that is how it was in my airbase."

Elizabeth laughed at the complaints of her girls. "Don't be silly," the Guardian said. "You girls are overreacting on all of this." Saying that, she pulled out three red and white folders with the Saint Helena High School Logo plastered all over the front. "High School is going to be great," the blonde Guardian said. "You all have a different homeroom. I've made sure that you all have gym class at the same time. I want you to keep on an eye on each other. Don't want more people to figure out who we are and what we do."

"That wasn't my fault," Grace said.

Elizabeth looked into Grace's black eyes. "No one said it was," the older woman said as she motioned everybody to get up and exit the coffee shop. "I was there, too. What happened could have happened to any demon hunter. My point is that we don't want to put more lives at risk."

"I think it's great," Nikki said. "Besides, I think Bryan has a crush on Grace."

Grace glared at Nikki while the comment brought Izzy out of her silence. "Why didn't you say that before?" the brown-haired girl asked.

"I wanted to wait until the first day in school," Nikki said as she opened the back door of the car.

Izzy looked at Grace, who just ignored the abuse. "I haven't met him. Is he cute?" Izzy asked.

"He is," Nikki answered for her sister. "Like a teddy bear."

Elizabeth smiled as she started her car and proceeded the drive up to the school. They were just a few blocks away, but the student body moved quickly up the road. Elizabeth smiled a bit, remembering her first day of high school as a demon hunter. She relished the memory for a few seconds until her daughter's voice brought her to reality. "Mom," Izzy called.

"Sorry," Elizabeth said, looking at her daughter through the rearview mirror. "What is it?"

"I asked about John," Izzy said. Maybe he could shed some light on her dreams. "He was supposed to arrive yesterday, and he never showed."

"There was a delay on his flight," Elizabeth said parking the car in front of the school. "Your father is working on his cover while he's helping in St. Helena. I think you'll see him for dinner tonight."

The girls started to get out of the car when they could hear a loud voice yelling. The demon hunters and the Guardian looked toward the commotion toward the football field. They could see a large man screaming in anger at what seemed to be his team. The tall coach's face was bright red as he unleashed verbal abuse on the boys on his squad. "You worthless maggots!" the coach said. "I expect nothing but perfection from you lazy pieces of crap! If you are unwilling to work out from the cesspool of mediocrity and live by a mantra of excellence, you better shoot yourself in the head since you have no reason to keep on living!"

"That's harsh," Izzy murmured.

"I agree," Grace said, looking at Elizabeth. "Was it like that when you were at school?"

"Can't remember," Elizabeth said. "I remember my principal was a pride demon, and my biology teacher was an evil witch. Just keep on the lookout. The coach can just be a terrible human being. Those are terrifying as well."

The three teenagers parted ways and walked toward the school entrance. Teens flooded past them like a river of people, screaming and shouting names. The school environment had an ordinary appearance by human standards, but a heaviness in the air covered a hidden darkness within the walls, like an open wound for all to see, but no one dared express a word about it. The three demon hunters reached their hallway lockers when Izzy turned toward Nikki. "Are we going to discuss the dream now?" the brown-haired girl asked. "Or are we going to wait until tonight?"

"Wow, O'Brien," Nikki said with a smile. "I didn't know you cared that much."

"This is serious," Grace said. "What the hell was that?"

"Could be a lot of things," the redhead said with a shrug. "I, for one, am aching for a good fight, and it seems that I'm getting one. My question to Izzy is, why are you holding yourself back?"

Izzy opened her locker and tried to recollect everything from the dream. Nikki and Grace did not see what she had seen. Their nightmare was a collective experience, but with individual points of view. "What was the last thing you saw?" Izzy asked as the memory of her dad crossed her mind making her winch.

"A dark silhouette fighting us while you dealt with yourself," Nikki replied. "I also sense a lot of fear in you. I just can't figure it out. We're supposed to be fearless. You told us that, remember? We're not damsels in distress."

Izzy was trying to avoid that particular part of the nightmare, but she couldn't. "This is something else,"

Izzy said, referring to her doppelganger. “That’s not me. It can’t be me.”

“It did seem like you,” Grace said. “Guilt and rage, bottled into one because of what happened. You can’t torture yourself like that. It’s like you want to be gripped by fear.”

Nikki stepped next to her friend and put her hand on her shoulder. “It’s okay,” Nikki said. “If you need time to deal with it, say so. We’ll understand. Whatever comes, Grace and I can take it. We’ll cover for you.”

“You didn’t see my dad?” Izzy asked as she turned around and faced her sisters. “He was there.”

Grace and Nikki shared a blank look. “You two have your own burdens,” Izzy said, closing back up as she stared directly into Nikki’s blue eyes. “Especially you. It’s a struggle every time your adrenaline kicks in.”

“I am dealing with it,” Nikki said as she leaned against the locker. “What I’m seeing is that you’re not dealing with your stuff.”

“I’m not as strong as you,” Izzy said, closing her locker door. Soon they were surrounded by more students, making the conversation impossible to continue. Izzy noticed Stephen a few feet away from her. She walked toward him, trying to push the awful memories down as the young man opened his locker. He immediately taped up the drawing Izzy saw him working on a couple of days before. “Looks like you finished it,” Izzy said behind his back while at the same time trying to clear her head.

Stephen turned around, showing a bit of surprise as the young girl inspected his drawing. “Yeah,” he replied. “It didn’t take long. Only two more days.”

"I assumed I would catch you in these halls," Izzy said. "Didn't expect it to be before class, though."

"And we've got all year," Stephen said with a smile as he put a few books inside his locker. He was about to say something else when a commotion caught the attention of both. The school football team had entered the hall, and they were obnoxiously loud as they walked. They seemed to be laughing and teasing other students. Izzy noticed some faces of the student body showed glimpses of fear and contempt. Very few showed signs of rage. She looked at Stephen, who just frowned at the football team's display. He closed his locker. "Guess I'll see you in art class," he said.

"Cool," Izzy said as Stephen walked away while her two sisters approached.

"Who was that?" Grace asked.

"Just a guy I met at the parish," Izzy replied. "He goes to school here."

"I see you met Stephen," Jaime said, walking up to the girls with Bryan at her heels. The chubby teen had a Canon camera around his neck.

"Hey, Jaime," Nikki said. "You haven't met our third sister. Isabella O'Brien."

"Nice to meet you," Izzy said, shaking Jaime's hand and then Bryan's. "Heard a lot about you guys. What's up with the camera?"

"School newspaper," Bryan said, looking at Grace. "I brought you a welcome-to-our-school gift," the teen said, pulling out a small box and giving it to Grace.

"Thank you," she said, opening it. It was a small pin with the St. Helena Saints logo. Grace smiled and looked at Nikki and Izzy, who both had stupid grins on their faces.

"Welcome to St. Helena," Bryan chirped.

"She's out of your league, nerd!" a football player yelled from across the hall. The scene produced laughter and soft giggles from the student body, which caused Bryan's face to go bright red.

Grace turned toward the football player with murder in her eyes, but Nikki and Izzy held her back. "Easy," Nikki said.

"Time and place," Izzy said.

"It would be awesome if everyone knew what you guys could do," Jaime said to the girls as everybody continued with what they were doing. "No one would dare mess with you."

"I assume Teresa and Anna explained what happens to people that know the truth," Izzy said.

Jaime was about to say something when the bell rang, interrupting the moment. Students started running toward their classes. Nikki, Izzy, and Grace looked at each other before bolting toward their respective homerooms.

The day crawled to a bitter end as the girls watched the wall clocks move slowly throughout the day. They were all done by three in the afternoon and wanted to get out of the cursed building. But a complication arose, and Elizabeth was unable to pick them up for another hour. So the demon hunters had made their way toward the football field to watch what seemed to be a 'normal' football training session from the bleachers.

The demon hunters sat on the red bleachers and waited while they witnessed the head football coach drill his players to the dirt. The older man screamed until his face turned bright red, as if he was going to burst. "I've seen drill sergeants be more compassionate than this guy," Nikki said watching the coach scream at what seemed to be the linebacker.

"Treating athletes like professionals doesn't make them professionals," Grace said as Bryan and Jaime approached them. Bryan seemed to be taking pictures of the training.

"Have you heard of this before?" Izzy asked Jaime. "The coach being this savage to the students?"

"Not at all," Jaime replied. "The coach has always been a very gentle and loving man. He was strict, but never at this level. A lot has changed."

"He's not the only one," Bryan murmured.

"What do you mean?" Grace asked.

"Some people today were just angrier," Bryan said. "Students and faculty alike. I know most of the freshman class, and something is wrong. They're not themselves. It's like something happened over the summer that has them acting strange."

"I didn't want to admit it, but it's true," Jaime said. "Not only the student body, but some teachers and other people across town.

"What else have you seen?" Izzy asked

"Being part of the school newspaper has its benefits," Jaime said. "I have to keep an eye on everything. Some store owners were so angry this morning when they opened up their shops, as if a bad mood has set in over everyone."

"Not everyone," Nikki said. "I've seen some cheerful people around. Namely us."

"It takes more than schoolwork to break our spirit," Izzy said, smiling at her sister.

"There are also mysterious disappearances of people," Jaime said, bringing the somberness back to the conversation. "The computer teacher was found dead about a week before you showed up. People just blamed it on the gang activity, but you know it's not that."

"There was also the break-in of the police station," Bryan interjected himself back in the conversation.

"A break-in?" Nikki asked. "Or a break-out?"

Bryan and Jaime just shrugged. "All we know is that a prisoner and a police officer are now missing as well," Jaime said.

"It was Sergeant Grant and the disgraced priest he arrested earlier that day," Bryan said.

"We don't know that," Jaime said.

"Wait," Izzy said. "Someone kidnapped a Catholic priest and a police officer from the police station?"

"That is what the sources say," Jaime said.

Izzy was about to say something when the roar of an engine and a crash caught everyone's attention. A red SUV plowed through the school fence, going top speed toward the football team. Students started screaming in panic while the players got out of the way. The car swerved and came to a stop right in front of the football coach. A thin man with glasses stepped out of the vehicle with his face filled with rage. He screamed as he fired a hard right punch toward the coach's jaw. The girls winced in pain, seeing the coach fall as the thinner man jumped over him and started punching and screaming. School security guards jumped into the scene with Bryan taking pictures of the commotion.

"I think that is your cover story for the school paper," Izzy said to Jaime.

Jaime nodded as she scribbled on her notepad.

Izzy looked to the side and saw her mom's SUV pull up, but Elizabeth wasn't behind the wheel. The brown-haired teen recognized her father behind his aviator sunglasses. "Dad's here," the teen said to her sisters.

Grace and Nikki grabbed their stuff and started walking toward the SUV with Izzy, saying goodbye to Jaime and Bryan. They had only taken a few steps when Grace walked back toward Bryan while she pulled out her cell phone, drawing a bright smile from the boy. Grace then ran back to join her sisters. "What's that about?" Nikki asked knowingly.

"Nothing major," Grace said. "It's been a while since I went out on a date."

Nikki just smiled as they reached Sean and the SUV. Izzy sunk her face into her dad's chest, giving him a big hug. "Thanks for coming," Izzy said as she looked at her father adoringly while Grace and Nikki hopped in the back of the vehicle.

"I must have done something right today," Sean said. "It's not every day my teenaged girl hugs me in public."

"I just needed it today," Izzy said. Sean caught a glint of sadness in her daughter's voice.

"Is everything okay?" Sean asked, genuinely concerned as he looked back at Grace and Nikki.

"I just had one of those bad dreams," Izzy said as she walked toward the passenger seat.

"Want to talk about it with me?"

"Yeah," Izzy said. "How has your day been? Where is Mom?"

"She's at home prepping dinner," Sean said, getting into the car and starting the engine. "She was also helping John set up some gear around the property."

"John made it to town," Grace said.

"Does Elizabeth cook?" Nikki asked, curious. "I knew about your culinary reputation, but not hers."

"For your information, Elizabeth has numerous skills," Sean said, looking in the rearview mirror and pulling out.

"And cooking is not one of them," Izzy said with a sly smile.

Sean just shook his head. "Your mother is fine," Sean said. "She can handle demons on the battlefield. A little light dinner will be a piece of cake. Now, let's talk about that dream of yours."

CHAPTER VII

Guardians' Home, Saint Helena, California; September 05, 4:15 p.m.

"IS THAT SUPPOSED TO smell like that?" John asked as he watched Elizabeth struggle in the kitchen.

"Not one word," Elizabeth called out removing a baking tray from the oven. She frowned at the overcooked meatloaf in her hands, then shrugged and walked over toward the table, where John was sitting. The young Guardian's focus was on a tablet in his hands. "Did you fix it?" the blonde woman asked.

John smiled a bit looking up. "Yes," he said pointing at the large screen overlooking the dining room and projected the security feed. "Here is the outside perimeter," John said. "You can switch from several angles, including the guest house in the back. Very few blind spots."

"We don't want to lose sight of you," Elizabeth said. "What about the interiors?"

"Also set up," John said, flipping to the inside feed. "Cameras at every door, as well as common areas. The basement gym has six angles alone." With that said, John switched to the video of the basement, showing the gym setup. Some wooden and steel weapons hung from the walls. There were also three wooden training dummies, which included a Wing Chun dummy. The floor had purple padding that extended through the entire basement surface, except for the back room. The basement's backroom had a built-in sound booth, with a piano and a violin placed neatly along the far wall. There was a single camera observing the interior of that room alone.

"Excellent," Elizabeth said admiring the setup.

"Is there anything else you guys needed me for?" John asked. "I think you guys have it covered."

"Yes," Elizabeth said stepping back and walking toward the kitchen. "I spoke to Sean last night before you arrived. You did an excellent job with the information you provided and the studies on Apocalyps."

"I heard that from Williams as well," John said.

Elizabeth stepped back into the room, carrying a large salad bowl. She paused for a second and set the container on the table, searching for what to say next. "You put my daughter in danger," Elizabeth whispered.

"I did," John said, unfazed by Elizabeth's hushed tone. Her anger was palpable as the room grew strangely silent. "Is Sean upset as well for my actions?"

Elizabeth tried to control herself as she looked at John. It was the first time a Guardian or a demon hunter could see the raw emotion going through her. "I wanted to kill you," the demon hunter said—she then seemed to control herself. "Then, I read what happened in Mexico. What you went through with

Angela." John remained silent and calm. "You gave her the information, and she sacrificed herself to save the world."

"That's what demon hunters do," John said. "How many times did you do it?"

"More than I can count," Elizabeth said. "Over a dozen times, not knowing if it would be the last time I would see my mom."

"Your mom died not knowing your secret," John said. Elizabeth remained silent while John spoke. "You have developed an excellent arrangement for everyone. Girls with the gift only serve three years. After that, their burden of demon hunting and protecting the innocent is over. They are released into the world, no longer exposing themselves to the dangers of what goes bump in the night. But they know what lies in the darkness. There is no stopping them from intervening when someone tries to unleash hell on earth. Other than that, I think it's a fantastic arrangement. Parents are always in the loop and involved in helping out the best way they can. But sometimes, an apocalyptic event occurs on that side of the world. Suddenly a family is shattered by the loss of a daughter, a sister, or a friend." Elizabeth kept quiet. "I understand your anger is not at me. Your rage is focused mostly on everything surrounding this blessing—or curse—that is fighting the forces of darkness. Even though you try to outmaneuver it, fate always gets you, one way or the other."

"I almost lost my daughter," Elizabeth whispered.

"But you didn't," John said. "She's out there using her gift, like countless others, for the force of good. Just like you."

"I don't want anything bad to happen to her," Elizabeth said.

"You share the same sentiment of other parents around the globe," John said. "That fear at the bottom of your stomach that keeps you awake at night. I guess that's why you brought me in—to help you in protecting these girls the best way possible." Elizabeth nodded softly. "I've lost one demon hunter," John said. "I will not let that happen again. Not on my watch."

Elizabeth was about to say something when she heard the SUV parking in the driveway. "The girls are here," Elizabeth said. "I trust that any information gathered in this Hell Spot will be shared as a team and not as individuals."

"As it should be," John said as the girls entered the dining room, with Sean trailing behind.

"Hey, John," Izzy greeted. "Dad got you out of the library, I see."

"It was more like an order than anything else," he said greeting Grace and Nicole.

"We have an early dinner," Elizabeth said. "Then homework, and then we hit the streets."

The dinner was pleasant, with all gathered around the table. The food was edible, and the conversation remained friendly as John explained how he managed to cram books into his brain. As the late afternoon progressed, the conversation got more serious regarding the events developing in town.

"These disappearances could be linked," Sean said. "Then again, these could just be vampire meal tickets."

"I'm intrigued by the taking of two humans from the police precinct," John said. "It does sound targeted.

Why bother taking two individuals from a heavily guarded location? It seems like too much trouble for normal demon activity."

"We scout the area?" Nikki asked.

"I think it's worth looking into that," Elizabeth said.

"What about the sudden mood swing in the townsfolk?" Grace asked. "Not that I am complaining, but we've got two papers due tomorrow, with a math quiz. And it's only our first day. That is enough evidence to prove the teachers are evil."

"I think that is just school," Sean said with a knowing smile.

"I don't think so," Izzy said. "Jaime and Bryan said that things have changed in the population now that Teresa and Anna are gone."

"It's all very recent," Elizabeth said. "The town reels from the death of popular and active students in the community. Not to mention the loss of an entire family, which was rooted here for more than fifty years."

"What about the constant bullying and harassing of students?" Grace asked. "Or what happened today on the football field? People acting like this is not normal behavior for what is supposedly a peaceful town."

Elizabeth looked at Sean, and both of them looked at John. "I will look around," the younger Guardian said.

"Yes, you will," Sean said. "I got you a job at the school."

"What?" John asked, almost choking on his last bite of meatloaf.

"You're the new computer teacher," Sean said. "Unfortunately, I have the gallery to open, and Elizabeth will be running the vineyard."

"It's just a temp job," Elizabeth said, reassuring the young man. "We need another set of eyes while we figure our footing in town."

"When do I start?" John asked.

"A week from now," Sean said as he started picking up the dishes. "In the meantime, take a look at the news feed. Maybe your brain can see something that we missed."

"Okay," Elizabeth said to the girls. "This is your first night out alone. I want constant communication with me. I'll monitor from here until you return."

"When do we train?" Grace asked. "I'm itching to try the new gym."

"It depends on when you finish your homework," Elizabeth replied. "Go!"

"Wait," Grace said; everyone stopped in their tracks. They all looked at Grace as she pulled out a small wooden box and gave it to John. "This was the last request from Teresa and Anna," the dark-eyed demon hunter said. "It seems to be a puzzle box, but we played with it last night, and we couldn't get it open."

"Did you try breaking it?" John asked as he inspected the small artifact.

"I did," Nikki said. "Almost broke my hand with it."

"I'll look into this," John said as he focused on the item.

"One last thing," Nikki said, making everyone look at her. "Can you do some digging on a demon that goes by the name of Solas?"

"The dark-skinned, blue-eyed demon?" Elizabeth asked.

"Who?" Sean asked.

"A demon who helped Nikki and Izzy a couple of nights ago," Elizabeth explained.

"Okay," John said. "When you say dark skin, do you mean Brent-style dark skin, or something more supernatural?"

"He looks human," Izzy said. "But he is a demon. His eyes flicker as if they're of blue flame. He was a short sword that is engulfed by blue fire as well."

"Sounds like he's part of the fallen order," John said.

"Fallen order?" Elizabeth asked. "Like Daristos in New York?"

John nodded. "It would be the first time I hear of a fallen-order demon so close to human beings without destroying them," John said. "Let alone a demon hunter. You said his name is Solas?"

Nikki nodded. "He also said that Teresa and Anna knew him. That he had worked with them before."

"Without the Guardians knowing?" Sean asked, seemingly upset.

"Okay, girls," Elizabeth said, trying to move things along. "Get your homework done, or else no gym tonight. Go!"

The girls hurried out, leaving John, Sean, and Elizabeth alone. Sean was visibly disturbed. One of the things he hated was being in the dark with a lack of information sharing. It made him feel as if he was tied up. "Demon hunters hide things from the Guardians all the time," Elizabeth said. "It is a symptom of lack of trust. You react badly to something, and the girls are going to be afraid to share."

Sean thought for a moment but let it go. When it came to treating demon hunters, who better to understand than his wife? The older man looked at John, who focused on the puzzle box in his hand. "Any ideas, John?"

"Interesting puzzle," John noted. "I have homework of my own, I see." The young man then turned toward the older couple. "Are you going to tell me now why I am here? I assume both of you wanted to say it at the same time."

Elizabeth and Sean looked at each other, agreeing to tell the new Guardian the plan. "Most Hellspots require one demon hunter," Sean said. "At the most, two."

"This is the only one that we've put three in," Elizabeth said. "After Teresa and Anna's passing, I felt the urge to protect this place at all costs."

"So you sent in your big guns," John said. "What has this got to do with me?"

"You're part of the arsenal," Sean said. "You're by far the most qualified Guardian to be looking over this place."

"But I have zero time on the field," John protested. "Clara and Joy would be more efficient out there in the middle of battle."

"We have the strength in the field," Elizabeth said. "We need you in the back end, supporting this area."

"You being in Ireland, you had your attention on too many spots," Sean said. "We need you to focus on one spot alone."

"And you played the odds game," John said, understanding the situation. "The probability of something transcendent happening here far outweighs it happening in another part of the world."

Elizabeth and Sean nodded as John stood up. "Don't

worry," John said. "I'll help you keep the girls safe. I owe that to Angela. Is there anything else?"

"There is," Sean said as Elizabeth looked at her husband intriguingly. "Izzy had a nightmare."

"She didn't mention anything to me," Elizabeth said, trying to hide the hurt in her voice. It wasn't the first time Izzy hadn't come to her first, but it always stung a little.

"It was about me," Sean said, looking at his wife. "It seems she saw me die, and a demon took over my body."

Elizabeth felt a chill run down her spine as she looked at Sean. Both husband and wife knew what the other one was thinking, but they didn't say it out loud.

"Not the first time she's dreamt that," John said, not noticing the change of mood in the room. "A common theme in demon hunters is seeing their loved ones die."

"Yeah," Sean said, turning his attention back to the younger Guardian. "The thing is that Izzy is dealing with a lot right now. With what happened in Ireland, which includes the death of the Weissers and Elsa, I can't tell if this is normal or something else."

John nodded as he observed the concerned looks on Elizabeth's and Sean's faces. "I'll keep my eyes open."

Both Elizabeth and Sean nodded as they walked away from the room while John looked at the couple, somewhat puzzled.

Elizabeth looked up adoringly at Sean. "You're in control, right?"

"I got it," Sean whispered back. "He's under control."

Saint Helena Two Vines Inn, California: September 04, 8:30 p.m.

Ian frowned at the laptop screen in front of him. He resisted developing new skills at his age, but being with an immortal vampire, he couldn't afford that luxury. He needed to be on top of his game as he focused on his reading. Sabine rested in the room next to him, and she expected results.

The laptop rang with an incoming call, drawing a smile from the older man as he pressed the green button to answer. A glint of joy reflected in his eyes as the image of a young twenty-year-old girl popped up in front of him.

"Sam," he managed to say as he looked at the young woman.

"Hey, dad," the girl said.

"How are things?" the older man. "To what do I owe this call?"

"Just wanted to surprise you," Sam said. "I passed the bar!"

"What?" Ian exclaimed. "When?"

"I got the results a few months ago," Sam said. "But I wanted to register before telling you."

"That's fantastic," Ian said with pride, but his daughter caught an ounce of sadness in his voice. "Objective clear," the older man said.

"Dad," Samantha said. "It's over. I can take your place now. You don't have to serve her anymore."

"Quiet," Ian said. "She's right in the next room. She can hear us."

It was now Samantha's face that reflected disappointment and a hint of sorrow. She looked to her side, trying to search for the words to say. In her mind, the scene had played differently from how her father had reacted at that moment.

"It's not over until she says it's over," Ian continued. "That is part of the vow."

"Then let's ask her," Samantha said as she pointed behind her father. Ian turned around to find the silky-haired, green-eyed vampire in the doorway.

"Samantha," Sabine said with a sweet voice. "I thought it was your voice that I heard."

"I just wanted to call my father," Samantha said. "I wanted to share some news."

"Yes," Sabine said. "You are now ready to practice law." Ian just lowered his head as Samantha looked at the vampire questioningly. "I've monitored your career very closely," Sabine said as she entered the room. Her stiletto heels clicked on the wooden floor as she strolled toward Ian's laptop. "Need to keep an eye on Ian's successor."

"My lady," Ian started to say something, but Sabine just gave him a look to remain silent.

"Do you think you're ready to replace your father?" Sabine asked the young girl through the monitor. "He sure wasn't when he had to take his father's place."

"I'm ready," Samantha said. She looked at her father, who spoke to her with his eyes. "I humbly ask you to take me in your service in my father's place," Samantha said, lowering her head a bit.

"Much better," Sabine said, seeing Samantha's respect toward her. "The McCallister clan has been under my protection for centuries. Are you ready to join your family's legacy?"

"My lady," Ian said. "May I say something before proceeding further with this discussion?"

Sabine walked toward the room window and peered into the night. The night called on to her to hunt. But over time, she had managed to control her primal instincts. "Samantha is over twenty years old," the vampire said. "More than capable of making her own decisions. Why would you deprive her of that luxury?"

"My daughter is still a child," Ian said. "She lacks the experience this job requires."

"Experience that only the field can provide," Sabine said. "We all learn by doing."

"My lady," Ian insisted.

"Samantha?" Sabine asked as she sat on a leather hotel chair and crossed her legs. "Do you have the information I requested?"

Ian looked surprised at the question. She turned toward his daughter on the laptop screen, who looked at him sadly. "I do have the information," the young woman said.

Ian looked shocked, while Sabine smiled. "Please go on," Sabine said. "Impress me." Sabine then turned toward Ian, who looked defeated. "Your daughter has a great intellect," the vampire said. "I had her hack The Guardian's database and get me some information. Can you share with us what you've learned?"

Ian looked at his daughter, trying to plead with his eyes. Samantha nodded as she looked at the vampire through the laptop camera. "Three demon hunters have been assigned to St. Helena. Their names are Isabella, Nicole, and Grace. They were top of their class for this year's demon-hunter gathering. They were also responsible for the events that transpired in Ireland a few weeks ago. Their Guardians are Elizabeth Somiere and Sean O'Brien. They're a married couple, dealing with the forces of darkness together for more than seventeen years. Sean is a half-breed, fully human with superior strength. Elizabeth is considered a legend to demon hunters and Guardians alike."

Ian looked shocked at his daughter's knowledge. "Anything else I should know?" the vampire asked.

Samantha looked at Sabine. "They have a new Guardian, a demonologist named John Simmons. He's prodigy-level smart."

"Smart like you?" Sabine asked.

"I hacked his systems without leaving a trail," Samantha said. "I'm sure he's not as smart as me."

Sabine stood back up and walked toward Ian's laptop. "The information you shared today does not leave this circle," Sabine said. "This is for me and me alone. Got it?"

"Understood," Samantha said.

"Okay," the vampire said as she started walking toward the entrance. "The question concerning who is under my service is simple. Your entire family is. Our agreement is explicit regarding what is needed. I need one of you at my side. The one on my side guarantees his successor, who shares the family name. In return, the McCallisters enjoy the comforts of my protection and fortune for as long as I decide to walk this cursed earth. Have I been clear on this?" Both father and daughter nodded. "Now," Sabine continued. "I hate being in the dark, so I will not let you be in the dark. My purpose is way beyond your understanding. You both have been asking the question. Why am I here? Why now? The response is simple—I'm here to make sure UrthaMal ascends."

"With your permission, my lady," Ian said, "but I don't fully understand. Only chaos of apocalyptic proportions will follow by bringing forth that demon to this plane. Humanity's existence would be at stake."

"Yes," Sabine said to the bewildered humans. "Thus, the reason this town has three demon hunters. Spilling their blood will be necessary before UrthaMal is released."

"But you've got a vow," Samantha said.

Sabine smiled. "You're a fast learner," Sabine said, while at the same time dismissing the subject. "I am also in need of the medallion of St. Helena for UrthaMal's coming-out party. Luckily I know where it is. So I am going out."

"My lady?" Ian called. "Do you need me out there with you?"

"I am an ancient one, Ian," Sabine replied. "I haven't needed anybody for centuries now. You, on the other hand, need to speak to your daughter and make a decision. Do you remain at my side? Or does she become your replacement, and you retire?" Ian lingered in silence as he looked at his young daughter on the screen. He could see an emotional shield trying to hide her naivete and fear.

Sabine peered into Ian's thoughts and smiled. The vampire turned toward father and daughter. "Even though he's not needed," Sabine continued, "I want your father to accompany me to the medallion's resting place. That will give him time to think before you engage in more dreaded conversation."

"I am ready to serve you," Samantha pleaded.

Sabine only nodded while she looked at Ian. "The day had to come one day," Sabine said to her companion. "Come on. A cold and dark mausoleum awaits me, while you ponder on your future."

CHAPTER VIII

Holy Cross Catholic Cemetery, Saint Helena, California; September 04, 11:00 p.m.

IZZY, NIKKI, AND GRACE walked through the dark graveyard with their senses at their peak while Aidan strolled behind them, giving the girls protective cover. Even with the blow they had dealt the underground demon network, the sensation of an overwhelming evil was still present in the air of the cursed town. St. Helena reeked of negative energy that propagated like a virus.

"First, we take care of the North Cemetery," John said to all the girls via their earpieces. "I recommend checking the graveyards clockwise for future incursions."

"Anything on the news feeds?" Izzy asked.

"Nothing," John replied. "I assume people are still frightened going out at night. Nothing on the police scanner as well."

Nikki stopped walking and looked at her sisters. "John," she said. "We are going to unplug you for a few minutes."

"Why?" John asked, not understanding.

"Girl talk," Nikki answered.

"I don't think that's a good...." John started saying before Nikki turned off her earpiece. She signaled both Grace and Izzy to do the same. The demon hunters obliged, looking confused at their red-headed sister.

"Do you think it was a good idea to tell our Guardians about Solas?" Nikki asked.

"The way Mom handles things," Izzy said as she looked at Grace. "She and Dad would have found out eventually."

"Never trust a demon," Grace said. "Even though they may act friendly, it's always with some ulterior motive."

"I think he's legit," Nikki said. "There was something in his voice when I mentioned Teresa and Anna. He's mourning them, and I think he does it sincerely. He genuinely looks broken-up inside."

"How would you know that?" Izzy asked, looking at her friend.

"I've seen that look in my father's and brother's eyes," Nikki said. "They've seen their share of death on the battlefield. Close friends that you're speaking to one minute, and the next they're gone."

Izzy just smiled softly at her friend. "You're not going to let this go, are you?"

"I have to give points to Nikki on this," Grace recognized. "She played that hand masterfully."

"Okay," Nikki said, stopping and sitting on a tombstone and looking at Izzy. "We have to clear the air on this now. What happened to Elsa wasn't your fault. You killed the guy responsible for this."

"Then why doesn't it feel better?" Izzy exclaimed at her friend. "Why do I feel like it's getting worse?"

"You can't push this," Grace said to Nikki. "No one can. Izzy has to deal with this on her own, and you know it."

"I just want to help," Nikki said to Izzy.

"Well, you can't!" Izzy snapped, making Aidan jump. "It's not you who lost a sister! It was me!" Izzy's words stung Nikki hard, and Izzy noticed. For a brief moment, she could see the hurt in the redhead's eyes. "I'm sorry," Izzy whispered. "Both of you have lost loved ones. I don't know how to deal. And I hate this. I hate not being able to deal with all of this. It seems that I'm just going through the motions. Yes. We won against Dante and his plan. We won that day. But now, with everything stopped, the reality that she's gone feels like a punch in the gut."

Nikki looked defeated. Izzy's words had hurt, but Grace was not about to give up on this. "There is nothing that can be said to make this better," Grace said. "You killed the vampire who killed Elsa. You stopped his plans. That will not bring Elsa back to life. All we can do now is continue doing what we are born to do. Take your time to deal. You can count on us for whatever you need during this."

Izzy looked at Grace and Nikki, who still looked hurt, but managed to agree with her dark-haired counterpart. "Whatever is coming, we can take it," Nikki said. "Just stop blaming yourself for everything. It's not cool."

"What about you two?" Izzy asked her sisters. "I just saw you two fighting a dark presence with red eyes in a dream."

"Fighting?" Nikki asked with a sad smile. "Or did you see our asses getting kicked?"

"That was my point of view," Izzy said. "What was yours?"

"I saw you trapped by your evil twin," Grace said. "I was trying to help you when I saw this red-eyed demon fighting Nikki. I tried to fight it, but it just threw me out of the way." The raven-haired demon hunter looked at Nikki. "It wanted you," Grace said.

"Yeah," Nikki said, stretching. "I sensed that as well. Did you feel a familiar vibe with this demon? Like we're all connected with her."

"Her?" Izzy asked.

"She's a female vampire," Nikki said. "I perceived it."

Grace was about to say something when she felt a human presence approaching from the North. "Two humans in our perimeter."

"Humans in the graveyard at this hour?" Izzy asked. She then felt vampires start to move in the darkness. "And the vampire's got the scent. Move!"

The demon hunters started running with Aidan alongside them, allowing their instincts to guide them through the dark. They dodged and jumped obstacles, reaching two teens in the middle of the cemetery. The demon hunters recognized Jaime and Bryan.

Grace was the first to get them, seeing the young man holding a bouquet of red roses. "What are you guys doing here?" the dark-eyed demon hunter asked as Nikki and Izzy joined her. "This is not the place to be."

Bryan looked down at the gravesite near his feet. Carved in the tombstone was the name *Margaret Donahue,* along with the details of her passing, precisely one year before. Grace understood but did not diminish the fact that there was fresh human blood present in a vampire-infested region. The young demon hunter could feel vampires starting to surround them. Red eyes emerged from the darkness. "There are a lot of them," Grace warned her sisters as she instinctively put herself in front of both Jaime and Bryan. "Stay behind me," Grace instructed the human teenagers, while Nikki and Izzy covered the rear and the front.

The demon hunters did not wait long as several more pairs of red eyes started appearing in the darkness. Their humanoid silhouette was visible to the girls' keen eyesight, who pulled out their stakes, ready to battle whatever came forth. The growling sound echoed in the night as a short blonde female vampire emerged, followed by a group of 3 vampires. As if cued, several vampires started appearing, surrounding the group. "Vampires have reproduced exponentially in this town," Izzy said as two dozen demons surrounded them. They seemed different from the batch they had disposed of before, with ragged clothes and dirt all over their bodies.

"Good evening," the female vampire said. Her appearance indicated she was twenty years old when she became a vampire. "Hello, little brother," the demon said, calling out to Bryan. "Have you missed me?" Grace and the demon hunters looked surprised at the young man, as his features had turned pale. Fear and disbelief were the only emotions visible on the boy's face. "I see you haven't forgotten to visit Mom," the female vampire continued. "Aren't you going to introduce me to your friends?"

"These are demon hunters Cassius spoke of," a tall albino-skinned, white-haired vampire said.

"Indeed," the female vampire said. "I apologize for my kid brother and his manners. Our deceased mother failed to provide good form into his upbringing. The name is Brenda."

"He's not your brother," Grace said as she gripped her stake tighter.

"Isn't he?" Brenda asked tapping the side of her temple. "My memories say otherwise."

"You killed Mom," Bryan said fearfully.

"I did," Brenda said, shrugging. "I was looking for her drunk and abusive ass of a husband, and she was just in the wrong place at the wrong time."

"Well," Nikki said as she twirled her stake, ready to act. Instinctively three vampires covered Brenda from harm. "Wow," the red-headed demon hunter said. "Being part of the undead does make you popular."

"This does not concern you," Brenda said. "Bryan and his family belong to me. Leave now, and I'll consider not taking your heads to Cassius."

"Was that a threat I just heard?" Izzy asked, getting a little annoyed. A young vampire with aspirations of grandeur always got on her nerves.

"Take it as you want," Brenda said. "The boy is mine, and there is nothing..."

Brenda's words were interrupted as Nikki sprang into action, jumping and landing in front of the vampire's entourage. She staked one on the chest while kicking the second one in the face. The third bodyguard was surprised, only seeing a red blur in front of him as Nikki struck several blows across his chest. She finished the third vampire, staking him and turning him to ash. "You talk too much," Nikki said.

Izzy cartwheeled to the right as Grace covered Jaime and Bryan. Several vampires made a jump toward the humans, only to find Grace spin-kicking them in the face. "Guess you want to get dusted tonight," Grace said as she plunged her stake into a vampire's heart.

Jaime shrieked as two vampires surrounded them. Izzy ran and jumped over a tombstone, extending her leg and connecting with the head of one of the vampires. As she landed, she jumped up, delivering a fierce uppercut to the second vampire. The undead creature flew in the air, only to feel a wooden stake pierce its back. It screamed before turning to ash.

Aidan growled, jumping over the teens and launching himself into a large, muscular vampire. The wolf started tearing the demon apart as the undead screamed in pain. The sound of ripping flesh made Jaime's skin grow cold, seeing blood spurt out everywhere.

Brenda took a step back as the demon hunters dispatched the group of vampires that protected her. The teen girls moved across the small field like blurred figures as dust and ash covered the area. Grace looked up at Brenda and walked toward her with purpose, with a stake in her hand. "Are you going to let her kill me?" the female vampire said toward her living brother as she turned off her demonic features and revealed her human form. Grace stopped for a second, looking at the vampire. The demon hunter then turned her attention toward Bryan, whose conflicted face reflected his heart's internal turmoil. With ease, Nikki and Izzy dispatched the rest of the vampires, leaving Brenda alone with the demon hunters. “Bryan,” Brenda called out to her brother. “She stakes my heart, and I’m gone forever.”

Bryan tried to say something, but no sound came from his mouth. Grace ran up to Brenda and thrust the stake into her stomach. Brenda gasped, feeling the wood pierce her soft flesh. Bryan’s scream caught the vampire’s and the demon hunter’s attention. “Stop!”

Grace looked at Brenda, who had an evil grin on her face. “I know what you are,” Grace whispered into the demon’s ear. The teenaged demon hunter removed her weapon from Brenda’s gut and kicked her in the stomach, pushing the vampire a few feet away. “Just this once,” Grace said. “You’re free to go. But if you get near Bryan or his loved ones, dusting will be the least of your worries.”

Brenda grunted in pain as she stood up and looked at her open wound. She looked at Bryan and smiled. “Be seeing you, little brother,” the vampire said running back into the darkness.

Grace turned back toward Bryan, who was kneeling next to his mother’s grave. Jaime stood beside him as Izzy and Nikki looked at each other awkwardly. “Forgot to mention my sister is one of those things,” Bryan said.

Grace walked up to the boy as she looked at her sisters. The demon hunters knew well the reality of what the demon was. “She’s not your sister anymore,” Grace said.

“Sure she is,” Bryan said as he wiped the tears from his eyes and looked at Grace. “It was her voice and her looks. She just has red eyes, and her face distorts.”

Grace looked at Jaime and then knelt next to Bryan observing the tombstone. The memories of her parents' gravestone lingered in her mind while she searched for the words to say. "That wasn't your sister," Grace repeated. "What you saw is something that has taken over the likeness and memories of your sister. She carries the flesh but not her soul." Bryan looked at Grace with his teary eyes. It was the first time the young demon hunter saw innocence in his eyes. For those instants, the boy seemed like a child and not a teenager like her. "What you saw is the thing that killed your sister," Grace said.

"She has been terrorizing Bryan," Jaime said. "It's like she's obsessed with him."

"They do that," Izzy said as she knelt, patting Aidan on the side. "The stronger the bond, the stronger the fixation on the victim's family."

"That bond can be positive or negative," Nikki said. "The memory of the love you had for your sister lingers inside that demon. They despise love, and will target the object of that love. Hence your mom and you."

"She said something about your dad," Grace said to Bryan. "Is he..."

"His dad is not a good person," Jaime said.

"Stepdad," Bryan corrected. "Brenda hated him."

Grace nodded as she helped Bryan up once the young man placed the roses on his mom's grave. There was a moment of silence before the boy turned his attention to the demon hunters. "Can you help me fight this thing?" he asked.

Nikki smiled. "It's what we do," the redhead chirped.

Grace smiled at Bryan and Jaime when piercing

pain ran past her skull. "Argh," Grace groaned as she fell to one knee. The agony in her head was crippling, feeling her strength leave her as pain throbbed in her forehead.

Bryan looked in fear as he knelt next to Grace and tried to help her back up. He looked at Izzy and Grace, who both were on their knees as well, clutching their heads. "Girls!" the boy called out.

"What is wrong with them?" Jaime asked as she rushed over to Nikki and Izzy.

"It's a vampire," Nikki gasped out, trying to fight the pain. "She's in the graveyard."

"Brenda?" Bryan asked.

Nikki just shook her head feeling the pain intensify, causing her to groan in agony.

Holy Cross Catholic Cemetery, Saint Helena, California; September 04, 11:15 p.m.

Sabine slipped the painkillers in her mouth feeling the headache intensify. She took a sip of water from the bottle given to her by Ian as she walked toward the white marble mausoleum in the middle of the graveyard, sensing the older man trailing behind.

Sabine's mind was not on the human walking behind her. She could feel the proximity of the demon hunters. The ancient vampire reached the entrance of the mausoleum. The raven-haired demon inspected the front gate for a few seconds before grabbing the sides and unhinging the door from its frame. Ian watched in awe as the vampire tossed the metal entrance to the side as if it were tissue paper. Sabine's vampire eyes looked beyond the darkness as she looked down the concrete steps into the tomb. "Stay up here," the vampire said to her human companion. "We'll have company soon." Sabine then made her way down with her stiletto heels, clicking the concrete with every step. As the demon reached the lower level, she admired the carvings on the wall. In the center of the lower level was a single stone sarcophagus.

Sabine smiled upon seeing the concrete chest. She grabbed the sides of it, only to wince in pain as smoke poured from her burned hands. The female vampire looked closely at the lid's finishings and saw catholic crucifixes and crosses engraved all over it. The vampire frowned looking at the cross at the head of the chest. Fear started overwhelming her mind and undead heart as she turned away. Looking away from the crosses, the vampire removed the lid from the tomb. She screamed in pain as her hands burned from touching the consecrated objects. Sabine looked inside to find a female skeleton with a round medallion around its neck. "Thank you, Saint Helena," Sabine whispered to herself as she pulled the circular ornament from the corpse, wincing again as it burned her hand.

The medallion had a soft blue pearl in the middle, surrounded by a thin, golden circular plate with engravings of two crosses on each side, a lightning bolt at the top, and a flame at the bottom. On the back of it, the Latin writing revealed the text "*Faith, Hope, and Love.*" The vampire slipped the medallion over her neck, grimacing as the metal chain burned her pale skin. The ornament itself rested on her chest, creating an oval-shaped burn mark. Sabine closed her eyes and absorbed the pain sensing the soft glow of the blue pearl. The vampire could feel the power surge through her body as the pain subsided. Soon the glow from the pearl disappeared. Sabine looked at where the burn marks should have been, but they were gone. "Excellent," Sabine said, feeling triumphant. All of a sudden, blinding pain made her gasp as she clutched her head, falling to her knees. "Dammit," the demon whispered to herself, searching inside her jacket pocket for her painkillers. She opened the lid and poured the pills inside her mouth. She chewed, vigorously ignoring the bitter flavor of the medicine. A few minutes passed before the vampire started to feel the ache in her head begin to subside. She stood up and looked at the medallion, confused at what had just transpired. "Bollocks!" Sabine exclaimed as she kicked the concrete sarcophagus in frustration. With her blow, the concrete exploded on the side, breaking the stone tomb in half. *It should have worked*, she thought to herself, trying to clear her thoughts.

"Lady Sabine!" Ian called down to her. "I may need your assistance up here!"

The vampire ran up the concrete stairs to find three vampires growling at Ian. "What is the meaning of this?" Sabine exclaimed at the fiends. Two male vampires were large, towering over six feet, five inches. The third vampire who accompanied them was a female with frizzled brown hair.

The vampires, seeing Sabine emerge from the tomb, stopped in their tracks, each falling to a knee. "Our mistake, Moroi Schulmeister," one of the tall, muscular vampires said. "We're under orders from Draco to protect you."

Sabine walked up to the strongest vampire and looked down on him. "I specifically requested not to be followed," Sabine hissed.

"We're aware," a female vampire said on the right. "But with demon hunters around, Draco didn't want to take chances."

Sabine grabbed the tallest vampire by the ear and stood him up until he towered over her. She dragged him toward Ian and forced the vampire to look at her companion. "Does this man look like a demon hunter?"

"No," the vampire whimpered as Sabine released him, watching him crumple down to the floor.

Sabine slowly walked toward Ian. "Go back to our place," Sabine ordered the human. "I don't want you here for what's about to happen."

Ian nodded as he ran away, while Sabine walked up to a white chest tomb next to the mausoleum she had just broken into. The older vampire sat on it and looked at the vampires while she crossed her legs. "Ready for today's lesson?" she asked the three minions, who all had confused looks on their faces. "This is why they sent you, right? Well, here is your chance." The vampire then pointed behind them as the three demon hunters appeared, followed by two human teenagers and a black and white wolf.

Izzy looked at the female vampire sitting on top of the chest tomb. She felt this strange aura, not like other vampires she had faced. The brown-haired girl looked at Nikki, who had a casual look on her face, as if she didn't have a care in the world. Grace, on the other hand, was covering Bryan and Jaime from harm. Izzy could see Grace was calculating their odds.

"Wow," Nikki said, breaking the ice. "First time a vampire doesn't blindly attack us. Kind of refreshing."

"Not my first run-in with demon hunters," Sabine said, shrugging a bit. "It is my first time with demon hunters stupid enough to walk with civilians while hunting the undead. What happened to the old demon hunter motto, which was to protect the innocent?"

"On your word, Schulmeister," the larger of the vampires growled as he measured the demon hunters. The words brought a shiver down Grace's spine.

"You might as well," Sabine said, somewhat bored. "Attack."

"Get out of here!" Grace screamed at Jaime and Bryan, pushing them out of the way as the three vampires launched themselves at them. Nikki intercepted the tallest vampire, striking two hard punches to his chest, bringing the massive demon to a stop. The redhead jumped and spun in the air, kicking the beast on the right side of his temple. The vampire screamed as he crumpled down in agony.

The frizzy-haired female vampire tried to attack the young humans, but only found Izzy in the way. The vampire growled at the demon hunter, who dodged and blocked her attacks. As the female vampire kicked high, Izzy went low, doing a foot sweep and bringing the demon down. Izzy plunged her stake into the creature's heart, making her combust to ash.

The second-largest vampire reached out to Grace, only for her to get close and thrust her stake into the beast's chest. The vampire groaned as he combusted into ash. Grace wasted no time making sure Jaime and Bryan were out of harm's way. They hid behind a tombstone while Izzy jumped over to help Nikki with the taller demon.

"Bored now," Sabine said as she stood up and squared off against Grace. The raven-haired vampire attacked, moving fast with precise punches and kicks. Grace was amazed at the vampire's speed. She had difficulty blocking the hard strikes as the onslaught made her step back toward the gravestone Jaime and Bryan were hiding behind. "Never bring innocents to the field of battle," Sabine said as she fired a hard, straight right-hand punch, penetrating Grace's defenses and striking the demon hunter on the side of her face.

Bryan gasped, seeing Grace get hit. The dark-eyed demon hunter regrouped and tried a sidekick, but the vampire just punched down on Grace's leg, making her grunt in pain. As the young girl grabbed her leg, the demon delivered a powerful uppercut, staggering Grace back against the tombstone. The female villain fired a straight kick that Grace managed to dodge. The strike broke the stone, revealing Jaime's and Bryan's horrified faces.

Grace recovered and ran, putting herself in front of the frightened teens. "Run!" the demon hunter exclaimed. Bryan and Jaime didn't need more motivation to bolt away.

"This is on you," Sabine said to Grace as the demon continued to attack. Sweat started to stream down Grace's temple feeling the vampire's attack speed increase. Each time she blocked an attack, the demon hunter felt as if iron bars were hitting her arms and legs. A combustion sound behind Sabine brought an ounce of hope to Grace as Izzy and Nikki ran up to help her.

As if the vampire knew, she just smiled and increased her speed, connecting with a right punch to Grace's side, followed by a left to the jaw and culminating with a spin-kick to the head. Grace grunted in agony as she fell, only seeing the vampire cartwheel out of the way when Nikki and Izzy joined the fray. "What took you two so long?" Sabine asked them. "It took two demon hunters to take down a single vampire."

Izzy helped Grace up, while Nikki measured the raven-haired vampire. "Time to stop playing," the redhead said.

"Good," Sabine said. "What are you waiting for?"

Nikki rushed the vampire, feeling Izzy and Aidan right behind her. She fired a spin-kick to the face, following a right hook and two jabs to the midsection. The vampire blocked the attacks without blinking. Izzy joined the fight, attacking from the side, trying to do a foot sweep, only for the vampire to jump out of the way while blocking Nikki's attacks. Both Izzy and Nikki started attacking the vampire with multiple blows, but the demon was too quick. Sabine blocked down on both and then jumped, spinning in the air, kicking both Izzy and Nikki in the face, making them stagger back. "Are you truly the best demon hunters the Guardians have to offer?" Sabine asked. "So far, I only see a couple of novices."

Aidan jumped toward the female vampire, only to receive a kick on the side of his body. Aidan yelped in pain, flying and crashing against a tombstone. "Aidan!" Izzy screamed as she ran toward her wolf.

Grace screamed as she jumped and fired a kick aimed at Sabine's chest; the vampire easily blocked the attack. Grace fought against the pain as she increased her speed. Her style flowed like lightning, making the vampire step back to defend. Grace attacked low, but the vampire was still one step ahead of her. It was as if she could read her moves before she made them. Sabine blocked the next attack and pushed the demon hunter back. The teenaged girl changed position instantly and attacked, trying to reach the vampire's pressure points. Sabine moved to the side and barely dodged as Grace's fingers almost got to her. Sabine did a backflip, extending her leg, her stiletto shoe connecting with the demon hunter's chin. The young girl staggered back, trying to regroup as she saw the vampire spin in the air while extending her leg and firing a spin-kick. Grace reflectively lifted her left arm to block the strike, causing Sabine's leg to hit the young girl's upper extremity with brutal force. A loud crack echoed in the night as Sabine landed gracefully.

Grace grasped her upper arm as the pain registered in her brain, and tears started pouring from her eyes. She screamed felling to her knees, clutching her broken limb.

Izzy looked in horror, seeing the raven-haired vampire stand over Grace. She turned her attention back to Aidan, who was breathing. Izzy's hands touched her wolf's side. She was somewhat relieved that she didn't feel broken bones, but she could detect severe bruising on her pet. The animal tried to get up, but had an ugly limp on him. "Stay out of this," Izzy instructed.

The wolf limped away from the battle as the brown-haired demon hunter quickly ran up to Grace. She and her sister looked up in fear at the vampire, who hadn't even morphed into her demon form. To the untrained eye, a human had just beaten Grace down. "I am severely disappointed," the vampire said as she placed her arms behind her back. "I expected more from you three."

Nikki jumped fast and fired a right hook, striking the vampire in the face. Izzy gasped in awe, seeing Nikki move that quickly. The blow staggered the vampire as she spat out blood. "Get out of here!" Nikki ordered Izzy and Grace, as the vampire cleaned the blood from her mouth.

"We're not leaving you to fight this!" Izzy said.

"You should," Sabine said as her face morphed into her vampire features. Her fangs grew, and her green eyes turned red. "Now, I have to destroy you." The vampire fired a hard right hook at Nikki, connecting with the redhead. Nikki flew to the side, her body cracking a tombstone due to the impact.

Izzy looked in horror at the vampire who was decimating them as she slowly walked toward her. She rolled out of the way just as Sabine kicked toward her face. The young demon hunter stood up, only for Sabine to stretch out and grab her throat, lifting Izzy off her feet. The vampire scrutinized Izzy's face as she observed her features from side to side, while holding her a foot off the ground. "I see now why your sister hates you," the vampire said. "You live this comfortable little life with your parents, feeling their love and protection, and yet you bitch and whine about loss and grief. What do you know about losing something when you have everything, and she has nothing? When she has lived in hell, and you have lived in paradise. You're a pathetic little girl drowning in fear over death. How sad." Izzy tried to process the information the vampire was revealing, but her mind was fading. The young demon hunter reached inside her jacket, pulling out a crucifix and shoving it in the vampire's face.

Sabine screamed upon seeing the holy object, releasing Izzy from her grip. She staggered back, trying to look away. The demon saw Grace throw a glass canister at her. Sabine lifted her arm to defend herself, just as the glass flask shattered against her arm. Holy water started to burn the vampire's arm as she screamed in agony. Nikki jumped from out of nowhere, striking the vampire on the face and chest. The red-headed demon hunter pulled out a stake and tried to thrust it into the vampire's chest, only for the demon to grab Nikki's wrist. "You're going to pay for that," Sabine growled as she twisted the girl's wrist painfully. Nikki gasped in pain, dropping her weapon. The vampire then violently punched Nikki on the side of her face, making the demon hunter spit blood across one of the graves. Her eyeglasses flew to the side, shattering against a stone tombstone. The vampire then kicked the young redhead in the chest, launching her several yards away.

Izzy tried to attack, but the vampire quickly moved out of the way. The demon grabbed Izzy by the back of her neck and smashed her head over a concrete tombstone, breaking the stone. Izzy's headache intensified as she clung to consciousness and fought to stay awake. The young demon hunter could feel a stream of crimson liquid running down the side of her head. The demon flipped Izzy over to look at her. The vampire had a stake in her hand and plunged it into

Izzy's left shoulder, where her clavicle and scapula met. Izzy screamed as the stake pierced her flesh and stuck right into her old wound. The vampire then kicked her in the face, drawing out more blood from her mouth and causing her to collapse to the grassy ground. Izzy groaned in pain as she saw the vampire grab Grace like a rag doll by her broken arm and fling her toward an old tree trunk, breaking the wood with the young demon hunters' body.

"That's it," Nikki said as she charged the vampire.

"Wait," Izzy whispered with a weak voice as she saw her sister charge the demon while she tried to get up, but was unable to.

Sabine received Nikki's onslaught head-on, blocking the best attacks Nikki had. "What are the Guardians teaching now?" the vampire said as she stopped and countered with a hard right to Nikki's stomach. Nikki spat blood from the blow and looked at the vampire with fear in her blue eyes.

"Are you going do something?" the vampire asked the read head. "Or just stand there and bleed?"

Izzy watched in horror as Sabine moved fast, punching with a left and right across Nikki's face, staggering the young teen. Nikki tried to counter, but her attacks were becoming slower, as Sabine demolished the young girl's body with strike after strike, making her step back toward the open mausoleum. Nikki tried to kick, but Sabine dodged and grabbed the girl by the back of the neck, smashing the young girl's head against one of the stone pillars that held the mausoleum upright. Nikki fell to her knees, defeated, as her blood streamed down the stone pillar. "Rule number one of demon hunting," the vampire hissed at Nikki exposing the young girl's neck. "Don't die."

"Stop!" Izzy pleaded, on her knees, looking at her battered friend.

Sabine's features turned back to her human self as she looked at the brown-haired girl. "Are you begging for her life?" the vampire asked holding Nikki by the throat. The vampire looked back and saw Grace trying to crawl toward them, unable to get up. "This is the first time I've seen a demon hunter do that. Most of them accept their fate and just die. Why should I spare her life?"

"I..." Izzy stammered.

"Say it!" Sabine ordered.

"I can't lose my friend!" Izzy yelled back. "Please! You won!"

"This isn't about winning," Sabine said as she looked at Nikki, who had now passed out. Blood streamed from the side of her head, covering half of her face with a crimson mask. "It's about teaching you girls a lesson."

"Sabine!" a male voice called out from behind Izzy. Izzy turned around, seeing Solas walk up to them. "That's enough! Let them go!"

"A demon comes to bark orders at me?" Sabine asked, almost amused. "This does not concern you, Solas. I'm still in a school session with these ladies." Sabine then picked Nikki up over her head and smashed the demon hunter across the concrete sarcophagus, next to the mausoleum. To Izzy's horror, Nikki went right through the stone as it exploded from the impact, rubble and dirt covering her. Grace looked helpless as concrete and soil engulfed Nikki's body as the tomb swallowed her. "Here ends the lesson," Sabine said with a calm voice as she walked away from her defeated foes. "Be seeing you, girls."

Solas ran toward the broken rubble Nikki was under as Izzy and Grace crawled toward their fallen sister. Izzy's eyes started to tear up seeing Bryan and Jaime pop out of their hiding spot and try to help Grace up. Grace winced in pain cradling her broken arm with her other hand. The brown-haired demon hunter saw Solas move the crushed stone away, revealing Nikki's injured and unconscious body. Blood streamed from the side of her head as well as the side of her mouth. Izzy's hand trembled as she turned on her earpiece. "We need help!" Izzy stuttered as Aidan limped to her side.

"Izzy?" John answered over her earpiece. "What's wrong?"

"John!" Izzy said. "Send Mom and Dad! Nikki is down!"

CHAPTER IX

Guardians' Home, Saint Helena, California; September 05, 11:55 p.m.

JOHN PACED IN THE second-level living room as he waited nervously for news. Izzy's frightened voice echoed in his mind, fearing the worst as memories from his past came forth. The words every Guardian dreaded rang in his mind again and again as the SUV pulled in the driveway. John saw a small crowd get out of the vehicle and move toward the main entrances as he prepped himself emotionally for what he was about to see. The young Guardian heard the front door swing open, and steps followed. John opened the door to Nikki's room just as Sean ran up the stairs with Nikki's limp, broken, and unconscious body in his arms. John's heart started beating rapidly as the older Guardian placed the teen on her bed. The young doctor looked and saw Elizabeth on top of the stairs, just nodding at him. John nodded back as he went to work, opening his medical bag. He examined Nikki's body, listening to her heartbeat and breathing. Everything seemed stable.

Sean stepped away, letting John do his thing. The older guardian walked out of the room, only for Elizabeth to bury her head in his chest. A mixture of emotions ran through Sean as he tried to comfort his wife. The man had seen demon hunters take damage in the line of battle. He had seen his fair share of death and despair, and it wasn't something an average person could get used to under any circumstance.

Sean kissed his wife on top of her forehead as he took her hand into his own. He then led the blonde demon hunter down the stairs, letting John work on what he knew best. As the older Guardians reached the lower-level living room, Sean took a second to assess the people around him. Izzy sat on the couch with a blank stare and dried-up blood on the side of her face and her upper chest. Beside her was Grace, with her left arm in a sling. Right next to them were two teenagers, a boy and a girl whom Sean assumed were Bryan and Jaime. Finally, looking out the window was the dark-skinned demon named Solas.

"Okay," Sean said as he looked at the group. "John is tending to Nikki. While we wait for him, let us start from the beginning. Why were two teenagers in the graveyard tonight?"

"That's my fault, sir," Bryan said, standing up. "I dragged Jaime into this."

"By what my wife tells me," Sean continued, "you are well aware of what goes on in this town and what we do. I'm not a fan of civilians being out there, especially if they know what goes on and crawls in the dark. Is this exciting for you? Are you looking for thrills in the night? Are you one of those kids that think this is one fun and crazy adventure?" As Sean spoke, he let his anger boil a bit, making his voice rise gradually.

"No, sir," Bryan said, his voice trembling.

"It wasn't our intention to get in the way," Jaime said. "We try to help, and stay out on the sidelines. That was Anna and Teresa's rule."

"A vampire defeated our demon hunters today," Elizabeth said seriously. "Was it because they were trying to protect you?"

Bryan and Jaime looked down at the floor, unable to say anything.

"It wasn't their fault that this happened," Grace spoke up, wincing a bit. "We did what we were supposed to do. We fought for those who couldn't fight for themselves."

"We're not blaming them," Sean said. "I want them to understand that civilians in the middle of a battle brings avoidable risks. People get hurt. People die because of this."

Sean was about to continue when he heard John walk down the stairs. Izzy and Grace looked up to see the young guardian remove his latex gloves. "Nikki is hurt badly," he said. "But she's recovering. Her body is healing itself as expected. It's a waiting game now."

"I should call her father," Elizabeth said as she stepped away from the group.

As the blonde demon hunter left them, Sean walked up to Solas. Izzy braced herself as Solas turned around, ready to face the older Guardian. The Guardian and demon faced off, being the same height and almost the same build. "What are you doing here, Solas?" Sean asked.

"Fulfilling a promise," Solas said.

"Bullshit!" Sean exclaimed. "I know you! I know what you're capable of doing! Your only interest is yourself!"

"Demons can change," Solas said, not backing down. "I'm not the same monster you met three hundred years ago. I've changed. Just as you have."

"Tell me what happened," Sean said as he backed down and slowly walked toward John.

"Vampire," Izzy said as she leaned back into the couch. "I've never seen one that strong. Not even Dante."

"She's an elder one," Grace said as she winced in discomfort, holding her broken arm. The dark-eyed demon hunter was processing the pain a lot better than she had in the previous weeks. "She's *Moroi Schulmeister*. The Vampire Schoolmaster. My dad always thought she was a male vampire."

"Do you know her?" Izzy asked Solas, who was standing back at the window. "She seemed to know you quite well."

"I've run into Sabine a couple of times," Solas said. "First time I've seen her fight demon hunters, though. She's always been a monster who operates behind the scenes."

"I don't get it," Grace said, shaking her head.

"What don't you get?" Sean asked.

"Sorry to interrupt," Bryan said, raising his hand. "Just wanted to clarify that we're not familiar with what you guys know."

"What's an elder one?" Jaime asked.

"An elder one is an ancient vampire," Grace said. "Vampires are normally immortal, unless they meet the end of a stake, or beheading, or holy water, or sunlight. Ancient vampires have walked the earth for millennia and are a testament to immortality."

"You mean to say this female vampire has walked the earth for more than a thousand years?" Jaime asked.

"More like two thousand," Grace said as she stood up. "No way to be sure. These vampires are not like the common ones. They live in the shadows, manipulating the darkness."

"How do you know so much about them?" Bryan asked.

"Her father studied the elder ones," Izzy said. "Right before one of them put an end to his life and the life of her mother."

The comment made Jaime and Bryan shut up. They realized at that moment that they were in way over their heads. Grace turned toward Sean as she spoke. "Elder vampires leave no one alive," Grace said. "They strive to keep their identity a secret. Their goal is to live in absolute obscurity."

"Sabine let you all live for a reason," Sean said. "Like Neil did with you."

Grace looked down at the floor and then at Izzy, who looked confused. It seemed Sean and Grace were on the same page regarding Sabine's purpose with them.

Abandoned Wine Cellar, Saint Helena
Outskirts; September 06, 1:30 a.m.

"I don't understand," Cassius said, trying to control his anger and confusion. He looked at Sabine, who only stared into UrthaMal's eyes. "You left the demon hunters alive?" Cassius asked. "You had them. You defeated them, and yet they still draw breath."

"They do indeed," Sabine said.

"I fail to understand why you are in charge instead of her," UrthaMal said. "She's the only one making sense in all of this."

"May I remind you that you are both guests in my home?" Cassius said, losing his patience. "My clan provides support and security. Without us, your plans don't come to fruition."

Sabine shook her head, somewhat tired of being surrounded by incompetence, just as Draco entered the room. The elder vampire looked at the tall enforcer and walked up to him. "How did my security do against the demon hunters?"

Sabine asked Draco, "Can you ask them?" Draco was about to answer when Sabine fired a straight punch into Draco's stomach, bending him over. As he fell over on his hands and knees, Sabine grabbed him by the neck and pushed his face down so he could see the ash on Sabine's black stilettos. "Ask them!" Sabine ordered as Draco helplessly looked at the ash. The older vampire released her prey and looked at Cassius. "You and your clan would be dust if I didn't do what I did," Sabine said.

"I fail to understand," Cassius said.

"She injected fear into them," UrthaMal said as she looked at the ceiling. "Fear extinguishes hope. And hopelessness feeds me." UrthaMal's body emitted a purple reddish glow as energy seeped out of her fingers and found its way into the ground. "My power is growing. But I still need more to be free."

"Keep doing what you're doing," Sabine said to UrthaMal. "Soon, you will ascend." Saying that, she motioned for both Cassius and Draco to walk out of the room with her. As soon as the vampires were outside, Sabine looked at the two demons before her. "What's better than a dead demon hunter?" she asked both of them.

"I can't think of anything better," Draco murmured.

Sabine slapped him across the face, making Draco growl at her, only to find a finely manicured finger pointing at his face. "Use your brains!" Sabine said. "It's not by brute force that we win this."

Cassius looked at Sabine intriguingly and then looked at the closed door. "A demon hunter living in fear is better than a dead demon hunter," Cassius said.

"Well done, Cassius," Sabine said. "Demon hunters are trained not to fear what goes bump in the night. When the champions cower in fear, all who admire them will lose hope and fall into despair—a perfect condition for UrthaMal to regain her strength and ascend." Cassius and Draco looked at each other, realizing Sabine's plan. "Now," Sabine said. "This is where your clan can do the most good. Go out and fetch UrthaMal a few humans for her to feed. Her influence will make them easy to spot. Demon hunters are not going to trouble you."

As the orders left her lips, footsteps from the stairs caught their attention. A lone female vampire walked down and knelt before the three older ones. "Schulmeister," she said as she lowered her head. "Master Neil is at our door seeking your audience."

Sabine's eyes lit up, hearing that name. "Why didn't you bring him down to us?" Cassius asked.

"I insisted," the female vampire said. "But he asked

for Lady Sabine to walk with him on the surface. He doesn't seem interested in staying with us."

"It's okay," Sabine said. "Whatever information Neil has will be useful. Go up and tell him I'll join him at once."

The elder vampire started walking toward the staircase when she stopped and looked back at Draco, who still glared at her. "Control that temper of yours, Draco. You should focus it on someone you truly hate."

"Can't think of anyone else at the moment," Draco seethed.

"How about if I give you Ankrnot?" Sabine asked with a sly smile.

Draco's red eyes lit up as he looked at Cassius and then at the female vampire.

"I knew that would get your attention," Sabine said. "Prepare your order. You will hunt him and offer him to UrthaMal."

Draco strolled toward Sabine and fell to one knee, looking at the ancient one. "It will be done, my lady."

"Atta boy," Sabine said as she walked up the stairs.

*****

Ian wiped the dust off the SUV as he looked at the elegantly dressed vampire in front of the buildings. His appearance was that of a young man in his early twenties, but judging by how other vampires looked at and revered him, he was far older. His demeanor imposed a certain amount of respect. The older man turned his attention back at the car, his thoughts on his daughter. She had no idea the job entailed saying goodbye to the sun. He dreaded the moment his daughter would replace him. But like all things in life, it was inevitable. "Of course it's inevitable," Neil said as he looked at the old man.

"Privacy means nothing to the undead?" Ian asked in a curious tone, more than a challenging one.

"Not all of the undead have the same gift," Neil said as he strolled toward the human. "But some thoughts are easy to grasp, especially if they're skin deep. Your love for your daughter is evident, and that is what betrays your mind. The more you rebound an idea in your head, the easier it's for us to grab it and manipulate it."

"So, that's how it works?" Ian asked as he put away the wiping cloth in his pocket.

"More or less," Neil said. "Although Sabine has honed her skill to an art form. That's the price you pay while you serve the immortal."

"Will my family ever be free from this?" Ian asked.

"All you have to do is ask," Neil said. "In the centuries I've walked beside Sabine, I've never seen a human who serves her held against his will. You continue here because you choose to. That same fate binds your daughter. Didn't she choose to study law to be in service of Sabine?" Ian's thoughts went back to his daughter. "Quod erat demonstrandum," Neil said as the door from the torn-down building opened, and Sabine walked out.

"Having conversations with a mortal, Neil?" Sabine said joining them. "So unlike you."

"If this mortal works for you, I trust your judgment," Neil said as he bowed and kissed Sabine's hand.

"Charmed to see you," Sabine said. She then turned toward Ian. "My friend. Please drive slowly behind us as we walk. Keep the lights off."

Ian nodded as he boarded the car. Sabine extended her arm for Neil to wrap his arm around hers. They slowly walked the streets in silence as Ian followed behind. "Care to tell me what happened in Ireland?" Sabine asked. "Messages from the clans are vague and unclear. I assume your first-hand experience in this matter will provide valuable information."

"Dark magic enhanced vampires all around the world," Neil said. "Dante used a mixture of essence from a Uroks-Nah demon, Grievous the vampire, and a demon hunter. That has fueled the strength of every vampire on the planet."

"That I understood," Sabine said. "What did the demon hunters do to counter it? There's nothing documented in their databases about the event."

"Not sure," Neil said. "All I know is that they unleashed Apocalyps from its resting place. Now a single demon hunter guards it in Ireland."

Sabine winced as a headache struck. Her knees buckled a bit as she held Neil's arm for support. The female vampire pulled a bottle of pills from her coat taking some and bitting furiously on them. "I need to know what happened," the female vampire said as the pain subsided. "It is not what Dante did that has crippled me so. It's what the Guardians did, releasing Apocalyps. That's when the headaches started. Can you find out exactly what happened?"

"I'll do my best," Neil said. "I assume that the medallion of St. Helena did not help with the headaches?"

Sabine opened her blouse for Neil to admire the relic. "The medallion is to protect me from UrthaMal's influence when she ascends," Sabine said. "I pondered the idea that it would protect me from this crippling effect that came from Ireland, but I was mistaken."

"Two unrelated mystic events," Neil said, referring to the medallion and Apocalyps. "I am surprised your mind contemplated the notion."

"I am desperate," Sabine said. "The headaches are getting worse."

"I heard what you did to the demon hunters," Neil said, changing the subject.

"Did you now?" Sabine said. "News travels fast in the underworld."

"Was it necessary?" Neil asked.

Sabine stopped and looked at Neil. "The plan still stands," Sabine said. "We need UrthaMal to ascend."

"Are you sure she's the demon you've been waiting for?" Neil asked. "What if she's not? What you did to the demon hunters could have been avoided."

"If it's not this demon, others can be," Sabine said. "What I did to the demon hunters was not avoidable. It's a means to an end. Certainly, you can agree that I should do it rather than any other enemy that they have."

"There are other ways," Neil said, looking at the sky.

"You're just upset because I hurt your favorite demon hunter," Sabine said with a smile.

"She's not my favorite demon hunter," Neil said as he looked into Sabine's eyes. "You're not the only person who has made vows. You're not the only vampire with a mission in this forsaken world."

"Interesting," Sabine said as she walked past him. "I respected your decision on taking care of the Wu

Guardians the way you did. I didn't ask for explanations. I just wanted results. Any news on The Tome?"

"We have a situation with that," Neil said. "After burning the book, the Guardians from Hawaii sent a digital copy to the demon hunters stationed here."

"The old demon hunters from St. Helena are dead," Sabine said. "The Guardian stationed back in Ireland did not record The Tome in the logs. That means the book was lost with the death of the twins, or The Guardian kept it for herself."

"The Guardian is not smart enough to keep something for herself," Neil said. "And the book did not perish with the demon hunters in the hell spot. I already looked."

"I assume you have a plan for this," Sabine said. "That book is crucial for the next step. It also contains information I would rather keep secret."

"I'll find it," Neil said. "Have I ever let you down?"

"Not in this lifetime," Sabine said. "Since the situation has become somewhat complicated, how about you and I rustle some feathers?"

Neil looked at Sabine with a knowing smile. "What do you have in mind?"

"Let's just say we'll lure out a big offering for UrthaMal," the female vampire said as she looked at the sky. "I may also get some information on what truly happened in Ireland as a bonus."

CHAPTER X

Guardians' Home, Saint Helena, California; September 06, 04:05 A.M.

NIKKI'S HEART WAS BEATING *at an alarming rate as she ran through the cave system's tight spaces. It was like a maze of rock and dirt, with no light in sight. Human and animal skeletons cluttered the ground everywhere she stepped. It was like making her way through an endless catacomb. The teenaged girl could hear the monstrous growling behind her. The smell of putrefying flesh and damp soil burned her nostrils.*

Nikki turned right, only to see a dark hall again, as the redhead tried to catch her breath but could not. The cave was collapsing. "Help!" Nikki screamed as she tried to crawl her way out of collapsing soil. The earth engulfed her. The young girl felt her heart was about to burst from her chest when she felt a hand grab her arm and pull her out of the collapsed tunnel.

Nikki took in gulps of air as she looked at her savior, seeing the elder vampire stare back at her with her shining red eyes. Sabine's raven hair floated as if it had a life of its own. "You reek of fear!" Sabine hissed. "You're no good to anyone!"

Nikki tried to crawl away, but the ancient vampire grabbed the teenaged girl by the throat, lifting her off her feet. Nikki looked directly into Sabine's eyes, seeing her red reflection. "You're supposed to protect the innocent!" the vampire seethed through her teeth. "You suck at it. You lack the strength and the will."

The fiend flung Nikki's body to the side. The teenager tumbled downhill, unceremoniously landing inside a wooden coffin. Before Nikki could utter a word, Sabine closed the lid of her tomb. "No!" Nikki exclaimed. "Stop! Please!" The sixteen-year-old started to hear soil dropping on her grave. "Get me out!" Nikki begged. "Please!"

Nikki woke violently, having difficulty breathing. She placed her hand on her chest and tried to calm down. The room didn't stop spinning as she lay in her bed. The girl was aware it was just a nightmare, but her mind replayed the scene repeatedly. Nikki sat up and tried to control her thoughts as flashes from the dream and the fight she had against Sabine crawled in her mind. The sheer power the vampire had was something she had ever witnessed. As a demon hunter, she had fought countless demons in all sorts of conditions. But this vampire had something else, and it shook the redheaded teenager to her core.

The young girl looked at her phone, which had been placed on her oak wood nightstand. She grabbed it and turned on the screen to see a single text message from her father. *Call me when you wake up,* the text read. Nikki closed her eyes and contemplated again what happened. She felt her entire body ache, and her head felt a thousand times bigger. She looked at her cell phone and started calling as the device's camera focused on her face. Nikki could see a large bandage on the side of her head. Dried blood stains on her face covered several bruises. She dreaded to hear from her father just as much as she longed for his voice. The call connected, and Nikki's father was on the other side of the video call. He looked tired, yet somewhat upbeat.

"Hey darling," Colonel Rogers said, smiling. "How's my firecracker doing?"

"I'm okay, Dad," Nikki quivered, feeling like a small child. "Just ran into a bit of trouble."

"Is that a fact?" Colonel Rogers asked. "It seems your face took on that problem head-on. Like always."

"Well, you know me," Nikki said, somewhat surprised at her father's positive reaction. "Can't figure out a better way to handle a situation."

"I assume your teammates were safe while you took on the heavy load?" Colonel Rogers asked.

"As you taught me," Nikki said, feeling a little bit better. Her father's voice soothed her fears a bit. "My wing women were safe as could be. No civilian casualties."

"I don't know if you look worse now than when we ran into that horde on the Indian sea," Colonel Rogers said, trying to remember. "You saved a couple of good soldiers and me that day."

"The difference is that I won that fight," Nikki muttered, almost under her breath.

Her comment drew a sigh from the colonel. "I'm glad you're okay," her father said. "When I got the call from Elizabeth, I feared the worst. But somehow, I knew you were fine. I can't explain the feeling. I still chewed out Elizabeth on her poor command, though."

"Dad," Nikki protested. "It wasn't her fault. She didn't have the intel. It all seemed like a normal patrol."

"I know," the colonel paused. "Just like when I send my pilots, and they encounter random enemy fire. It's part of the job we carry out for the greater good. Still, the talking down on Elizabeth was necessary. It keeps her on her toes. But that's not what this call is about." Nikki feared the worst as her dad went quiet on her. "It's about you coming clean to me. How are you feeling?" Nikki looked at the image of her father. She then noticed her left hand was shaking. The young girl tried to control the involuntary trembling but couldn't. "I see it in your eyes, Nicole," her father said. "I see you losing your edge. It's completely normal, if you ask me. I've seen my best pilots give up their wings because of a malfunctioning engine or a close encounter with an enemy. It happens to the best of them."

Nikki remained silent. She tried to contain the tears slowly dropping from her eyes. "Elizabeth gave me the option to pull you out," Nikki's father said.

"What?" Nikki cringed at the idea.

"Valid and very responsible response from a leader that has lost two of her best soldiers in the field," Nikki's father said.

"Doesn't she trust me?" Nikki asked, fidgeting with her fingers, trying to stop the shaking on her left hand.

"It's not about trust in you or not," the colonel said. "It's about giving us a choice. The choice is yours and mine. Especially yours. Elizabeth is giving you an out if you think you need it. No one is forcing you to do this."

Nikki thought for a long, hard second. Her left hand didn't stop shaking. "I can't leave them," Nikki said. "I can't leave my sisters."

The colonel nodded, silently recognizing his daughter's will. "You have a great little squad there," Nikki's father said. "Grace is a brilliant and cunning warrior. That intellect of hers is unmatched. On the other hand, you have Izzy and her big heart. You are the strength. As in any chain, your squad will fail if one of you tumbles."

"We won't fail," Nikki said, having a hard time believing her own words.

"This new enemy has made a dent in each of you," the colonel said. "You must overcome your fears and recover the lost edge before you face her again. It's all about getting back on that fighter jet. For all of you three."

Nikki smiled a bit as the shaking in her hand lessened. "Thanks, Dad," Nikki said. "You sure know what to say to make me feel better."

"Hey," the colonel said. "It's my job. If you need to talk, I'm always here. And so is your brother."

"I know," Nikki said. "I have to go now. Something tells me it's going to be a long day today."

"Keep me posted, my little firecracker," Colonel Rogers said. "I'll be waiting for your call."

Nikki hung up the phone and tried to stand up. Her sore body complained at the sudden movement. Everything hurt as the young redhead walked over to her balcony door and opened it. It was still dark out as the teenager made her way toward the handrail of the balcony. The cold floor brought a shiver down her spine. She turned around and saw Izzy playing her violin in her room with Aidan lying on the floor at her side. Grace read a book lying on her bed. Nikki turned around and looked at the property's vineyard as she closed her eyes and called to her sisters with her mind. Soon she heard both doors open and felt the warm embrace of her friends on each side.

"I guess I had you worried," Nikki said as she looked at Izzy. "Sorry you were terrified."

"It's not your fault," Izzy said as she looked at the vineyard. "The thing that is to blame has a face."

Nikki smiled and looked at Grace. "You thought you were getting rid of me that easy?" the redhead asked.

"The thought crossed my mind," Grace said. "But I've no idea what to do with myself without you causing me daily grief."

"How's the arm?" Nikki asked, referring to Grace's limb in a sling.

"Healing," Grace said. "Not as fast as I want, though. I am improving on how to deal with pain, though, so I take that on the positive column."

"Okay," Nikki said as she turned toward Izzy. "How is Aidan? I saw him take a wallop."

Izzy turned toward her wolf, who had a sad look on his face as he laid on her bedroom floor. "He's got some bruised ribs, according to John," Izzy said. "But he'll be fine. He won't be seeing action any time soon, though."

Nikki sighed. "We got our asses kicked. What now?" she looked at Izzy for an answer.

"I guess we regroup," Izzy said. "This vampire took something from us out there. We need to get that back before we face her again."

Grace nodded. "This new fear you're experiencing is the same one that Neil planted in me. I've been dealing with it for longer than I can bear."

"But you've dealt with it," Izzy said. "We need a crash course on how to deal with these vampires. The elder ones are here for a reason. We need to figure out what it is."

"What do we know from them?" Nikki asked. "The vampire said a lot of things." The redhead turned toward Izzy. "What sister was she talking about? Do you know?"

Izzy shook her head. "I've no idea," the brown-haired demon hunter said. "There are these dreams. A girl plagues them. She's vengeful and full of hate toward everyone and everything that I love."

"I don't think that falls into this picture, though," Grace said. "Sabine used all the knowledge she has on us to shake our core. Even though this missing sister is important, I don't think it's related to the elder one's presence in the town."

"If this sister exists, we'll find her," Nikki said, touching Izzy's shoulder. "But Grace is right. We have a bigger fish to fry."

Izzy nodded. "Can you think of anything about the elder ones?" Izzy asked Grace. "Anything at all?"

"They're secretive," Grace said as she paced in front of her sisters. "That's their whole point. They're exclusive. They think they're above the average vampire." The dark-eyed demon hunter flinched as she tried to use her disabled arm. "They leave no one alive, so I'm surprised we made it out of there. Especially knowing what Sabine looks like."

"Back in Ireland," Nikki said. "You said Neil was in the cave, but he didn't engage in the battle at the castle. Any idea why?"

Grace thought for a moment. "Didn't want to get his hands dirty. Not unless it's something personal and intimate. The death of my parents was like that. They knew something he wanted to keep hidden." Grace's eyes lit up. "Bryan mentioned something, though."

Izzy and Nikki couldn't help smiling. "You talked to Bryan?" Izzy asked.

"You like the boy," Nikki teased.

Grace shrugged. "I'm into down-to-earth guys. Unlike some who prefer to live dangerously, bonding with the undead."

Izzy looked at Nikki, whose cheeks had started turning red. "I knew it!" Izzy said. "You have a thing for Solas, don't you?"

"We're not talking about this right now," Nikki said, trying to redirect the conversation. "What did Bryan say?"

"He mentioned how the vampires dressed," Grace said. "Their clothes looked dirty and poorly maintained. Sabine looked different. Her clothes looked elegant, as if she has them dry-cleaned every day."

Izzy looked somewhat confused as she tried to add up the ideas. "It would seem Sabine is not staying with the pack."

"It would make sense," Nikki said. "Not getting involved, but watching from behind the scenes."

"Saint Helena is a great tourist town," Izzy said. "She could be living on the surface, renting a vineyard or a room in a hotel or inn."

"With access to dry cleaning," Grace said.

"It's a start," Izzy said. "Let's run it by my parents. After an encounter with a vampire of that caliber, I doubt they're letting us do investigations on our own."

"What do we do when we find her?" Nikki asked. "Don't get me wrong. I am all for a second round, but with this one, I think we need a little extra."

"Let's bounce ideas off of John," Grace said. "Maybe he can think of something."

Guardians' Home, Saint Helena, California; September 06, 06:05 A.M.

John Simmons entered the house with a large mug of coffee in one hand and an English muffin in the other. He walked toward the study and opened the door, revealing the massive screens with a small server plugged in. He started the gear up and took a seat in the comfortable office chair, placing his cup of coffee on the desk while he took a bite of his breakfast. The computer systems rebooted right where the young guardian had left them a few hours before. He started with a security overview of the entire property, while out of the corner of his eye, he saw his translator program going over the USB Grace and Elizabeth found. He'd had a few hours of sleep, but it was enough for him to function. The young Guardian had spent most of the night investigating all the information related to the ancient vampires. The data was scarce and vague; with little advantage, they could pull out.

Elizabeth and Sean walked into the study and looked at John. The Guardian couple were wearing workout attire, and their bodies glistened in sweat. "Are you a robot of some sort?" Sean asked. "Don't you ever stop?"

"It's a compulsion," John said as he grabbed the TV remote and turned on the morning news. He then turned toward the Guardians. "I could say the same about you," John said. "How long have you guys been working out? A couple of hours?"

"Just about," Elizabeth said as she focused on the news. "It seems it's going to be a long day." The blonde demon hunter grabbed the remote control and turned up the volume of the news.

"A developing story in town," the newscaster stated. *"Multiple crimes have been reported in the last twelve hours. A flood of calls reporting crimes ranging from theft, robbery, and murder was made to nine-one-one operators last night. Police seem baffled, as no apparent motives or patterns are present in more than a dozen crimes."*

"That doesn't seem to be supernatural," Sean said. The older man then stopped talking about what he saw on the screen. The female correspondent continued her report, but in the background, two women were fighting to the ground. Behind them, a couple of teens were kissing passionately. "That matches the outbursts at school," Sean said.

"Well," John said as he turned toward one of the computer screens. "The news feed reports school and other businesses are open as usual. Whatever is happening, it doesn't seem like the town is fully aware of what's going on."

"Thoughts?" Elizabeth asked her male counterparts. "I was hoping to do some digging around the police station. See what they know."

"That leaves John and me to hold the fort," Sean said as he looked at John. "I would like the girls to miss school today. With all that's happened, it would be better if they regrouped. Have them train here and decompress."

John looked at Elizabeth and Sean. "Okay," the young Guardian said. "I will try to cross-reference the activity in the town. Going to see if a pattern forms."

"Interesting," Elizabeth said as she moved toward her laptop and projected the underground tunnels from the town. "Can you cross-reference unusual activity in town and superimpose on our tunnel grid?" the blonde demon hunter asked John. "It would have to be the last twenty-four hours."

"With the news developing this fast, it could take a couple of hours," John said as he started his magic on the keyboard.

"What about this Elder One?" Sean asked Elizabeth. "In the centuries I've walked the earth, I've never heard of this vampire. I don't want the girls to face her unprepared."

Just then, the Guardians heard the teenaged girls walking down the stairs and enter the study. They were all dressed and ready to start the day. "Good morning," Izzy said. "I think we have a lead."

Sean looked surprised and at his watch. "So early," the older Guardian said. "Should I cook breakfast first?"

Elizabeth, on the other hand, looked concerned, seeing the battle scars on her demon hunters. "Are you sure you want to get back out there?" the blonde demon hunter asked. "You have options, you know."

"Yes," Nikki said, looking at Elizabeth. "My dad was very clear about that."

Elizabeth nodded as she crossed her arms, not

backing down. “The choice is there,” Elizabeth said. “It always is. No pressure from your Guardians or your sisters.”

Nikki smiled at Grace and Izzy. “As I said to my dad,” the redhead said. “I am not going anywhere.”

“Good,” Elizabeth nodded her head agreeing with Nikki. “Your assignment for today is to stay in and train. All three of you.”

“What?” Izzy demanded. “You’re benching us?”

“I am not risking your lives with some unknown vampire out there,” Elizabeth calmly responded.

“I am okay,” Nikki lied, trying to look into Elizabeth’s green eyes. “I can handle it.”

Elizabeth took a step forward and looked down on the girls. “You barely made it out yesterday,” the older demon hunter said. Her tone made Izzy flinch, recognizing the demon hunter general in her mom. “You made a choice. But I pull rank. And I say you’re sitting this one out.”

“We can’t risk it,” Sean intervened. “We’re aware of your skills as demon hunters and have seen you in action, so we know that you can take care of yourselves. The fact that this Sabine is not an ordinary vampire puts us all on edge. We have nothing on her other than she wiped the floor with all of you three. Whether it was intentional or not that she left you alive, we can’t expose you to her again.”

“Not only that,” Elizabeth said. “You put innocent kids in danger.”

“That wasn’t our fault!” Izzy protested. “They were already there! It’s not like we took them on the hunt!”

“You should’ve gotten them out!” Elizabeth snapped

back. She tried not to yell at her girls, but her voice sounded louder than she intended. "When you face a powerful opponent who dwarfs your abilities, you run away and regroup! You don't engage! You broke rule number two, and you almost broke rule number one in demon hunting! Not to mention endangering the lives of two innocent kids!" Grace, Izzy, and Nikki looked down on the floor, not saying a word. They knew the senior demon hunter was correct. She had earned the right to dictate terms to them. And they needed to follow those terms. "No more incursions on your own until I say so," Elizabeth continued. "If you go out at night to hunt, you go out with either Sean or me. Do I make myself clear?"

The teenaged girls nodded as Elizabeth walked out of the room. Sean looked at the girls and sighed. The girls looked up to him, not knowing what to say. "The fear in you is palpable," the older Guardian noted. "You can't hide this fear from us. It doesn't help in our cause."

"What can we do?" Grace asked.

Sean looked at the girls and then at John, who waited for an answer. "Sometimes fear is good," Sean said. "Fear keeps us on our toes. It keeps us from becoming complacent in what our job entails. It can save you girls from becoming crappy demon hunters." The older man started walking out of the room and looked back at the girls. "The trick with fear is that you can't let it consume you. You must allow it to wash over you. And when the fear passes, you'll see how it forged you." With those last words, Sean walked out.

Izzy, Nikki, and Grace looked at each other with nothing to say. The truth spoken by Elizabeth and Sean didn't bring comfort to their hearts. John pondered for a moment before he spoke. "Being defeated on the field sucks," the dark-haired Guardian said, looking at the disheartened girls. "Doubt creeps into your thoughts. You feel your confidence shattered, trying to process what happened. I know you're trying to go through this sequence of emotions as fast as you can. It doesn't work like that. It takes time."

"What if we don't have time?" Nikki asked. "What if more lives are lost while we're cowering in here?"

"You can't protect the innocent if you're dead," John deadpanned, shrugging a little. "Elizabeth and Sean have made the right call."

Nikki headed toward the far wall and leaned against it, while Grace sat on a wooden chair. Izzy just rubbed her arms, not knowing what to say. John looked at the troubled girls and smiled a bit. "Why don't you share this idea that you had?" the young man said as he started typing on the computer. "The more information we find on Sabine, the better."

The girls looked at each other with doubtful glances. "It's stupid," Grace said, feeling inadequate. She was the only one who had previously faced an ancient vampire. They were experts in demoralizing the victim's spirit. And Sabine had succeeded with a single fight.

"Hey," John said, turning back to the girls. "There are no bad ideas. What's your lead?"

"We suspect Sabine is not staying with other vampires," Izzy said. "She's staying somewhere on the surface."

"What makes you say that?" John asked as he pondered at the concept.

"Elder vampires are loners," Grace said as she tested out her broken arm, wincing a bit. "They stay away from the action and the main nest."

"Her clothes were too clean for her to be underground," Nikki said as she started pacing around the study. "She must be staying in a lodge or an inn—something near dry cleaners.

John listened to them attentively as he processed the idea. "What do you think?" Grace asked. "Can you do a background check on who has registered into town in the past two weeks?"

"Of course I can," John said as he turned toward the monitors and started typing. "Anything else you want me to look into?"

"Headaches," Izzy said as she looked at her sisters with a shocked look. "I can't believe we forgot about that. Every time we seem to be close to this vampire, we get splitting headaches."

John frowned as he looked at the demon hunters. "Could that be your instinct telling you danger is near?"

"It's not the same," Nikki said. "This vampire is connected to us somehow."

"She was in our dream," Grace added.

"In your dream?" John asked. "How? Only demon hunters can have a shared dream experience."

"This is where you come in," Izzy said. "She must have some magic element with her that permits her to invade our dream state."

"With her being an elder one," Grace said, "her access to magic potions or amulets is practically infinite."

"Okay. I'll look into that as well," John said as a list of locations appeared on the screen. "These are the locations that have seen activity with people checking in. It's a long shot, since this town is a tourist attraction for wine enthusiasts."

The girls looked at each other, surprised at the efficiency of the young man. "That was quick," Nikki said.

"I try," John replied as he got a response from the USB translation with a text box on the screen. He opened a window and frowned as he looked at the text. It was a book written in a strange language.

"What is that?" Grace asked.

"It's the contents of the USB drive you found with Elizabeth," John replied as he looked at the four-hundred-page document. "The drive was heavily encrypted. I just hope that my program didn't damage the contents of the document."

"It didn't," Izzy said with a smile as she stood next to John and looked at the screen. "It's a combination of Aramaic and Latin." Grace, Nikki, and John looked at Izzy with shock in their eyes. "It's a word salad," Izzy said, reaching for the computer mouse just as John grabbed it.

As Izzy touched John's hand, both looked at each other awkwardly. "Sorry," the girl said.

"My bad," John replied, letting Izzy take over. "Force of habit, me controlling the computer."

Izzy smiled as she maneuvered the mouse pointer and focused on the characters on the screen. "The characters are re-arranged to generate a code. You have to reverse the system to get what it says." The girl typed a few more commands and decoded the book's first line to reveal the title: The Tome.

John's face went pale as he looked at the title. "This

can't be," John said, placing his hands on his head.

"What is it?" Grace asked

"It's an ancient text," John said as he programmed Izzy's code into his software, typing furiously on the keyboard. "A text more than two-thousand-years old. Few considered it to be real."

"What does it contain?" Nikki asked.

"Legend has it that it's the first chronicles of vampires and demons documented by humans."

"Wait," Grace said. "That means that..."

"It's the first Guardian manual?" Izzy asked.

"You could say that," John said as he turned around and looked at the girls. "Do you know how the Smith twins got a hold of this?"

All three demon hunters shook their heads as Sean entered the room, freshly showered and sharply dressed. "Okay," the older Guardian said. "I will be cooking breakfast, and then we will hit the gym."

"I'll continue decrypting the thumb drive," John said as he turned toward the screens and started working. "I will debrief The Guardians in Ireland concerning the book Elizabeth and Grace found. The girls will fill you in on it."

"Sounds like a plan," Sean said. "Let's go."

CHAPTER XI

Police Department, Saint Helena, California; September 06, 9:30 a.m.

ELIZABETH WALKED OUT OF the police department, visibly flustered. Even though the front desk sergeant was friendly beyond words, law enforcement's negative aura was evident. The feeling of confusion and powerlessness was palpable, creating a foul mood in most officers and detectives. They were all living in fear, and their worst emotions were beginning to flourish. With people disappearing in every age group and the kidnapping of one of their own, tensions were high. Yet, they refused to believe something supernatural was afoot. The blonde woman pulled the strands of hair from her eyes and tucked them behind her ears as she took out her cell phone and dialed home.

"Hello," John answered on the other end.

"John," Elizabeth said. "Dead end with the police station. Other than police officers living on the edge, I have zero leads. What have you found out?"

"I went over the theory the girls had come up with," John replied. "My system pulled out several addresses that might lead to something. It seems like a long shot, but we might as well follow this to see where it takes us. I handed the list to Sean. He is training with the girls downstairs."

"Okay," Elizabeth said. "Have him follow up on that. I will be home shortly to spend some time with the girls. Anything else?"

There was a pause on the other side of the line. "It seems you and Grace found The Tome when you uncovered that thumb drive."

Elizabeth froze, pondering for a second the news John had shared. Her former Guardian, Williams, had beaten her to death talking about that ancient text. The underworld, as well as the Guardians, knew its value and significance quite well. "Are you sure it's the correct text?" Elizabeth asked. "How did it come into the twins' possession? Why didn't they share it with their Guardian or Clara?"

"Someone encrypted the file in the thumb drive," John said. "Maybe the girls didn't know what they had. How they obtained it is the question that boggles my mind. The Tome didn't fall in their lap from thin air."

"Keep digging," Elizabeth said as she reached her black vehicle. "There must be something we're missing."

"Will do," John said, hanging up.

Elizabeth boarded her SUV and started the engine when an older dark-skinned man in a gray suit approached her window. "Mrs. Somiere?" the man said.

Elizabeth was surprised at first, but then realized he must have been someone working at the police station. “Yes?” Elizabeth responded.

“My name is Ian McCallister,” Ian said, extending his hand. “I’ve read so much about you, and it’s a pleasure to meet you in person.” Elizabeth’s surprise and confusion disappeared as her demon hunter instincts were activated. She looked at the man from head to toe, measuring him. He was about six feet tall and looked human.

“How can I help you?” Elizabeth asked, keeping her guard up.

“You can take a walk with me,” Ian said. “My employer would like to have a word with the demon hunter of legend.”

“Just a word?” Elizabeth asked, getting out of her car. Ian smiled as he guided the blonde woman down the main street. Elizabeth could feel her instincts tingling, sensing two vampires near. The dark aura surrounding the demons was different from others Elizabeth had experienced before. One of them was powerful and ancient. The other one seemed to be the same, only that it vibrated on a different frequency. Suddenly a splitting headache stopped Elizabeth in her tracks.

Ian noticed Elizabeth stagger and stopped walking. “Are you okay?” the concerned man asked.

Elizabeth looked at the elder’s eyes and took note of the puzzled look in them. “I am fine,” Elizabeth said as the pain in her head subsided. “Let’s meet your employer.”

Ian continued walking, reaching a coffee shop. The store was closed down and boarded up for renovations, but the door was unlocked. “My employer said that there is no fooling you," the older man said. "There are only two vampires inside. Just so that we're fully transparent."

"I appreciate that," Elizabeth said as she opened the door. The inside of the coffee shop was dark, with tables and chairs covered in plastic. Particles of dust and wood covered every flat surface. An elegant, raven-haired, twenty-year-old woman dressed in a white suit sat in the far corner of the coffee shop while she stirred a cup of tea in front of her. A black-haired man in his twenties dressed in a crisp, dark gray suit stood behind her. There was no denying their nature. They looked young, but the energy they projected was a dead giveaway. They were a pair of ancient vampires. The female vampire's dark aura was the one that vibrated on a different level. Something was off from a regular vampire, but Elizabeth was unable to pinpoint it.

"Elizabeth," the female vampire said, looking up from her cup of tea. "It's an honor to meet you at last. Your reputation and legend are known far and wide through the underworld."

"I am familiar with that concept," Elizabeth said, measuring everything in the room, considering a possible confrontation.

"We're not here to fight," the female vampire said. "We're only here to talk. Please come and sit." As the vampire said this, she extended her pale hand at the chair in front of her.

Elizabeth's face remained emotionless. The older demon hunter measured the odds in her mind as she calmly approached the vampires. Her chances were abysmal if she needed to fight both demons.

The female vampire smiled as she took a drink of her tea. "It's okay," she said. "If we wanted to kill, you would be dead already."

As the words left her lips, Elizabeth couldn't help but feel a shiver down her spine. *Did she read my mind?* Elizabeth thought to herself.

"It's a gift from the curse of immortality," the woman said, shrugging as she placed her cup of tea back on the table.

The dark-skinned man appeared from behind the pair of immortals. He placed a cup of tea across from the female vampire. "Honey peach is your preference, is it not?" the man asked Elizabeth.

Elizabeth nodded as she sat down across from the vampire.

"Thank you, Ian," the female vampire said. "Please wait in the car. We won't take long."

Elizabeth looked into the vampire's green eyes. She was indeed beautiful in her human form. "Sabine, I presume?" Elizabeth said as she took a sip of tea. The blonde demon hunter was trying to control her thoughts. While her instinct dictated to run, her mind advised against it. She needed information.

"The one and only," Sabine said, flaunting a bit with a soft smile as she heard her name. "My companion is Neil. Grace has spoken to you about him, has she not?"

"She has," Elizabeth said, putting her cup down. "He's responsible for the death of her parents. They were fine Guardians as well."

"Death is a necessary evil, I am afraid," Sabine said. "Neil and I are burdened with that knowledge. Their death, even though tragic, was a necessity."

"I am sure they and your countless victims wouldn't share your sentiment," Elizabeth said, staring straight into Sabine's eyes, unafraid.

Sabine paused for a moment as she looked into Elizabeth's green eyes. "Your reputation is worthy of admiration," Sabine said. "Here, you sit across from a powerful vampire, while you wrestle with the thought of running away or sticking a stake in my heart."

"I've met vampires like you," Elizabeth calmly said. "Flaunting this air of superiority, underestimating what I can do."

Sabine's smile grew ever so slightly. "Darling," the female vampire said. "You've never faced someone like me. I, on the other hand, have met my fair share of demon hunters. You are the first one I've met who made it past the age of twenty, though."

"I am that good," Elizabeth said, putting her cup down.

"I agree," Sabine said. "What makes you different from the previous demon hunters is that you see things in degrees of gray," Sabine said. "You of all people should know that not everything is black and white. You think before you stake. I like that in a demon hunter."

Elizabeth tried to read Sabine. *Why does she feel so different from other vampires*? Elizabeth thought to herself. "It was pretty black and white what you did to my demon hunters last night," Elizabeth said calmly.

"They're alive, aren't they?" Sabine said. "With what they described, do you think I am someone who toys around and leaves my victims to tell the tale?"

"The question did pop up," Elizabeth said. "I assume

this meeting is related to this higher purpose in your vampire calling."

"I am not your enemy," Sabine said, looking directly into Elizabeth's eyes.

"You could've fooled me with what you did to three sixteen-year-old girls," Elizabeth said, not buying for a moment the sincerity she felt in Sabine's voice.

Sabine looked at her almost-empty cup of tea. "There's more than meets the eye," Sabine said.

"Really?" Elizabeth said. "Are you going to enlighten me, or are you just going to stare at your empty cup of tea?"

Sabine looked up at Elizabeth, and the friendly demeanor of the vampire was gone. Her facial reactions remained human, but with a scowl drawn on her face. "Why did you unleash Apocalyps?" Sabine asked.

Elizabeth froze for a moment, taken off guard by the question. Her mind tried to block the thoughts, but it was too late. Sabine planted the seed, and the memories triggered automatically. The image of Izzy entering the nightmare dimension to retrieve Apocalyps, followed by her unleashing the sword's power among all the demon hunters. The idea of her daughter holding the forbidden weapon was taken from her.

"It was Isabella," Sabine said, putting the cup of tea down. "Somehow, she linked the legacy of Apocalyps to the demon hunter line."

"Is this why you brought me here?" Elizabeth asked. "What's your endgame in all of this?"

"Not your concern," Sabine said. "People are going to die, Elizabeth. There is no stopping what's in motion. It will start tonight, and there is nothing you, your other Guardians, or your demon hunters can do about it." The way Sabine said those words brought a chill down Elizabeth's spine. Sabine composed herself and looked at Neil behind her, whose expression had not changed during the entire conversation. Sabine looked back at Elizabeth. "The demon UrthaMal is stuck between this world and the hell dimension," the vampire said. "She's feeding off of humans to gain her strength and ascend. That's why you feel this town's stench in fear. Once she transforms into her true form, nothing will stop her."

"Why are you telling me this?" Elizabeth asked.

"Because you were in the dark," Sabine said. "I hate it when my opponents are in the dark. I just love a fair playing field. Besides, you have something that I need. If you hand it over, I may consider lowering the number of human casualties."

"What do you want?" Elizabeth asked.

"The Tome," Sabine replied. "You have it, and I want it. Hand it over to me tonight in the cemetery where I demolished your champions. Eight sharp."

"I don't know what you're talking about," Elizabeth said, trying in vain to hide her thoughts.

Sabine stood up, with Neil putting a white trench coat over her shoulders. "You can't lie to me," Sabine said. "Your mind is an open book. I know where you and your demon hunters hide. Don't worry. I am not a blabbermouth, and I will keep the information to myself until I see fit. In the meantime, you will bring The Tome to me."

"What if I refuse?" Elizabeth asked, for the first time feeling a drop of fear in the pit of her stomach.

Sabine approached Elizabeth, so her green eyes stared down at hers. "I'll finish what I started with your girls," the vampire said. "And I will begin with your daughter." Sabine and Neil exited the coffee shop through the back, leaving Elizabeth alone with her thoughts and those last words lingering in the air.

Guardians' Home, Saint Helena, California: September 06, 11:30 A.M.

John Simmons tried to let the warm water from the shower wash away his worries. After decoding The Tome and going over its pages, his brain was on fire, trying to process everything he read. The usual satisfying sensation of discovering new knowledge was nowhere in his heart. Instead, fear and powerlessness crept in the pit of his stomach as the young man turned off the water. He stepped out of the bathroom of his room, taking a glance at his clothes nicely pressed on his bed. The medieval actions the Guardians committed in ancient times for the greater good bounced in his mind as he looked in the mirror while he combed his hair. "Death is a necessary evil," John said to himself, repeating a sentence from The Tome. The young man dressed in casual attire of light blue jeans and a white button-up shirt. As he got ready, his thoughts wandered anxiously about what ancient demon hunters felt two thousand years ago.

There was another factor to take into account—Elizabeth's meeting with Sabine. The blonde demon hunter had called and informed him and Sean of the situation. The fact that the vampire wanted The Tome meant the fiend was several steps ahead of them on everything. They just couldn't figure out what that was.

The young Guardian slipped on his glasses and stepped out of the guest house he was staying in, feeling the sunlight bathing the wooden deck. He walked down the wooden steps into the Vineyard Sean and Elizabeth took care of now. It was just a few acres, but enough to produce wine as one of the Guardian's many businesses. No one would suspect the small vineyard was just a cover for an organization that protected the living from the undead.

John entered the main house at the front of the property and went into the study once again. He sat on the chair and hovered the mouse over the translated text to open it when a folder on the side caught his eye. John moved the mouse and opened the digital dossier, revealing a list of video files. There were around a hundred files, all dated. John opened one that had a date from the beginning of August. The video started playing, revealing two dark screens side by side. Suddenly, a young blonde girl appeared on the right, while Elizabeth's younger sister, Clara Somiere appeared on the left.

"Clara," the blonde girl said.

"Teresa," Clara looked at the screen and seeing the young eighteen-year-old blonde demon hunter on the screen. "Just arriving from patrol?"

"Correct," Teresa said with a bright smile on her face. "Just getting in the house. Anna's getting some food; we're starving."

"A lot of vampires?" Clara asked with a worried tone.

"Vampires, and demons and..." Teresa started.

"Ooohhh my," Anna said behind her twin sister as she brought a carton of ice cream and a spoon. She had a huge smile. Like she did not have a care in the world.

"Give me," Teresa said to her sister as she took the carton and started eating while Anna grabbed the laptop.

"Nothing we couldn't handle," Anna said, fixing her hair in a ponytail. "What's new in Old Ireland?"

Clara smiled as she heard Anna`s fake Irish accent. "Nothing new," Clara responded to the question. "Getting ready for the hunter-gathering. Remember yours three years ago?"

"Awesome times," Anna said, laughing. "Remember when Alex shot his crossbow accidentally and almost hit Sean in the butt?"

Clara laughed out. "You should be ashamed," Clara mocked. "He's a senior Guardian."

"Too brooding," Teresa said. "He's married to the love of his life, has a sweet daughter, and yet every day it seems it's the end of the world for him."

"Don't you let them hear that," Clara warned while she laughed. "He hates it when you call him out on it."

"We know," Anna and Teresa said at the same time and started laughing. "Will you be delivering the new demon hunters to this Hell Spot?" Teresa asked. "We would love for you to come."

"Yeah," Anna said. "Even if it is not Guardian business. You can come down and shop with us and talk about Teresa's boyfriend."

"Anna!" Teresa said, punching her sister in the arm. "No one means no one."

"It's Clara," Anna said, getting serious for a moment. "She's cool."

"Boyfriend?" Clara inquired. "Do tell."

"Nothing to tell," Teresa said, blushing a little with a bit of embarrassment.

"Oh, Oh," Clara said with a knowing smile. "I've seen those eyes before. Spaced-out, dreamy-looking eyes."

Teresa's face got even redder while Anna grew quiet. "You should see him, Clara," Anna said, trying to hide her emotions. "He's a six-foot, heaven-made, bald, blue-eyed football player."

Teresa punched her sister's arm. "He's not a football player," Teresa stated. "He thinks it's a pastime for kids."

"For kids?" Clara asked, a little bit concerned. "He's older?"

"Much older," Anna said. "Centuries older."

"Anna!" Teresa exclaimed. "Clara... It's not what you think..."

"What am I thinking?" Clara asked.

"He's not a vampire," Teresa defended herself.

"That was a bit cliché for you," Anna teased. "You had to top that."

"Anna!" Teresa exclaimed, getting exasperated with her sister's antics.

Clara smiled and was about to say something when something off the screen caught her eye. Clara turned her attention back to the camera, "Girls," Clara called. "It's late. Get some rest, and I'll talk to you tomorrow. I want to hear more about this mystery guy. After stopping the impending end of the world, I'll arrange a social visit."

"Cool," Anna said. "Promise?"

"I promise," Clara said. "Good night, and take care."

"Bye, Clara," the twins said simultaneously as the video came to an end.

John closed the video file and thought for a moment about what he saw. He was about to open the last file on the list when Elizabeth's voice interrupted his actions.

"Is that the only video you've seen?" the blonde demon hunter asked.

John twirled around, seeing Elizabeth at the entrance of the study. She stood there with her arms crossed and a concerned look on her face. "Yes," John answered as he turned back toward the monitors. "I was about to continue reading The Tome when the video list caught my eye. Did you know about that conversation?"

Elizabeth entered the study and stood next to John as he opened the last file on the list. "Clara told me she was always talking with the Smith twins," she said. "I didn't know the twins were recording the conversations."

"It wasn't the twins," John said. "The file stamp has Anna's name on it." John opened the following file and saw one of the blonde twins pop up. She looked tired but alert. She seemed to be alone in her room.

"It's August fourth, and we just arrived from patrol," Anna said. "Teresa is in bed, so that gives me time for this recording. We did some reconnaissance again on the gate for the hell spot. It all seems set. Joy and Teresa are hopeful that we have the bases covered. I still have my doubts. Something lingers in the back of my head, driving me crazy."

The blonde demon hunter took a drink from a cup next to her laptop. "Solas and Teresa have been going out hunting on their own for three months now. I see him trying to help. I sense he has genuine feelings toward Teresa, but something is off with him. I can't fully trust him. The fact that Teresa has kept her relationship with him a secret from Joy and the other Guardians doesn't sit right with me. I've tried talking to her, but she just shrugs me off. My sister tried to shrug me off again and wanted me to cover the warehouse in the south while she and Joy took the gate on their own. Joy told her she was crazy. After Joy left, Teresa explained that Solas would make a better partner on the field than me. I wanted to slap her, but she said something about wanting to come clean with Joy without compromising the warehouse. After yelling at her face for having Solas in her head too much, she finally accepted that these were not the best conditions to come clean about that relationship."

There was a slight pause before Anna continued. She seemed to be reflecting on something before she spoke. "The thought of me being jealous has crossed my mind. But my distrust for this demon pretending to be good just tugs too much on my instincts. I think Teresa is too much in love to see it. I hope he is legit, and his feelings are pure. If they're not, and he is using Teresa, no hell will compare to the torment I will put him through."

The file stopped there. John looked at Elizabeth, who just stared at the video, seeing one of her demon hunters' memories. "I don't know what to do," Elizabeth admitted to the younger Guardian as she sat on the wooden chair put aside, placing her head in her hands, trying to process everything that was going on. "These are private memories. Like a diary. Why did she leave this here? What was her intention?"

"You knew her," John said. "You groomed her to be one of the best demon hunters on the planet. What does your instinct tell you?"

Elizabeth nodded as she wiped her eyes that had become teary. "Send the last video to the girls, to their phone," Elizabeth said. "Explain how you found it. Then encrypt the rest and set up a private server so I can review the files one by one."

"Will do," John said as Elizabeth composed herself. "The girls are downstairs training while Sean is checking out the addresses we pulled out. No luck on that front."

"Okay," Elizabeth said. "Have you told the girls about my meeting with Sabine?"

"No," John said. "I assume you have some reassuring words for them after meeting this beast."

Elizabeth slowly shook her head. "This vampire is something else," she said. "I've faced all types of master vampires. None compare to her demeanor and posture, so I've got nothing."

"What is she like?" John asked.

"I don't know where to begin," Elizabeth said. Her worried voice put John on edge. He considered Elizabeth the best demon hunter ever, and having her concerned about a vampire didn't seem right.

"She's not all-powerful," John said, trying to make sense of the little information they had. "She needs The Tome. That means Sabine needs us for something. She also asked you about Apocalyps. Could she be another vampire in search of the sword?"

"I don't think so," Elizabeth said. "She was more interested in why we unleashed Apocalyps. What did you find out? Did you read The Tome?"

"I did," John said with a frown on his face as he opened the document. "The actions of the first Guardians and demon hunters are troubling."

"How so?" Elizabeth asked.

"They showed no remorse in sacrificing human life for the greater good," John said. "The Guardians of old considered human life worthless. They instilled that thought into their demon hunters, making it easier for them to sacrifice their lives for the greater good."

"It's that bleak, huh?" Elizabeth asked.

John shook his head. "It just hits you hard when you contrast what we do today. We measure the success of every incursion on how few civilian casualties we lose. In the past, that was irrelevant. Take out the demons no matter the cost of human lives."

"I'm afraid to ask details about what took place," Elizabeth said.

"They were atrocities, Elizabeth," John said. "The first Guardians bound a monster from hell into a human girl to create the first demon hunter. According to The Tome, these men and women dabbled in dangerous dark magic, implying blood pacts, human sacrifices, and other barbaric acts."

"I am going to regret asking for examples," the blonde demon hunter said.

"There are several," John said. "The one that stands out is the sacrifice of the town of Atribates. Demon hunters led an ascended demon into the village. While the monster ravaged the men, women, and children, The Guardians bound the beast, using the souls of the dead, and cast it down to hell."

Elizabeth was stunned by what she just heard. She knew The Guardians were vicious in their actions, but she could never imagine taking it that far. "Is that our legacy?" Elizabeth asked. "This is where we come from?"

"We have improved," John said. "You were the catalyst for something better. But the dark past can't be denied. The legacy of darkness surrounding the demon hunters and the Guardians will haunt the organization long after we are gone, even if our current motto is to protect the innocent. Yes, we protect those who can't fight the forces of darkness by themselves, and defend the defenseless. But our past is forever tarnished by the actions of our predecessors."

"Okay," Elizabeth said. "That doesn't explain why Sabine wants this. What is the connection between this, her, and UrthaMal?"

"I don't know," John said. "UrthaMal is a purebred demon who missed getting out of hell when Anna and Teresa closed the hell portal."

"Sabine mentioned something about UrthaMal ascending," Elizabeth said. "Does that ring a bell?"

John looked at Elizabeth and thought for a moment the words he was about to say. "It's not natural for demons to live in this plane," John said. "You can't break the rules of this earthly dimension. That is why most demons that our girls battle are half-breeds. They're demons, but not purebred hell monsters. A beast from hell ascending in our dimension means that it becomes its true monstrous nature, bestowed with all the powers from hell. Still bound by our reality, but free to unleash devastation unlike you have ever seen. If we have a chance to defeat this foe, we need to do it before it evolves."

"What does she do?" Elizabeth asked. "I faced purebred only once in my lifetime. Apocalyps was the only thing that could take it out. Maybe Sabine needed to know if the sword was here in California."

"You used Apocalyps against The Hell General Daristos," John said, referencing Elizabeth's past heroics. "He was a purebred warrior, so you needed a weapon for that caliber. UrthaMal is nothing like that. She's a corrupting demon."

"A she?" Elizabeth asked.

"The writings describe her as female," John said. "She influences the unhealthy desires of weak-willed humans to push off the brink after infusing the area with fear and anguish. Once they perish, the demon feeds off their souls. That is how she gains strength."

"That explains the strange behavior of the population," Elizabeth said, understanding the news segment she saw earlier in the morning. "She's injecting fear into the population, driving them to be slaves to their hidden pleasures."

"Correct," John said. "As she gets stronger, her area of influence expands. If UrthaMal is set free, her negative impact will cause every single human to self-destruct as they fall prey to forbidden passion."

"Why haven't we been influenced?" Elizabeth asked.

"It's all in the will," John said. "I assume that your condition as demon hunters protects you to a certain degree. Can't say the same thing about Sean or myself."

Elizabeth started pacing in the study, feeling something in the back of her mind. But she couldn't pinpoint it. "I am still drawing a blank on Sabine's true motives," the demon hunter said. "What would be the reason to bring forth a demon that consumes humans?"

John shrugged as he looked at the open texts on the monitor. "I could be reading the information wrong. I will go over the texts again."

"You better hurry," Elizabeth said. "I will give a copy of The Tome to Sabine tonight."

"Okay," John said. "Guess I have a deadline."

The young man opened the document on the screen. Elizabeth glanced at the words he had highlighted while reading it. *Death is a necessary evil.* "Wait!" Elizabeth exclaimed. "Why have you highlighted that text?"

John looked up at the phrase. "It's the old Guardian's motto," John said. "They lived by that."

Elizabeth pondered for a second the idea that had popped into her head. "You and I will go out to meet Sabine tonight," Elizabeth said. "I may need your expertise when we talk with her."

John looked confused as Elizabeth left the study.

CHAPTER XII

Guardians' Home, Saint Helena, California;
September 06, 11:40 A.M.

NIKKI SMASHED HER FIST against the punching bag with brutal force, channeling her frustration and anger with each strike. She was trying to shake the failure from her system and was failing to do so. Elizabeth's words from the morning still stung in her mind and heart, and John's video of Anna talking about Solas didn't help. "How could I be so stupid?" Nikki recriminated herself as she struck the sandbag hard, with a strong spring kick. "Contemplating the notion that a demon could be good just because he helped us."

Izzy was helping Grace remove the arm sling that held her damaged arm. "We make mistakes," Izzy said as she rolled Grace's bandages off her hand. She and the dark-haired demon hunter had also seen John's message, so they understood Nikki's feelings. "Sometimes, our instincts betray us," Izzy said.

"I just feel like a huge dolt," Nikki said, punching the bag.

"It's not a stretch from your natural state," Grace said with a soft smile.

"You are begging for another broken arm," Nikki retorted, visibly angry.

"Nikki!" Izzy called out. "She's kidding."

"Not in the mood right now," Nikki said, visibly upset as she continued punching the bag.

Grace shook her head silently as she removed the last sling from her arm. She flexed her arm, wincing a bit. "It still feels stiff," Grace said to Izzy. "But I feel the bone back in place."

"Demon-hunter healing has a great upside," Izzy said. "I am surprised it took such little time. You healed faster than I did back in Ireland."

"Are we evolving?" Grace asked. "I felt something different in my speed a few nights ago. That didn't help with this vampire, though."

"I don't know," Izzy replied. "We should take it easy for now, until we figure out what's going on."

The sound of ripping leather and falling sand caught Grace's and Izzy's attention as they saw Nikki standing over a destroyed bag with a pile of sand at her feet. The young red-headed demon hunter adjusted her new eyeglasses as she inspected the damage. "Strength is there," Nikki said. "So that wasn't the issue." The girl started ripping off her grappling gloves as she headed toward the wooden dummy.

"I thought I took it badly when I lost a fight," Grace said, crossing her arms.

"It's not the defeat that gets me," Nikki said. "I've

gotten my ass kicked on more than one occasion. I can handle a loss."

Izzy shook her head as she tried to process everything that happened to them. She looked at Grace, who returned the stare. "It's fear," the dark-eyed demon hunter said. "The sensation of dread at not being in control."

Izzy contemplated her inner turmoil. An image of her and Elsa running around in Amsterdam hunting vampires and demons with smiles on their faces crossed her mind. They made a great team while clearing a vampire nest. Her thoughts were eclipsed by the memory of Elsa's body's turning to dust as demons used her essence to fuel a new wave of vampires.

Izzy looked at her new sisters. "I can't lose you," Izzy mumbled at Grace and Nikki. "Seeing you fight this vampire and get taken down just brought the same sensation I felt when I lost Elsa. I can't go through that again." Nikki looked at Grace and Izzy, trying to understand. "I know we have this line of work," Izzy continued. "I know death snaps all the time at our heels. But I've never felt it so near to me. Not because I may die, but because I may see you two fall. The fear is overwhelming, haunting me in my dreams."

"Death is part of what we do," Grace said, looking at Nikki. "That was what my dad used to say to me. It's the only lesson I never learned from him. I simply lost control that night, vowing it would never happen again. I guess I suck at keeping vows."

Nikki remained silent as she looked at her sisters. Izzy looked at her friend intriguingly. "I considered you fearless," Izzy said. "So calm and collected. It is surprising to see you like this."

Nikki smiled a bit at the compliment. "Death is part of the job," the redhead said. "I lived with two air force pilots. All my life, I considered that when death came knocking on my door, it would be in a blaze of glory."

"What happened?" Grace asked.

"I was five when my mom died," Nikki said. "Cancer had eaten her body up, and she was in that same hospital room for more than a month. I remember Dad didn't want me to see her, but I didn't listen. I snuck into her room and hid inside a closet, looking at her unconscious body. That is when it happened."

"What?" Izzy asked.

"A pulmonary embolism," Nikki said. "Machines started making noises, bringing in a swarm of doctors and nurses. They boarded the closet door, and all I could hear were the last gasps of air my mom made before dying." Grace and Izzy looked at each other, shocked at what they'd just heard. "Doctors did all they could," Nikki continued as she closed her eyes. "I can feel the walls closing in. The labored breathing."

Nikki and Grace saw her sister's facial features change as the memory started triggering an attack. They both reached Nikki as she fell to her knees, trying to control her breathing. Both girls could hear Nikki's accelerated heartbeat. "We're here," Izzy said, grabbing Nikki's hand.

"I know," Nikki said as she tried to process what was going on. She felt as if the ground had swallowed her whole, with no light around her. After a few more seconds, the sensation passed. Nikki opened her eyes and saw Grace and Izzy staring back. "I had gotten used to it," the redhead said, "but now it has come back."

"Fear never leaves us," Elizabeth said, interrupting her demon hunters. All three girls turned around, seeing the blonde demon hunter at the door. They had no idea how long she had stood there. "Fear is a tricky thing," the older woman continued. "It's ingrained into our minds to produce one of two reactions—run or fight. The problem happens when it grabs hold and paralyzes us. Nothing worse than being frozen in fear." Grace and Izzy helped Nikki back to her feet. "You girls have gone through a lot," Elizabeth said. "But you're not the first, and you certainly won't be the last."

"What do we do?" Nikki asked. "How do you deal with fear?"

Elizabeth thought for a moment before answering. "Recognizing it is the first step," the older woman said. "All of you are there now. I believe that the best thing after identifying what you fear is rationalizing it. You are not afraid of an elder vampire. Sabine just brought out the fear in you and exploited it."

"But how can I stop being afraid?" Nikki asked.

"We don't," Grace said. "It's something that will live in us forever."

"We either let it help us or break us," Izzy said.

Elizabeth nodded. "It's something you have to deal with," the Guardian said. "And it seems we don't have time."

"What do you mean?" Nikki asked. Elizabeth then proceeded to explain her meeting with Sabine, including John's information on UrthaMal.

"What do you think?" Grace asked, processing the fact that Neil was in town.

"I have a theory about Sabine and the other elder vampires," Elizabeth said as she paced in front of the girls. “If I am correct, a lot of innocent lives are at stake.”

“John said that UrthaMal needs to feed,” Izzy said. “She starts first with those with a weak will. She will come for those.”

“She can’t escape, so she needs vampires to cater to her,” Grace said. “And vampires are accommodating to this demon’s bidding.”

“They will take more tonight, you said,” Nikki pointed out. “Where exactly?”

“A place where weak-willed people are ripe to be taken?” Izzy asked. Suddenly her cell phone beeped once. The brown-haired girl opened the phone and read the text as her eyes widened at the message. “There is an event tonight at school,” Izzy said. “Clubs and other extracurricular activities will be open for registration.”

“Who sent you the text?” Nikki asked with a knowing smile.

Izzy blushed a bit at the question, but answered confidently. “Stephen,” the brown-haired girl said. “There is the music program he wants me to check out. He also wants me to take a gander at the after-school art program.” Izzy turned toward her mom. “Plenty of weak-willed teens in a single place. It seems like a great spot for vampires to strike.”

“I am afraid so,” Elizabeth said, agreeing with her daughter.

“Only an invitation grants vampires access to the school grounds,” Grace said.

“School is a public space,” Elizabeth said. “The undead don’t need an invitation to a place like that. At what time does the event start?”

"Seven," Izzy replied.

Elizabeth thought for a moment as she looked at her girls. "You have to go," the older demon hunter said. "Sean will be your backup."

"And if we're wrong?" Nikki asked. "What if the attacks are somewhere else?"

"Let's pray it isn't," Elizabeth said. "Let's train for a bit and brainstorm an adequate defense for tonight."

Saint Helena High School, California; September 06, 6:50 p.m.

"We should have called a bomb threat," Izzy said as she looked out the window of her father's SUV. Students flocked to the front entrance of the school. "I feel like we're using human lures to bring out the undead."

"We don't know if the attack will be here," Sean said. "But we'll protect it. John checked, and there is no other conglomeration of people tonight other than this."

"What about you?" Grace asked from the back seat. "You are not immune to UrthaMal's influence."

Izzy's insides tugged a bit, hearing Grace's warning. She looked at her father adoringly. "Please be careful," the brown-haired girl said.

"I am pretty strong-willed," Sean replied, rubbing his daughter's back while looking at the rearview mirror, seeing the football team approaching. "Just watch out for those who may need you the most."

"Ugh," Grace scoffed. "Do we have to save those jerks?"

Sean smiled and looked at each of the demon hunters. "Protect those who can't fight the forces of darkness on their own. Go. Now." Grace and Izzy stepped out of the car, but Nikki remained in the back seat, unable to move. Sean turned his head around and looked at the red-headed demon hunter. "Are you okay?" Sean asked.

"I don't feel one-hundred percent," Nikki said.

Izzy and Grace looked at each other, approaching the window to look at their sister. Sean nodded and thought for a second. "I am going to check the underground tunnel that leads to the school," he said. "It might be cramped down there. Do you want to help me out? I could use a strong demon hunter at my side." Izzy smiled a bit as she heard her father's words and his intentions. Nikki looked at Izzy and Grace, who both gave her an encouraging nod. Sean smiled, knowing the girls were speaking with their thoughts. "Okay," Sean said as he motioned Nikki to jump to the front seat. "Nicole and I will take the tunnels. You two watch the front and back entrances. If something goes down, focus on getting the innocent to safety. Please be careful."

Nikki jumped to the front seat and smiled at her sisters. "Jot my name for any sport that is available," she said. "Nothing that has close contact."

"Will do," Grace said.

Izzy looked at her father and then at Nikki. "Please watch out for him," Izzy said to her friend.

Nikki took a deep breath and looked at Sean, who smiled at her. "I'm sure he'll be watching over me."

"Don't worry," Sean said. "You two, be careful." With those final words, he drove off.

Grace turned toward Izzy as she saw the football team enter the school out of the corner of her eye. "You think they'll be alright?"

"As long as they're together," Izzy said as she and her sister started walking toward the school. "He's taking her to face her fear. He knows what he is doing."

They entered the double doors and saw several tables lined up in the main hall. As the girls made their way, they noted the students were signing up for all the different after-school activities. The sports programs included football, baseball, soccer, and gymnastics, while the more academic and artistic activities were the decathlon, chess, theatre, music, and journalism.

"How is Aidan holding up?" Grace asked. "Will he be joining us today?"

"I don't know," Izzy replied. "When I woke up this morning, he was gone. He does that sometimes when he takes a beating. He goes into the wild to lick his wounds. Unfortunately, he never leaves a note saying when he'll return."

"Can you feel him when he is near?"

"I can," Izzy replied. "I think we are in sync with each other now. Not sure if it's part of my demon hunter abilities, or he's just a special kind of wolf."

"Hope he helps us out tonight," Grace said. "With all that can happen, we could use him." Grace stopped in the middle of the hall and looked around. "Where's Stephen? I was expecting him at the art table."

"I know," Izzy said as she saw Jaime and Bryan approaching. "But we don't have to wait for your friends to show up."

"Hey," Jaime said as she reached both girls with Bryan at her side. "I didn't think you'd show today."

"We made time," Izzy said. "We need to get used to our surroundings."

"How's your arm?" Bryan asked Grace discreetly. "Things went south really fast last night."

Grace smiled, reassuring the boy. "It's fine," she said. "We heal pretty fast. The important thing is that you're okay."

"Why aren't you guys at the journalism table?" Izzy asked. "I thought you would be taking a lot of names."

Jaime laughed a bit. "The class from last year closed down the school paper," the girl said. "With all the things that go down in this town, no one is interested. We just got the permission to open it up during this past summer."

"So, it's just you two?" Grace asked.

"Yes," Bryan said. "Jaime is an excellent writer. And I've been obsessed with photography for the past three years. It seems like a great idea."

"Want to check out what we have?" Jaime asked as she guided the girls further down the hall. They passed the football team, who were waving and hollering, paying attention to no one but themselves. Turning right, they opened the door to a small office. There was only a whiteboard, a desk, and pictures posted all over the wall. "This is our office," Jaime said.

Grace slowly walked toward one of the photographs hanging from the wall. It was from the football training session. "Is this the football coach?" Grace said, inspecting the high-definition picture. The detail of the photo was mesmerizing.

"Yeah," Bryan said. "Coach Richardson. He got us to the state championship five years ago. But his winning streak has been dry for a while."

Grace inspected the photo and looked at it closely. The Coach's eyes were fiery red. It seemed peculiar for a professional image. "Why does the coach have red eyes?" Grace asked, showing the picture to Izzy, who inspected it.

"You noticed that, huh?" Jaime said. "I can tell you it's not the camera, and it's not Bryan. He is good at what he does."

"Mr. Haberman also has red eyes in the pictures I took," Bryan said as he pulled a photo from the wall. "That is the man who attacked the coach on the field."

"Any more red eyes on pictures?" Izzy asked.

"I've seen a few on the students," Bryan replied. "The pictures I took of the football team have a few. That includes some cheerleaders as well. I also saw some in students in the media club and the decathlon team."

"What are you thinking?" Grace asked Izzy.

"I think that you are catching something paranormal with these pictures," Izzy said. "But it's just conjecture. Red eyes appear in pictures all the time."

"Not in mine," Bryan defended himself.

"Not everything is paranormal," Grace said to the boy. "Your photos are exceptional. You have a gift."

Izzy inspected the articles posted on the wall, and the St. Helena Catholic Church caught her eye. "What's the story with the priest they arrested a few days ago?" Izzy asked. "Do you know?"

"I think your friend Stephen is the one you should ask," Jaime said as she walked toward the back of the desk. "He is the key witness in that case."

"What case?" Izzy asked Jaime.

"It's an abuse case against the former pastor," Jaime said. "Stephen's father committed suicide last year. It all points to actions performed by the priest. Stephen will testify against him."

"For abuse done to his father?" Grace asked.

"It seems Stephen found an old diary from his dad," Bryan said. "It's kind of sad, because Stephen is the hardcore Catholic in the school."

"I would have nothing to do with that faith if I were him," Jaime said.

"I understand the sentiment," Izzy said, stepping back from the article. "Well, I guess I have to find the art club." With that, the brown-haired girl stepped out of the room.

"Was it something I said?" Jaime asked Grace, who continued inspecting the photographs.

"Izzy takes her Catholic faith very seriously," Grace said with a sad smile. "You can't beat the undead without consecrated weapons."

"What?" Jaime asked, looking at the doorway.

"It's okay," Grace said. "You didn't know. So how do you join this club?"

"You want to join?" Bryan asked.

"I think it's perfect," Grace replied. "I get a perfect cover. When grown-ups ask what I am doing at night in the graveyards, I just say it's part of a story for the school paper."

"Like Clark Kent!" Bryan chirped, while Jaime tried to hide her embarrassment.

"Yeah," Grace said with a smile. "Like Clark Kent."

Saint Helena Tunnels, California; September 06, 7:10 p.m.

Sean drove his car in silence as he looked at the side where Nikki contemplated the scenery from her passenger window. "Are you hungry?" Sean asked the demon hunter. "We could get a burger or something before heading into the cave system."

"I'm okay," Nikki replied dryly.

Sean nodded as he took the next left. He drove a hundred yards before reaching the edge of the woods. Both Guardian and demon hunter got out of the car and inspected their surroundings. "Do you feel anything?" Sean asked as he walked to the car's trunk and pulled out an automatic crossbow with a cylinder clip full of wooden projectiles.

"Nothing," Nikki said as she joined her guardian. She pulled out a stake and two daggers.

"Packing light?" Sean asked.

"I can manage with this," Nikki said. "Too much gear slows me down."

"Okay," Sean said, closing the car door and guiding the red-headed girl into the woods. "There is a small entrance to the cave system over here."

"How do you know?" Nikki asked as she let he Guardian guide her through the trees and bushes.

"Guardians have been keeping tabs on this town for a while," Sean said. "We've mapped out the cave system. We know every entrance and corner. This one is closest to the school."

Demon hunter and Guardian continued making their way through the trees until they reached a large wall of stone and granite. "Dead end?" Nikki asked as Sean inspected the right side of the wall.

Sean smiled as he removed some bushes from the rock face, revealing a small entrance with a three-foot diameter. The Guardian pulled out a pen flashlight and illuminated the passageway. "We only crawl fifteen feet," Sean said. "After that, it's a quarter-mile walk to the school basement. The perfect way for the undead to enter the school without alerting anyone." The Guardian looked at Nikki, whose face had paled. "Come on," Sean said. "Get in."

"Is this the only entrance?" Nikki asked with a bit of anxiety in her voice, as she looked at the enclosed space she needed to make her way through.

"There're plenty of entrances to the cave systems," Sean said. "But the hike is too long. This passageway is our best bet. Let's go."

Nikki looked inside the tight space. She could hear the rumbling of soil and dirt crumbling down. It almost sounded like an echo. "I can't," Nikki whispered as she took a step back.

Sean nodded as he looked at the sixteen-year-old girl. "Feels strange to be paralyzed by fear, doesn't it?" Sean said. "I talked to your father about a week ago, when I informed him of moving you to this location. He speaks highly of you. Especially the incursion on the Indian sea."

"Fathers do that a lot," Nikki said, looking down.

"Indeed we do," Sean said. "You took out a dozen vampires and three fire demons."

"I had help," Nikki said.

"You had backup," Sean corrected. "The special forces were guiding the civilians to safety while you took on a large pack of demons. Only fifteen, and you already had nerves of steel. Your father's voice beams with pride, speaking of that event."

"I've heard him tell the story," Nikki said.

"And yet here we are," Sean said, looking at the cave.

"You have no idea what I'm going through!" Nikki exploded. "This feeling of powerlessness! Of not being in control!"

"Control," Sean repeated, while nodding his head slowly. "Is it the tight space that scares you? Or is it the fact that you seem to lose control in that space?" Nikki looked at the older man with a questioning look. "I am a former vengeance demon," Sean said. "Saving the world granted me the opportunity to have a human life with a demon's strength, but the beast dwells in my body still. The monster inside me aches to get out and unleash destruction and chaos."

"I thought you were free of that," Nikki said.

"Every day, it's a battle to control the beast inside," Sean said. "My biggest fear is to fail, and the monster is let loose upon my wife and daughter."

A shiver ran down Nikki's spine, hearing those words. She had read about Sean's former demon self. The monster was formidable in strength, but most of all, in psychotic nature. The way he tortured Elizabeth and her loved ones in the past was no secret among the demon hunters. In some circles, there were Guardians and demon hunters who did not fully trust Sean. But he had gained control of his beast, and the respect of his peers. "How do you do it?" Nikki asked. "How do you keep control while you have that thing deep inside?"

Sean looked at the sky for a moment. "I recognize its strength," Sean said. "I see how formidable the beast is and remind myself that today may be the day it beats me. But then I take that same strength and make it my own. I understood that being paralyzed in fear only gave the demon more power. So I welcomed the fear. I made it part of my strength to battle it every day." Sean paused and looked at the teenaged girl. "That is half the battle," the old man continued.

"What's the other half?" Nikki asked.

"The love I have for my wife and Izzy," Sean replied. "Love drives away the fear." Nikki nodded as she looked inside the cave. "You didn't leave your mother alone," Sean told Nikki. "Even though you were scared to death hiding in that tight closet, you were there with your mom. And she knew you were there, too. The same source of your fear is also the same source of your strength and courage. It's all about love, Nikki. That is the core of your strength. The love for your mother."

Nikki took a moment to reflect on Sean's words. She placed her hand on her heart and took a deep breath as she walked toward the entrance. The girl looked inside, seeing giant rats and spiders crawl away from the little light that came through the opening. "It's just fifteen feet," Nikki said to herself while she climbed inside the tight spot. The young redhead slowly made her way to the other side when a flash in her mind stopped her. She could feel the cave collapsing as her heartbeat increased. Nikki gasped for air, only to hear Sean's voice behind her.

"It's okay," her Guardian said. "Breath it in. Bring on the fear. You can do this."

Nikki tried to focus, feeling like the ground was collapsing around her, making the cave feel tighter. But she could move freely. The teenaged girl crawled slowly, ignoring the rodents and insects, reaching the end of the tunnel. Her army boots touched the ground again, and she took a deep breath as her heartbeat slowed down. A few seconds later, Sean was beside her. "Well done."

"Does it ever go away?" Nikki asked as she looked at Sean, who was inspecting the cave.

Sean smiled and looked at the girl. "No," he replied. "It's part of you. You only learn to live with it." Sean turned right to the tunnel and started walking. "This is the way to the school," Sean said. "It's the only underground access they can use."

Nikki walked behind her Guardian, alert to her surroundings. She felt nothing out of the ordinary except the dampness of the cave. "Are you still haunted by what you did in the past?" Nikki asked. "What's the difference between then and now?"

"Few demons capture the soul of a human," Sean said. "As a vengeance demon imprisoned my soul and acted out of the impulse of rage, the beast magnified by tenfold all my negative human thoughts and carried them out. Even though it trapped my soul inside, I was well aware that the actions were mine. Driven only by hate, my only desire was to cause suffering. The demon suppressed my consciousness for over four hundred years."

"That changed when you killed a demon hunter," Nikki said, recollecting the stories of The Guardians. "The Guardians brought out your conscience so that the pain tormented you for eternity."

"You've done your reading," Sean said. "But to answer your original question, the only difference is that now the human side is in control and not the demon. My crimes are not easy to erase, though. The burden of four hundred years of devastation haunts me still."

"What is the difference between you and Solas?" Nikki asked.

"Solas is older," Sean said. "Much older. I think he

is over eight centuries old. While I was a vengeance demon, Solas is a hellspawn. For the centuries I knew him, he has behaved like a normal hellspawn—a warrior forged to serve the powers of hell. He is a foot soldier for the underworld, product of a rage demon. The main difference between us is that my demon took over a human body. Solas is considered a spawn of a purebred."

"Meaning what?" Nikki asked.

"There is no humanity in him," Sean said.

"How can that be?" Nikki asked. "Purebreds can't walk this plane."

"He's a spawn of a purebred," Sean corrected. "Still, he must have sacrificed part of his dark powers to remain on this plane in that carcass of a human form. That does not make him less dangerous."

"What's the difference between a rage demon and a vengeance demon?" Nikki asked. "They sound similar."

"In many ways, they are," Sean said. "Both prey on the volatile emotions of humanity. Vengeance uses hatred as fuel. Rage's fuel is anger—both powerful emotions, and very common in the human race." Sean looked at Nikki. "Both demons are manipulative and take advantage of their opponent's weakness. They are not to be trusted."

"Solas helped Teresa and Anna," Nikki said. "He helped us as well, a couple of nights ago."

Sean listened carefully to Nikki's voice, sensing the subtle emotion she was trying to hide; she failed miserably. "I see no reason to trust him," Sean said. "Solas is known for playing the long con game. He could be manipulating the scenes to reach his true objective."

"And what could that objective be?" Nikki asked.

Sean stopped walking and looked at his demon hunter. "Solas is a foot soldier. Very rare for him to be on his own. A hellspawn usually hunts with a pack. Still, even if he is a lone wolf, his mission could be to gather information on the Guardians and the demon hunters—what better way than to that than gain their trust?"

Nikki frowned as she continued walking alongside her Guardian toward the school. There was something off in his explanation, but she let it go.

CHAPTER XIII

Holy Cross Catholic Cemetery, Saint Helena, California; September 06, 7:50 p.m.

John fidgeted nervously with his fingers as we walked alongside Elizabeth in the hallowed grounds of the cemetery. Strolling in haunted territory looking for the undead was the last thing he imagined he would be doing for the Guardians.

Elizabeth smiled at the young man's nervousness. "Don't worry, John," the older demon hunter said. "I got your back."

"And who has yours?" John asked. "No offense, but I don't see the strategy in my coming along to meet an ancient vampire."

"You need the fieldwork," the blonde woman said. "Besides, I need your brain."

"Really?" John asked. "Why is that?"

"This vampire can read minds," Elizabeth said. "I want to see what she can do when she meets a superior intellect."

"Okay..." John doubted.

"Besides, this is your opportunity to walk along with a demon hunter," Elizabeth said. "Demon hunters need their Guardians at their side while they hunt. It's part of the job."

"I thought my job was being inside a library and doing reports," John said.

"You needed the promotion," Elizabeth said as they reached the broken sarcophagus tomb where Sabine had fought her girls. Elizabeth could smell the bloodstains on the broken concrete and grassy soil. The older woman crouched and inspected the tracks on the ground, reviewing the battle in her mind. "She's good," Elizabeth whispered to John. "She's on another level."

"You can see what happened last night just by looking at the battlefield?" John asked.

"When you've had countless fights, it becomes easier," Elizabeth said, standing up straight. "She'll be here soon. Remain quiet at all times. If she speaks to you, keep your sentences short and straightforward. I am hoping your brain short-circuits her mind-reading skills."

Elizabeth and John stood their ground and waited in silence for a couple more minutes. Elizabeth could now sense the dark aura she'd felt in the morning. Sabine had arrived, and she was not alone. Three pairs of red eyes appeared in the darkness. John swallowed hard as three large, muscular vampires emerged from the shadows. They were all at least six-feet-four in height, with disfigured facial features and large fangs. Their clothing was dark and worn out. Behind them, an elegant and beautiful raven-haired woman appeared. Her attire told a different story from what her lackeys wore, as it was a leather pants-and-jacket ensemble with a simple white blouse. A small rose in her right breast pocket matched the color of her ruby lips. Sabine was ready for battle. A man dressed in a dark gray suit followed the woman, unfazed by his surroundings. "Elizabeth," Sabine said, taking note of John. "I see you brought company. I wanted to see Sean, but I guess you have him babysitting your little girls."

"I found your book," Elizabeth said, pulling the thumb drive from her jacket pocket. "Fascinating read."

"I am sure you haven't read a single book since you graduated college," Sabine mocked as she looked at John. "That's why you have your Guardians." Sabine peered into John's mind, only to see a thousand memories moving from one side to another in no particular order. The Vampire flinched, having a hard time grasping a clear thought.

"Yes," Elizabeth said. "He's my Apocalyps expert. No one on the planet knows more about the sword than him."

Sabine smiled, focusing back on Elizabeth. "Except your daughter," the vampire said. "She's had first-hand experience."

"You'll get the same information from her as you have from me," Elizabeth said, unfazed by Sabine's threat.

"We'll see," the vampire said, crossing her arms.

"The Tome," Elizabeth said, waving the thumb drive. "You want this, right? What guarantees do I have that you'll keep your word?"

"You have none," Sabine snapped back. "Now, hand it over." Elizabeth nodded as she threw the thumb drive toward Sabine. Neil extended his right hand and caught the device, inspecting it for a few seconds. He nodded at Sabine. The female vampire smiled and looked at Elizabeth. "Pleasure doing business with you," Sabine said as she turned her back and started to walk away.

"Why did you betray the Guardians?" Elizabeth asked. The question stopped Sabine in her tracks as she whirled around and glared at the blonde demon hunter. "Does the vampire clan know that the elder ones were once Guardians who haunted them down?" Elizabeth asked.

John's eyes widened as he looked at the three lackey vampires who shared the same surprised look.

"Schulmeister?" one of the vampires asked. "What's the demon hunter talking about?"

"Sabine, Neil, and all the elder vampires are former Guardians," Elizabeth said, crossing her arms. "They turned themselves into vampires to keep the vampire clans under control for generations."

Before anybody could flinch, Neil pulled a small crossbow and fired three arrows, aiming at each vampire. The vampires screamed as the wooden shafts perforated each chest cavity, piercing their hearts and turning the demons into ash. Elizabeth and John froze as the vampire pointed the crossbow at them. "I truly underestimated you," Sabine said to Elizabeth. "How did you find out?"

"The way you speak is the way you write," Elizabeth said. "You wrote The Tome, didn't you?"

"The current generation of Guardians were never to have access to the book," Sabine said.

"The question remains," Elizabeth said. "Why?"

"Mortal minds can't fathom the magnitude of events that have and will transpire," Sabine said. "While you have been saving the world for just over fifteen years, my brethren and I have worked for over two millennia."

"You sacrificed over one hundred demon hunters," John said. "Condemned an entire village to damnation."

"That was not the first time," Neil said with a shrug. "And it hasn't been the last."

"Death is a necessary evil," Sabine said. "When you've lived as long as we have, you begin to grasp the concept."

"Not caring how many innocents die in the process?" Elizabeth asked.

"Wake up, little girl!" Sabine yelled. "No human is innocent! UrthaMal is proving that at this moment! She is bringing human desires to the forefront. A weak race, dominated by unhealthy passion and fear, guiding themselves to an eternity of suffering. A small price to pay to keep the world spinning."

"Why?" Elizabeth asked. "Why do you need UrthaMal to ascend?"

"I thought you read the book," Neil challenged John, drawing a look of surprise from the young Guardian.

Sabine glared at Neil for the comment. "This is not your concern," Sabine said, turning her attention back to Elizabeth. "What should be your top priority is saving your girls from what is going down tonight."

"My girls can take care of themselves," Elizabeth said.

"I'm sure they can," Sabine said with an evil smile. "But can they make difficult choices? Would they choose to save innocent kids in peril, or their Guardian?" A chill ran down Elizabeth's spine as the words left Sabine's lips. "I guess I'll see Sean soon after all."

Sabine and Neil started walking away as Elizabeth pulled her cell phone. "Call Nikki and Grace!" Elizabeth ordered John. "It's a diversion! They're after Sean!"

Saint Helena High School, California: September 06, 7:40 p.m.

Izzy's fingers softly played the keys of the piano inside the music room. The notes that filled the air brought comfort to her troubled mind and heart. The memory of her playing music inside a demon-infested saloon while her best friend dispatched the undead surrounding them was a treasured thought to the young teen. She tried to shake off the memory and focused on the present as she slowly changed her tone. She had searched for Stephen in the art group, but had failed to spot him in the room filled with more than a dozen students signing up for the extracurricular activity.

Giving up, Izzy had strolled into the music room, only to find out that the music teacher had rescheduled the signups for the music club. That is when she spotted the piano and decided to indulge herself a bit. Music was indeed a means of escape from the burdens of demon hunting. The young teen continued for several minutes before feeling eyes watching her. Without stopping, she turned her head to see Stephen in the doorway.

"That's beautiful," Stephen said. "Where did you learn it?"

"The Netherlands," Izzy said as she continued playing. "Inspired by a close friend."

"What happened to her?" Stephen asked as he walked into the room and stood next to Izzy.

"She died," Izzy said, looking straight ahead.

"I see. I am not the only one death has visited," Stephen said.

"I read about you," Izzy said. "After our conversation in front of the church."

"Checking up on me?" Stephen asked.

"Curious," Izzy said while she continued playing.

"About what?"

"On how you knew about the Catholic priest," Izzy responded. "I was also intrigued by you being the only one in the building praying in front of the Tabernacle. In my experience, church-going is reserved for senior citizens."

Stephen snickered a bit at the comment. "Are you excluding youth from the faith?"

"Living in Europe has narrowed my view a bit," Izzy said. "These past few days, I've begun to question everything."

"A reasonable response when tragedy strikes," Stephen said. "I learned that last year."

Izzy stopped playing the piano and looked at the boy. "I read about that," the brown-haired girl said. "How did you cope?"

"Realizing the truth," Stephen said. "We live in a twisted and mean-spirited world filled with bad actors across all the spectrum, full of faulty role models, including our parents, teachers, political and spiritual leaders who guide the innocent and naïve to perdition. But that is not new to anyone who pays attention. The bad weed grows alongside the wheat. Faith has nothing to do with that reality."

"I've read that story," Izzy nodded. "That doesn't explain why the good suffer tragedies. Like you, for example. I am sure your family did not deserve what happened to you."

"And you did not deserve to have your best friend taken from you," Stephen said. "And yet, it happened."

"I don't get that," Izzy said. "Why does it feel that good people get the bottom end of what this life has to offer?"

"Suffering forges the best of us," Stephen said, shrugging. "We may not see the greater good beyond today."

"I find that stupid," Izzy said, standing up to walk out of the room, exasperated with the conversation.

"Most do," Stephen called out. "Very few things pale in comparison to the pain my father's tragedy brought to my family. There were days that I wanted to give up on everything. But that wouldn't help anyone. I realized those events in my life would be the source of my strength. It gave me the courage to fight against injustice. I didn't realize it would strengthen my faith, as well."

Izzy stopped and looked at Stephen. In his hands, he held the prayer beads of the rosary. "It seems you have found your calling," Izzy said.

"Blessed are those who find it at a young age," Stephen said with a soft smile. "Do you have a calling?"

Izzy was about to respond when her cell phone started ringing. "Sorry," Izzy said as she looked at her phone and saw a picture of Elizabeth. "Hey, Mom," the brown-haired girl responded.

"Izzy!" Elizabeth said. "It's happening tonight! They're after your father!"

Izzy's face went pale, hearing the urgency in her mother's voice. Suddenly the lights in the school went out, and the emergency lights turned on. Screams of excitement from the student body echoed through the halls. Izzy turned toward Stephen, who had a confused look on his face. "We need to get out of here!"

Saint Helena Tunnels, California: September 06, 7:59 p.m.

Nikki could feel the dark essence increasing from the tunnels. "We have incoming," Nikki said as she pulled out her stakes, regretting not bringing her short sword.

"Can you tell how many?" Sean asked.

"Two dozen," the redhead said. "Could be more." Her demon hunter vision peered beyond the darkness, not seeing anything running down the tunnel. Then she saw the silhouette of a few demons marching toward them. Nikki turned toward Sean, who loaded his automatic crossbow while he guarded the entrance that led to the school's lower level.

Nikki then focused her attention on the cave's ceiling. "They're on the surface," Nikki concluded.

Sean was about to respond when a loud and low voice echoed in the darkness. "Ankrnot!" a demon growled. "It's time for you to pay for your crimes, traitor!"

Sean frowned as he stepped forward. "Nicole," he whispered. "Go upstairs and help out your sisters."

"What?" Nikki exclaimed. "I'm not leaving you alone down here!"

"Your sisters are outnumbered!" Sean snapped, drawing a look of surprise from the redhead. "That's an order!"

Before Nikki could move, she saw a six-foot-nine dark-skinned vampire emerge from the darkness, followed by four warrior demons. Nikki took a close look at the monsters, recognizing that they were not of the vampire kind.

The first was a bald, thin, albino-skinned six-foot-two monster with large purple eyes and long fingers which ended in sharp claws. A skin-tight black leather suit protected its entire body while the beast was barefoot, exposing large black nails on his toes.

The second demon was a short, red-skinned dwarf demon. Its black horns curved like a goat, giving the chubby-looking fiend an impressive height of five-foot-three. Its silver eyes glared at Nikki as he clanged his sword and shield.

The third demon that accompanied the vampire was a female-looking blue-skinned, red-haired demon that seemed amphibious. The creature lacked a nose, but it had gills that vibrated as its naked chest moved. Only a brown leather skirt covered the lower part of her body.

The final beast was a thin, well-built humanoid in a white suit, with long white hair that reached his waist. Metal coils wrapped his white hands, while his eyes seemed to flash with light blue electricity.

"We meet again, Ankrnot," the vampire said, talking to Sean. "I have longed for this moment."

"Sorry to keep you waiting, Draco," Sean said as he fired an arrow from his automatic crossbow.

The projectile whistled through the air, only for the vampire to catch it with his hand. "Kill the girl," the vampire ordered his four demons as he snapped the arrow in two. "Ankrnot is mine."

The first three demons charged Nikki, who stood her ground while the suit-dressed fiend released the coils from his hands, extending them as large metal whips. Crackling bolts of electricity emanated from the weapons as he waited.

The albino demon slashed upward with its arms and threw two spinning kicks, hoping its claws would connect with the demon hunter. Nikki blocked the first two attacks and backflipped, avoiding the kicks while keeping one eye on the sharply dressed monster. *He is waiting for the other three to wear me down,* Nikki thought to herself.

The small troll slashed sideways and lunged its short sword, only for Nikki to dodge and grab the little demon's right arm. "Thank you," she said as she kneed the troll's right extremity, causing the beast to release the sword while screaming in agony.

Nikki grabbed the sword's grip, only to wince in pain as the weapon burned her hand.

"Silly girl," the troll growled. "Only I can wield my weapons." The monster charged the teenaged girl with his shield.

Nikki grabbed the sides of it, screaming again as the weapon burned her palms. She wrestled the shield from the troll's grip and smashed his face with it. She then threw the shield, spinning it toward the albino demon, connecting with its chest.

Out of the corner of her eye, she saw Draco tackle Sean to the floor. The vampire seemed stronger than Sean on so many levels. But her Guardian held his own smashing the demon's face with the crossbow. The strike only angered the beast, as he wrestled the weapon from Sean's hand and threw it to the side. He then punched Sean down, drawing blood from the man's mouth.

The amphibious beast attacked Nikki next, as it tried to punch her face. Nikki dodged to the left and right as the monster continued its assault. The demon then flipped her head, extending long red tentacles in place of her hair, wrapping around Nikki's wrist. The demon hunter grunted, but stood her ground as the monster tried to pull her into her striking range.

These demons are not average, Nikki thought to herself as she glanced back at Sean, who punched Draco and was now on top of the vampire. The Guardian was trying to reach his weapon while keeping control of the massive beast. Nikki looked at the demon dressed in white. He smiled sadistically as the metal coil whips glowed with energy.

The demon hunter turned her attention back to her opponents, who were now recuperating. The teenaged warrior grabbed the hair-tentacles that trapped her wrist and pulled hard, ripping them from the demon's head.

The amphibious beast howled in pain, black blood dripping from her head. She saw the demon hunter twirling the tentacles in her hands like two small whips of her own. She cracked the tentacles, striking the female demon in the face, drawing out more black blood, this time from her cheek.

Nikki spun her arms, striking the troll demon on the hand with the tentacles, not allowing him to pick up his sword. The young girl jumped and turned in the air, extending her right leg, connecting with the troll's head with a vicious ax-kick. The demon's skull caved in with a sickening crack, as its body twitched one last time before falling lifelessly to the ground.

The albino demon had recovered and spun like a top, with its long claws extended. Nikki deflected his attacks with the tentacles, only for its nails to slice them into several pieces.

Nikki backflipped away, but as her hands touched the cold floor, she felt a stinging sensation across her stomach. Her army boots landed hard on the floor, and the girl winced, sensing a small gash on her belly.

"Demon hunters bleed," the purple-eyed monster hissed. He jumped with its claws exposed, ready to skewer the red-headed teen.

Nikki saw everything in slow motion as she jumped forward, extending her leg connecting with the fiend's chest before his extremities reached her. The demon hunter grabbed his wrists and snapped them with one swift motion.

The demon howled as Nikki turned his broken wrists back toward his purple eyes. She lunged its claws backward, stabbing the monster with its own black nails through his orbital sockets.

The amphibious demon looked at her fallen companion, then at the white-haired demon. The monster nodded at her. The blue-skinned demon turned her attention back to the red-headed demon hunter and let out a high-pitched screech.

The demon hunter could visualize the sound wave from the demon's mouth, but it was too late as the howl reached her ears. Nikki screamed in pain, grasping her ears and falling on her knees as the blue-skinned being walked toward the incapacitated girl, unrelenting on the sound wave.

Nikki felt as though her head was going to explode. She winced in agony, looking to the side, seeing Draco had overpowered Sean and was beating him down to a pulp, while the white-haired demon cracked his metal coils, releasing bolts of electricity in the air. The girl felt her eardrums were about to give way when she spotted Sean's automatic crossbow just a few feet away. Nikki grimaced as the amphibious beast increased her howling pitch, intensifying the pain as she walked forward.

Nikki screamed, jumping to the side, grabbing the crossbow in the process. The demon followed the girl with her sonic blast to see the demon hunter fire a single bolt from her weapon. The arrow flew through the wave, right into the monster's open mouth. The projectile pierced right through the back of the demon's throat as the metal head popped out of its neck. The beast gasped for breath, only to see the teenaged girl airborne as she brought the crossbow down across her skull, splitting the head in two. Gray matter and blue blood spilled across the floor.

Nikki's ears hadn't stopped ringing as she looked, somewhat dazed, toward the white-haired demon who cracked the metal coil toward her. The red-headed girl arched back, feeling the power of the metallic whip and seeing the blue crackles of electricity running through it. She somersaulted back as the beast cracked the whip again, trying to connect.

He's keeping me at bay with that thing, Nikki thought to herself, dodging the attacks. She fired from her crossbow, only for the demon to strike the arrow with his weapon.

The demon cracked both whips down, pushing Nikki back, then jumping forward with a flying kick. His foot connected with the red-headed girl's chest, launching her against the stone wall. Nikki gasped in pain. She turned her head seeing Draco lift Sean over his head, throwing him against the metal door that led toward the school. He walked toward the human with murder in his red eyes.

Nikki's body tensed, sensing the imminent doom about to befall her Guardian. She felt energy swell up from inside as she had never felt before. "This's going to hurt," Nikki whispered to herself as she saw the white-haired demon strike down with both electric metal coils. The demon hunter lifted her hands, bracing herself for the pain that was to come. The metal hit her palms causing her to scream in agony feeling the electricity run through her body. She battled through the pain, holding the whips and swinging hard to the left. The monster did not anticipate this and lost his balance, feeling the demon hunter's sheer power as she lifted him off his feet and swung him toward Draco.

Draco saw only a white blur as the full weight of the demon collided with him, bringing them both down to the floor with the metal coils landing on them. Electric bolts surged through both their bodies making them twitch in agony.

Nikki collapsed against the wall reaching for her crossbow and aiming at Draco. She fired a single arrow, piercing the vampire right on the temple.

The vampire screamed while grabbing the smoking arrow sticking out of the side of his head.

Nikki stood up and half-walked, half-ran toward her bloodied-up Guardian, helping him up. She fired another arrow, this time aiming at the white-haired demon, only for Draco to grab it and snap it in two. "No one can kill us!" he screamed, snapping his fingers. "The Order of Karratt will never die!"

The demon hunter, even in her daze, could feel a small horde of vampires starting to run down the tunnel. She put Sean's arm around her shoulder as they both started making their way toward the school's lower-level entrance. As they entered, Nikki dropped Sean on the floor and looked back, seeing a dozen vampires running toward them with Draco's sadistic smile beaming.

Nikki closed the metal door and locked it. She then grabbed a metal pipe and barred the metal entrance with it.

"Dead or alive, you're coming with me, Ankrnot!" Draco screamed from behind the metal door as the vampires smashed it. Their combined strength bent the metal entrance, making the hinges creak in response to the punishment.

Nikki blinked hard, trying to shake off the sonic and electric attacks. She looked at Sean, who was now standing up and cleaning the blood from his battered face. She was about to say something when her cell beeped once with a notification. The redhead opened her mobile, and Izzy's message drew a cold drop of sweat from the side of her head.

They're after my dad! Get him out of there!

CHAPTER XIV

Saint Helena High School, California; September 06, 8:05 p.m.

IZZY LOOKED AT HER cell phone, waiting for Nikki to respond, as the students' commotion was at a fever pitch outside the music room. It seemed an eternity passed before Nikki replied with a text.

He's with me. He's hurt. We're coming up.

Izzy looked up, seeing Stephen had not left her side when Grace entered the room, with Jaime and Bryan trailing behind her. "We've got company!" the demon hunter said.

"My dad is in trouble in the basement!" Izzy said. "We need to get him out of here! They're after him!"

The sound of windows shattering and students screaming made teenagers jump. "A lot of vampires are coming into the school," Grace said. "I can't protect the entire student body on my own."

Izzy walked toward the doorway and looked in the darkened halls. Students were screaming, trying to get out of the school in total pandemonium. "I need to find my dad," Izzy whispered as the familiar fear tensed up every cell of her body. The nightmare flashed again before her eyes.

Grace grabbed Izzy by the arm. "Students and staff are going to die!" Grace exclaimed. "Your dad can take of himself! And he has Nikki! We need to help everyone get out!"

Izzy looked at the commotion in the darkened halls. She then looked at her sister and nodded. "Hit the fire alarm," Izzy instructed. "I will clear a path to the outside grounds and cover the students out there. You get the students out and clear the vampires in here."

"Sounds like a plan," Grace said as she pulled on the fire alarm. She looked at Stephen, Jaime, and Bryan. "Follow Izzy out of here. She'll protect you outside."

Grace then started running toward the dark halls as the fire alarm blared throughout the building. Izzy looked at the teenagers with her. "Follow close to me," Izzy instructed as she began jogging toward the nearest exit. Students screamed as chaos ensued and they pushed and shoved to get out of the darkened halls. Izzy looked back, seeing Stephen, Jaime, and Bryan following behind, trying not to separate.

Izzy turned right and saw the exit sign just a hundred feet away when a high-pitched scream came from a room on the left. "Let her go!" she heard a female voice scream.

The brown-haired demon hunter barged into a room to see two males and a female vampire holding the biology teacher prisoner, while a female student was sprawled on the floor crying.

Izzy looked at the teens following her. "Head toward the exit!" she ordered. "I'll join you in a few minutes!"

The teens did not need further instruction as they kept running while Izzy pulled out a small stake from the back of her jeans. "Let her go!" the demon hunter ordered the vampires.

A female vampire with curly dark hair growled at Izzy. "Who the hell are you to bark out orders?"

The short-haired blond male vampire licked the neck of the Biology teacher while looking at Izzy. "She's just a scared little girl pretending to be tough."

Izzy ran toward the vampires before the thought of injuring the civilians crossed their minds. The teenaged girl jumped on one of the desks and flipped over it, covering the space that separated her from her foes. The demons did not have time to reach her when Izzy stuck her stake into the blond vampire's eye.

The beast howled in pain and only saw a blur as the young girl moved to the side. The vampire could only hear flesh pounding flesh and his brethren grunting and moaning. Soon he saw both his companions on the ground and the young girl escorting the biology teacher and the young student out of the room. "Get up!" he ordered. "She's getting away!"

As soon as the women had exited the room, Izzy closed the door, turning toward the vampires and gripping her bloodied stake. "Do I look scared to you?" she asked.

The three vampires rushed the teen as she kicked one of the desks in front of her, tripping the blonde one-eyed vampire, causing him to fall flat on his face. The remaining fiends tried to reach the demon hunter with their claws, only for her to stop them with a spin-kick to the face. She pounced on the second male vampire and plunged her wooden stake into his chest, turning him to ash.

The female vampire screamed at Izzy, flinging wild punches that the teenager blocked easily, taking steps back from the onslaught. She felt a pair of arms restrain her from behind, feeling a putrid breath down her neck. "I've got you now, little girl!" the one-eyed vampire hissed.

Izzy lifted her right leg, kicking the female vampire on the knee, making her buckle. Without dropping her leg to the floor, she kicked the vampire twice more in the chest and face. Blood streamed from the female vampire's nose as Izzy's boot broke it. The demon hunter then smashed the back of her head into the vampire who held her arms, causing him to grunt in pain. She lifted both her legs around the female vampire's face while the male vampire still had her arms. She twirled her body to the right, shifting her weight, causing her momentum to bring both vampires down on the floor. Izzy recovered and staked the female vampire, turning her to dust.

A piercing scream from outside the school caught Izzy's attention. She could see the football team trying to deal with a small horde of vampires and demons on the outside. Izzy looked to her side and saw the panicked look of the remaining one-eyed male vampire. "Can you fly?" she asked.

The vampire did not have time to process the question as the girl grabbed him by the scruff of his jacket, twirling and launching him through the glass window. The vampire sprawled unto the grassy field and tried to get up, only for the demon hunter to jump on top of him, plunging her stake into his chest and turning him to ash.

Izzy looked around, seeing most of the student body and staff had gotten out of the school and were all to the side of the building's main entrance. But six students who seemed to be part of the football team had wandered toward the desolate east side where she was. They were now trying to fend off a small horde of a dozen vampires, and they were losing. Izzy could hear the faint sound of sirens in the distance.

"Hey!" Izzy exclaimed, calling for the vampires' attention. Her face fell, seeing a massive seven-foot-tall male vampire stand up and look at the girl. His ripped leather jacket barely contained his massive physique. A large scar adorned the whole side of his chiseled, bearded face.

"Take these kids to Cassius!" the large vampire ordered. "I'll handle this little nuisance."

Izzy ran toward the vampire with her stake in hand, as the massive demon, in a fantastic feat of speed, spun and extended his leg, connecting with the young girl's chest. Izzy felt her chest cavity was about to explode as the impact caused her to fly to the side, making her release her stake. Her body sprawled awkwardly on the grassy soil. She started coughing as she got on all fours, trying to get back the wind that had been knocked out of her.

The bearded vampire walked toward the young girl, who was not getting up. He stood just at her side, listening to the girl gasp for breath. The vampire then sent his massive fist downward, colliding with Izzy's back. The brown-haired girl screamed in pain as she fell face-first flat on the ground. The vampire then grabbed the girl's head and pressed down, causing her to muffle faint whimpers.

Izzy's heart raced, feeling the painful pressure increase on her head. *Not like this!* She thought to herself. She could feel a new wave of energy flow through her body—something she hadn't experienced before. The young demon hunter felt this surge of power intensify throughout every cell of her physique as she lifted her upper body, to the surprise of the large vampire. The vampire pressed down, but it was like pushing down on steel. The vampire released his grip and fired a right punch downward, aimed at Izzy's face.

The demon hunter felt everything move in slow motion; sensing the blow coming, she moved to the side and flipped on her back just as the fist collided with the soil. The teenaged girl wrapped her legs around the monster's arm and kicked the beast's face with the heel of her boot. The demon screamed as the teenager moved her legs up to his arm, reaching his throat, trapping the vampire in an armbar. The demon grunted, trying to free himself, shifting his position to alleviate the pressure, but it was too late as a loud crack echoed in the night.

The bearded vampire screamed as Izzy twisted the dislocated arm one more time. Izzy released her hold and rolled over on her back seeing the large vampire fall on his knees. The demon hunter rolled forward and kicked the vampire right in the face, hearing a satisfying crack in conjunction with the demon's howls of agony.

Izzy rolled to the side one more time and reached for her dropped stake. She then lunged at the large vampire's chest, piercing his heart. The beast screamed as he exploded into ashes.

The young demon hunter took a deep breath and saw the horde of vampires had disappeared, along with the students she tried to protect. "Damn," Izzy whispered to herself as she got up. She then saw Stephen and Jaime running toward her.

"Are you okay?" Stephen asked, his voice filled with concern.

"I'm okay," Izzy said as she noticed Bryan was not with them. "Where's Bryan?"

"We got separated just as we reached the exit!" Jaime exclaimed. "He's still trapped inside the school!"

Izzy was about to say something when she saw the police and the fire trucks arrive. "Stay with the rest of the students and the police," Izzy ordered. "I'm going back inside!"

Saint Helena High School, California; September 06, 8:20 p.m.

Grace walked the darkened halls of the school as the fire alarm blared in the background. She could feel the dark essence infesting the school all around, but her heart remained calm. It seemed most of the faculty and student body had evacuated, but the pit of her stomach told her otherwise. Screams and growls echoed in the halls with the creatures of the night searching for humans led astray.

The dark-haired demon hunter recalled her Guardian's words about focusing. Grace let her instinct guide her when she felt something tug deep inside.

The sixteen-year-old broke into a sprint, running further down the halls and into the school. The only light source inside was that of the emergency lighting that flickered, creating dark shadows at her side. She was a moving target now, as her footsteps caught the attention of the vampires and demons inside. She could feel them closer now.

A wooden door burst to the side as a long-white-haired vampire emerged, growling at Grace. The young girl anticipated its movements as she grabbed him by the shoulders and smashed him against the metal lockers, denting them. She stuck her stake into him, turning him into dust.

The demon hunter moved to the side as a fist smashed against the school locker. She turned around and kicked upward, connecting to a second vampire who had appeared. Her strike caught the beast off guard as he staggered back and the girl plunged her wooden weapon into his heart. The monster exploded into a cloud of ash and dust.

Grace turned her attention to the hall and saw ten vampires emerging from the doors, all glaring at her. But that wasn't what held her attention. At the end of the hall, she saw the blonde vampire, Brenda, smiling gleefully at her while wrapping her arm around Bryan's throat and dragging him down toward the basement.

Grace started jogging through the hall, feeling everything move in slow motion as the vampires flooded to attack her. A new wave of energy she hadn't felt before flowed in every cell of her body. The demon hunter let her instincts take over as one beast threw a haymaker at her face. The girl ducked and thrust her stake in his heart as she kicked an oncoming demon on the chest. She ducked under a kick of a third vampire foot sweeping him and bringing him to the floor. As his body crashed down, Grace cartwheeled over him, staking the demon in the process and kicking two oncoming vampires. The teenaged girl grabbed the second vampire she struck and threw him to the other two vampires she'd kicked, watching them collapse in a heap of limbs.

Two more vampires ran forward, trying to grab the girl, only for her to dodge under their massive arms and move right behind them, staking both of them in the back with her wooden weapon. She cartwheeled back as two more vampires tried to kick her face, effectively avoiding the attack and reaching the three previous vampires who had gotten to their feet. She did a spinning roundhouse kick, connecting with all their heads backflipping, avoiding two vampires that were still swinging at her.

Grace's back was against the lockers as both vampires kicked up, while the teenager ducked and rolled forward. The demons' legs crashed against the metal, denting the cabinets. Grace stood up and plunged her stake into both vampires as she jumped, somersaulting without her hands touching the ground and landing right in front of the vampires she had just kicked, staking all three of them in the chest.

The demon hunter moved toward the last vampire, and before he could attack, she thrust her stake in his chest. She pulled it out and twirled it as she continued running toward the basement entrance, only hearing behind her the vanquished demons exploding into ash and dust.

Grace reached the entrance of the basement and proceeded downward. She could sense a trap set up for her, but she couldn't let Bryan's sister take him. The lighting in the basement was just as bad as it was on the surface. The spaces were tight, which made it ideal for her in a fight, so the vampire was luring her to an open area.

As the girl walked down the hall, following her instincts, she could feel a familiar presence in her heart. She turned around, seeing Nikki's silhouette, followed by Sean's solid frame. As the dim light illuminated their bodies, Grace gasped, seeing Sean's battered and bruised face. He was leaning heavily on a tattered and worn-down Nikki, who still carried a stake and a crossbow.

"They're about to break the door," Nikki whispered.

Grace proceeded to help Sean stand up straight. "I heard these monsters are after me," Sean commented weakly. "Do we know why?"

Grace shook her head. "Elizabeth didn't mention it. She just warned us to get you out of here. But Brenda got a hold of Bryan and dragged him down here. I need to get him out."

"Vampires are about to swarm this place," Nikki warned. "Two members of the Karratt Order are leading them."

"You can't leave the boy down here," Sean instructed. "Let's find him. The metal door won't hold the vampires for long. Where's Izzy?"

"She helped evacuate the building," Grace whispered as she continued walking. "She trusted us to get you out of here, which we will do."

"Find the boy," Sean said. "Then we get out of here."

Grace continued leading, feeling the dark energy around her. Vampires flooded the underground caverns around the school, but only a few had entered the premises. She could also feel Izzy's energy dispatching monsters inside the building. The dark-haired demon hunter continued walking to the end of the hall when she heard soft laughter echo in the darkness. "You can't have him!" Brenda hissed. "He's mine!"

Grace bolted down the hall, sensing Nikki and Sean trying to keep up with her. The demon hunter ran faster than she had ever run before, making a right, then left, as she pulled out her stake. She turned the final corner, reaching the boiler room—seeing Brenda hold Bryan's neck exposed, ready to sink her fangs into him. Behind her, five vampires moved toward Grace with deadly intent.

The dark-eyed demon hunter pulled out a glass canister and threw it, aiming at Brenda's vampiric face. The female vampire screeched as the flask exploded and holy water burned half her visage. She released Bryan, to Grace's relief, as she jumped and spun over the five vampires who attacked. She pulled out a small quarter-sized brown package from her pocket and threw it up at the ceiling. "*Luceat lux clara!*" she exclaimed as the pack exploded into a blinding white light.

The vampires screeched, shielding their red eyes just as Nikki got into the room. She jumped into the fray as Sean leaned next to the wall, while his demon hunters blurred through the small pack of vampires, coating the boiler room with ash and dust.

Grace turned her attention toward Brenda, who cradled her burnt face with her hands as Bryan ran toward the demon hunter. "You don't remember our last conversation?" Grace asked.

Brenda bitterly looked at Grace and started giggling. The vampire's laughter brought a shiver down Grace's spine. "You simply don't get it," Brenda said. "It's not you we want."

Grace turned toward Sean and Nikki when she felt the surge of dark energy all around. Vampires were now inside the basement with them. The dark-eyed girl looked around and saw an adjacent hallway, opposite the entrance where they had come in. She started running toward that exit when a dozen vampires streamlined through, growling at her.

Grace covered Bryan, while Nikki covered Sean. Both demon hunters could feel demons had broken through and were coming toward them.

"Cassius wants the human," Brenda said, acknowledging Sean. "Killing two demon hunters and turning my brother will be a bonus."

Nikki and Grace looked at each other as they firmly grasped their weapons, just as they heard a voice in their heads scream at them, "*Move to the side!*"

Grace pushed Bryan to one end of the boiler room, while Nikki pushed Sean to the other. A loud explosion came from the ceiling as pieces of concrete and steel flew to the sides, ricocheting off the walls. The demon hunters looked up and saw a three-foot-diameter hole in the ceiling, through which Izzy had jumped with two flaming glass chemistry beakers in each hand. As the brown-haired demon hunter landed, she flung the beakers at the mob of vampires. The glass exploded, releasing balls of flame that set ablaze the undead.

"I hope I don't get expelled for this," Izzy murmured.

"Three demon hunters are no match for Cassius, Draco, and the Order of Karratt," Brenda hissed, pointing at the original entrance.

Draco entered the room, followed by his white-haired enforcer and more vampires.

"You're coming with me, Ankrnot!" Draco bellowed as he pointed at Sean.

The white-haired demon prepared his whips when an arrow whistled through the air, striking the beast on the shoulder. Nikki looked toward the origin of the shot and saw Solas by the second exit with a crossbow in one hand and a flaming blue sword in the other.

"Not today, Draco!" Solas exclaimed.

Grace pushed Bryan toward the second exit, covering him while Nikki pushed Sean. Izzy grabbed hold of her father while the red-headed demon hunter started firing her crossbow at the remaining vampire horde. Blessed bolts started flying, and vampires howled in agony.

Bryan and Grace exited first, followed by Sean and Izzy, who thanked Solas before leaving. Nikki stood next to the dark-skinned demon and fired another clip at the beasts. "Careful with the white-haired demon," Nikki said. "He gave me a shocking experience."

Solas smiled at the joke as he fired another bolt. "Let's get out of here!"

Solas and Nikki started running as more vampires emerged on the opposite side. Both demon and demon hunter felt the horde on their heels. A final right guided them toward the stairs that led to the football field. As soon as the cold air hit their faces and their feet touched the grass, Grace and Izzy closed the door and barred the exit with a metal pipe.

Izzy hugged her dad as they walked away from the entrance when a loud bang bent the metal door outward. "Dad! Get out of here!"

Before he could respond, the metal doors burst to the side and Draco emerged, followed by his white-haired enforcer. "Kill the demon hunters," he ordered. As the words left his lips, a flood of vampires came out from behind him.

Grace covered Bryan as she pulled out her stake, seeing Nikki and Solas eager to engage as they went to Izzy's side and covered Sean, who was ready for battle.

The vampires charged in full at Izzy's side, who stuck her stake to the first one while spin-kicking the second one. Her heartbeat was racing, not because she feared the undead, but for her father's safety. Two vampires tackled her to the ground, but she rolled with the attack and dusted one while kicking the other one in the face.

Nikki double-fisted a vampire on the chest, following her attack with a kick to the face. She grabbed the vampire and threw him on the upcoming horde when three more jumped toward her. Nikki was about to attack when Solas jumped in front of her and slashed with his fire sword on the new incoming fiends, turning them to ash.

"Thanks," Nikki said to Solas as she fired a one-two combination to a tall vampire. "But I'm not a damsel in distress that needs rescuing."

"I know," Solas replied. "But, an assist is good from time to time."

Brenda and two vampires rushed Grace and Bryan at full force. "I'm sorry," Grace said to Bryan. She then stepped forward and split-kicked the two vampires on the face, bringing them down. Brenda tried to kick the dark-haired demon hunter, but was too slow to connect. Grace quickly blocked the strikes and punched hard on Brenda's chest, pushing her back.

The two vampires kicked up and struck Grace on her chest with synchronized blows; the demon hunter gasped and stepped back as both demons threw spin-kicks at her face. The teenaged girl ducked and rolled under them, staking both vampires and turning them to dust.

Grace looked forward and saw Brenda already in the air as she connected with Grace's bruised chest with a flying kick. The teenaged girl grunted feeling the stake slip from her fingers as she landed on her back. Brenda jumped again and stomped hard on Grace's stomach, causing the girl to scream in agony.

"My first demon hunter," Brenda hissed as she straddled the sixteen-year-old girl who laid on the ground. "They say your blood tastes like fine wine." The demon went to bite Grace, only for her to arch her back in pain.

Grace looked surprised as she realized that Bryan had stuck her dropped stake onto Brenda's back. He had missed her heart, but it was enough to distract the demon. Brenda looked at her younger brother with a pained look. "Why?" she asked, just as Grace pushed the beast to the side.

Brenda grunted in pain, feeling the wooden stake dislodge itself from her back. She kicked up, only for Grace to jump on top of her, piercing her heart with the stake. Brenda gasped before turning to ash.

Grace turned toward Bryan, who fell on his knees with tears in his eyes, seeing his sister die again. The demon hunter then jumped up and launched herself at a vampire that was about to attack Bryan. She grappled the beast, plunging her stake deep into its heart.

Sean kicked two vampires, grabbing a third and throwing him toward Draco, who stepped to the side.

Izzy smiled, feeling better now that she was fighting alongside her sisters and her father. It was awesome seeing her old man kick butt in his brute style; he seemed to have found a second wind. Izzy staked two more vampires, turning them to dust.

Draco scowled, seeing the demon hunters pulverize his vampires. "Enough games!" he exclaimed as he patted his white-haired demon. "Bring me Ankrnot!"

The white-haired demon nodded as he cracked the metal coils from his hands. He whipped to the one side, isolating Grace and Izzy. He then slashed at Solas, only for Nikki to tackle the dark-skinned demon.

Izzy saw in horror what was about to happen. She jumped to the side, avoiding the electric coils, and reached out to her father but fell a couple of feet short.

Sean extended his hands to his daughter when the metal coils wrapped around his torso. Electricity flowed through his body, causing the man to scream in pain.

"No!" Izzy screamed as Draco's lackey pulled Sean toward him, dragging him through the grass.

As Sean was pulled to the dark-skinned vampire, the massive beast smashed his fist against Sean's face, knocking him out. Draco looked at the demon hunters. "Be seeing you," he said hoisting Sean's unconscious body over his shoulder and running down to the school basement.

Izzy stood up, in time for the demon dressed in white to whip his electric bolts at her. She dodged and moved just as the beast turned and followed his master. Izzy dusted the remaining vampires and followed after the monsters, with Grace and Nikki right behind her.

They went back into the basement only for the white-haired demon to slash upward, bursting the pipes from the ceiling, bringing metal and concrete down.

Izzy's heart fell seeing the demon block the corridor behind him, looking helpless as the fiends took her father from her. "Dad!" the teen girl screamed, falling to her knees.

CHAPTER XV

Abandoned Wine Cellar, Saint Helena
Outskirts; September 06, 9:00 p.m.

SABINE MADE HER WAY down the stairs, reaching the lower level of the abandoned warehouse. Vampires knelt as she passed them, with Neil trailing behind her. The raven-haired vampire ignored the undead, focusing only on the pounding of flesh and grunts of pain echoing in the darkness. She passed by the room where UrthaMal was locked in and headed to the black door at the end of the hall. Draco's number one enforcer was guarding the entrance, which brought a frown on Sabine's face as she looked straight into the blue-eyed, white-haired demon. The lightning coils crackled around his arms, ready to do battle.

"The surface requires your attention," Sabine instructed the suit-wearing demon. "The demon hunters will come for Ankrnot. Please make them feel welcome."

The demon nodded without saying a word and walked up the stairs as the ancient vampire opened the black door.

She saw Cassius gleefully grinning, while Draco battered a chained-up Sean down to a bloody pulp. Crimson liquid dripped from the vampire's dark-skinned hands.

"Gentlemen," Sabine called out. "If you don't mind, I need him alive."

"Why?" Draco growled at the ancient one. "He betrayed darkness! He deserves to pay tenfold before I extinguish his life."

Sabine sighed and shook her head. "I don't want to leave the Order of Karratt leaderless yet again," she calmly said.

"I am sick of this!" Draco exclaimed as he towered over Sabine. "You speak in nothing but riddles, with no clear path on a course to take!"

"Draco!" Cassius reprimanded. "That's enough!"

"Yes!" Draco said as he looked at his employer. "It's enough indeed! While we play charades with a so-called ancient one, the demon hunters on the surface draw breath. They're responsible for the death of Athena! The time for vengeance of the Order is now!"

Sabine rolled her eyes and swiped at Draco's throat. Her concealed blade pierced the soft flesh, almost cutting straight through the giant vampire's neck. Dark blood spurted out as Draco's hands instinctively attempted to seal the wound. His lacerated vocal cords were unable to make a sound as he fell to his knees.

Sabine sidestepped the dark-skinned vampire and looked at Cassius. "Even though a vampire's heart beats no longer, it's amazing how much blood can be lost when a throat has been slashed."

Dark blood stained the floor as Draco fell to his hands and knees. "Please, Neil," Sabine said, not looking away from Cassius's eyes. "Put that piece of trash out of its misery." Neil pulled a wooden stake from his suit and thrusted it into Draco's back. Dust and ash sprinkled down onto the dark vampire blood.

"Now," Sabine said to Cassius. "You better tell Draco's enforcer of his leader's untimely demise. Inform your clan their time is at hand. UrthaMal will rise within the hour. Nothing will stop you now."

Cassius knelt before Sabine and kissed her hand. "It will be done, Moroi Schulmeister."

The vampire walked away. Neil caught Sabine's eyes and walked out of the room, closing the door behind him, leaving the beaten and chained-up Guardian alone with the female vampire. The raven-haired demon sat crossed-legged across from Sean and admired his battered physique. "Sorry for the hostility," she said. "I'd wished your final moments on Earth would be pleasant ones."

Sean smiled as he tried to clean the crimson liquid from his battered face. The black chains rattled as he tried to get comfortable. "I can't outrun death forever," Sean said. "I only wished it would be more significant, though."

"Oh, but it will be."

"How so?" Sean asked. "Being soul food for a hellspawn? Trust me, my mind had a more creative way for me to go."

"If you knew what I knew," Sabine said, "You would realize your death has a glorious purpose."

"What is it that you gain?" Sean asked. "Can you at least give me that bit of decency? A reason?"

"We have a couple of minutes," Sabine said.

"UrthaMal can sense you. She's aching for your soul. Your strong spirit will be enough to free her."

"What's your endgame?" Sean asked again. "Releasing a higher demon on this plane will cause the extinction of the human race. Without humans, how will you feed?"

Sabine smiled as she looked at the ceiling of the underground cellar. "I've lived for two millennia," Sabine said. "I've seen countless demons take a higher form. I've seen warriors of light battle and fall, battle and be victorious. It is not the first time I've done this, and it will certainly not be the last."

Sean looked at the vampire inquisitively as numerous ideas formed in his mind, while Sabine admired the Guardian trying to put everything together. "When I first encountered the Guardians," the elder vampire said, "They were all believers–like you, before you let the demon Ankrnot take over. That belief gave the Guardians and the demon hunters purpose. It grounded their mission into something. Just like other organizations, they believed in the higher good, no matter the cost. Humans longed for the physical salvation of the creatures of the night. And their blind belief shielded them from the horrors the Guardians are guilty of."

"Past tense," Sean said. "We're not like that anymore."

"Can you truly be free from that legacy?" Sabine asked. "How can you look at your demon hunters in the eyes and tell them you are better now just because you run things? How much suffering and pain has your organization caused to countless girls and their families just because they have a 'gift'?" Sean remained silent, but his thoughts betrayed him, and Sabine took advantage of his weakness.

"You know what the funny thing is," Sabine said as she stood up. "The Guardians believe that you can save humans from his mystical darkness, but it's impossible." Sean looked confused for a moment. "Think about it," Sabine continued. "At the turn of the twentieth century, we had the intellectual enlightenment of the human race. Society put religion, myth, and superstition aside, with logic and reason taking their place. What was the result of that? More war, famine, and disease that has wiped out more than one hundred million human lives."

"So, what's your point?" Sean asked bitterly.

"I find it astonishing that organizations like yours fight to keep this suffering-infested world spinning," Sabine said with a shrug. "What's the point? UrthaMal is living proof of that. Right next door is a demon who feeds exclusively on the human's darkest passion. She's just revealing what is rotten in this pathetic race, dominated by the flesh. Human beings are destined to destroy each other. They're selfish creatures thinking about their own needs, not taking into consideration the damage they cause themselves and others."

Sean winced in pain, straining under the weight of the chains that held him down. "You feel her, don't you?" Sabine asked as she continued pacing around the broken Guardian. "She feels you, too. She feels your hatred. Just like an average human Sean, you can't avoid what truly defines you. The hate inside you fuels that vengeance. What caused it? What is the genesis of that dark emotion? Can you share that with me?"

Sean struggled against the chains, feeling a dark essence reach out to him from the dark and searching for his emotions. Sean tried to hide his thoughts, but the black energy was stronger and relentless.

"Don't fight it," Sabine whispered, searching Sean's mind. "It's part of you. Be free. Tell me your hidden passion."

Sean screamed in pain as the memories flashed inside his mind. The past flooded his every thought.

The Guardian looked at his young twenty-two-year-old hands. The white candles lit the dining from his home country in Ireland. Sean turned to the side, seeing Sabine with him and his thoughts. The young man looked at the closed door before him, only hearing female screams from the other side.

"What's behind that door?" Sabine asked.

The door opened, revealing an older man. His unbuttoned white shirt covered his moist upper torso while he buttoned up his brown trousers. As the man walked, his bare feet felt like stomps on the wooden floor echoing in Sean's mind. "Are you angry, boy?" Sean's father asked.

Sean trembled in rage, seeing past the older man and toward the beaten body of his younger sister. "She didn't put out much tonight," Sean's father said, referencing the young man's sister. He smiled cruelly at his son. "You seem upset, boy. Where's my supper?"

Sabine nodded as she looked at the memory. "You lacked the strength and the will," Sabine said, understanding. "So you made a deal."

Sean looked at his hands. Knife wounds adorned his palms with blood drops falling on the wooden floor. A nine-pointed star was drawn at the base of his feet; orange light surrounded the young man as a six-foot-five brown-skinned demon with white eyes placed his long, clawed hands on Sean's shoulder. Sean screamed sensing the monster taking control of his body and vengeance warping his mind and heart.

Sean's father screamed in horror as Ankrnot started tearing him apart limb from limb. Blood splattered on the wooden walls with human flesh and bone ripping from side to side.

Sabine just nodded at the vengeance demon's carnage as five servants tried to pry off the monster from their master, but the same fate awaited them. The demon grabbed each servant and bathed in their blood, to Sean's sister's horrified look.

Sean looked at his sister, and new emotions filled the demon-controlled human: disgust and contempt. Ankrnot leaped from the pool of blood he stood in and slashed the life out of his sister.

"That is how vengeance works," Sabine said as he looked at Sean's broken and defeated face. "It's never enough, which drives my point home. Human beings are rotten. No matter how much you try to save them from the impending darkness and doom, somehow they find a way to destroy themselves.

The black door behind Sabine opened, and Neil stood on the door frame. "UrthaMal is ready," the male vampire said.

Sabine nodded and looked at Sean. The Guardian's spirit was broken and ripe for the taking. "Her meal is ready," the raven-haired vampire said, just as two more vampires walked in and dragged Sean's body out.

Sabine slowly followed the vampires into UrthaMal's

resting place. The vampire looked at the demon, who had an ecstatic look on her face. "This one is perfect," UrthaMal purred as she admired Sean's bloodied body.

"We'll leave you to it, then," Sabine said, motioning the vampires to step outside. "See you at your coming-out party."

Sabine walked out and motioned Neil to follow her. "How long do we have?" Neil asked as they made their way up the circular staircase.

"Thirty to forty minutes," Sabine said as they reached the upper level. "Maybe less."

As soon as they reached the front entrance, Cassius looked at Sabine with expecting eyes. The rest of his clan had gathered there, which seemed like three dozen vampires. Draco's white-haired enforcer awaited orders. "Is it done?" Cassius asked.

Sabine nodded at the clan leader. "It's done, Cassius. In a few minutes, all you have wished for will come to fruition."

The elder vampire turned toward Draco's enforcer. "I assume you have a name?"

"Hepheenious," the demon replied as blue and white electricity ran through his body, flooding his eyes.

"You are now the leader of The Karratt Order," Sabine said. "Your former leader broke your sacred code, prompting his immediate termination."

"Our contract is our word," Hepheenious said, understanding. "If he rescinded, he was unworthy of his title and position. He alone sealed his fate."

"Glad you see it that way," Sabine said. "The contract you have with Cassius and his clan is still in play. But with Draco's demise and your depleting numbers, you have the option to leave and still preserve your honor. I leave the choice up to you."

Hepheenious looked at Cassius and nodded. "I'll remain and fulfill the contract. But the rest of the order will regroup."

"Excellent," Sabine said, stepping outside into the night and catching a glimpse of her driver next to her SUV.

"You leave us now?" Cassius asked cautiously as the female vampire walked toward her car. "In our moment of triumph?"

Sabine turned toward the vampire and smiled. "I wouldn't miss this for the world," she said. "Get your vampires ready. We'll have company soon. You'll bathe in a glory that your former ward could only dream off."

Cassius looked extremely pleased as Sabine walked toward her driver, with Neil behind her. Ian saw his employer approach as he pulled out a long, black rectangular case from the vehicle's front seat. "What you asked for, my lady," the older man said.

Sabine looked at Neil and nodded to him as the male vampire walked toward the SUV and got in the back. Sabine opened Ian's case, revealing a beautiful dark katana, protected by a smooth black saya. The elder vampire removed the weapon from its resting place and pulled out the blade. Its suka had a lovely golden dragon carving, coiled from the pommel and concluded right before the guard. "You've done well, my friend," Sabine said to Ian as she twirled the katana. The blade generated a soft tune as it cut through the air.

Ian nodded, closing the case. "Anything else you need from me tonight?" the older man asked.

"One last thing," Sabine said. "Drive away from this town, taking Neil with you. He'll tell you where you will drop him off. After that, go home to your daughter. Spend time with her."

Ian looked confused at the last instruction. "I beg your pardon, my lady."

"Your thoughts are not secret to me, my friend. You've longed for this moment. Your services are no longer needed. Go home."

"But, my family has a vow," Ian stammered.

"Yes," Sabine said as she put away the katana and strapped the sword on her back. "Always reminding me of those pesky vows. Trust me, I'm aware. The vow still stands. If your daughter chooses to continue her family's legacy, it will be her choice. Not mine, nor yours."

Ian processed the information and nodded at the vampire. "Thank you, my lady."

"Go," Sabine ordered. "Clock is ticking."

Ian nodded as he got into the SUV and started the engine as Sabine walked back toward the abandoned warehouse, where Cassius anxiously awaited.

"Any last recommendation?" the younger vampire asked.

"Just relax," Sabine said. "You lead this clan. You'll know what to do once UrthaMal ascends. She'll grant you everything you desire. In the meantime, you should prepare a solid defense. Four demon hunters will be here any minute now, and they will stop at nothing until they rescue their Guardian. I'm afraid they'll be too late, though."

Cassius nodded and looked at his clan. "Protect the perimeter," the vampire ordered. "Once UrthaMal has risen, nothing will stop us."

Sabine smiled and entered the warehouse. Sean's screams echoed within the dark and abandoned structure. The ancient vampire pulled out her bottle of pills, feeling a headache coming. The raven-haired demon popped half a dozen capsules and chewed hard. She needed to be ready and in top form to face what was coming.

CHAPTER XVI

Saint Helena High School, California;
September 06, 9:00 p.m.

ELIZABETH MANEUVERED HER SUV into the high school parking lot, noticing police patrol vehicles as well as two fire trucks at the scene. Flocking the entire area was a crowd of students and concerned parents. Elizabeth turned toward John, who shared a nervous look. They were running out of time. Elizabeth parked her car and closed her eyes, calling out to her girls with her mind. The blonde Guardian and demon hunter could feel their fear, despair, and hopelessness. Elizabeth opened her eyes and motioned John to get out.

As both Guardians stepped out of the vehicle, Izzy, Grace, and Nikki ran up to them with Solas, Jaime, Bryan, and a third teen boy Elizabeth hadn't seen before.

"They took Dad!" Izzy exclaimed as she hugged her mom and started to cry. "We couldn't stop them! I couldn't stop them."

Nikki stood behind Izzy during the entire time. She felt devastated by how the events had transpired, sensing the weight of responsibility on her shoulders. There was no excuse she could think of.

"They came in numbers and were prepared," Grace reported. "It was all to get to him. He was the target all along."

"I know," Elizabeth answered, trying to control her voice. Even though she was successful in not letting her voice crack, she couldn't help but feel a sense of doom in the pit of her heart. She looked at John, hoping for a solution out of this mess. His face was not reassuring. "Why Sean?" Elizabeth asked.

"The strength of his will," John concluded. "It has to be. UrthaMal feeds off of souls that fall for their most profound passions. Sean's will to control Ankrnot inside him is the main course for this demon."

"What happens to my father if UrthaMal feeds off his soul?" Izzy asked, dreading the answer as she wiped the tears from her eyes.

"Only Ankrnot will remain," John concluded.

"Wait," Grace said, looking at Elizabeth. "The Guardians have always contemplated the possibility of this demon breaking free. You have countermeasures for this, right?"

Elizabeth nodded as she walked toward the back of the SUV and opened the trunk. The two red boxes with a white cross stamped on them were to the side of a large wooden chest. The blonde Guardian opened the first box, revealing a golden Irish crucifix. Beside it was a crystal orb filled with blessed water and oil. "I hoped I'd never resort to this," Elizabeth mainly whispered to herself. The Guardian opened the second box, extracting silver chains from it.

She brought out the elements and handed the orb and crucifix to Grace. "I need your expertise on this one. Your father designed the ritual."

Grace's eyes widened as she looked at the objects in her hands. She looked at John, not knowing what to do.

"I'll send you the instructions to your phone," John said to the dark-haired demon hunter. "It's not only the elements and procedure, but it also requires the strength of a demon hunter to perform the rite. The Guardians tasked your father in developing this in case Ankrnot was ever set free."

"What about the chains?" Nikki asked Elizabeth.

"The only thing that can bind Ankrnot," Elizabeth replied as she wrapped the chains around her chest. "Specially made by the Guardians."

"We capture Ankrnot and keep him alive," Izzy said. "Will this ritual work even though UrthaMal has fed off of my father?"

John sighed as he looked at Elizabeth, who feared the worst. "There're a lot of variables," John said. "Once UrthaMal extracts Sean's soul, she will be strong enough to free herself from where she is and ascend. She will be a purebred demon walking on this plane, with all the hellish power at her disposal. It will be mere minutes before she corrupts the citizenry of this entire town." John paused as he looked at Elizabeth. "That means I'll be affected as well. It will only be you, demon hunters. UrthaMal's power will give her control over lesser demons. Depending on how many creatures are there with her, you will fight not only her, but also her army."

"What do you mean you'll be affected?" Nikki asked.

"The entire human population of this town will succumb to their deepest desires," John said. "With UrthaMal's influence, she will unleash our deepest passions until we succumb to them."

"Succumb?" Nikki asked.

"Hard to say," John said. "Consider our deepest passion being used to an extreme, where it causes your destruction: rage, selfishness, lust, among other hidden emotions, pushing us to our limit." The Guardian paused for a moment. "We either kill each other, or we take our own lives. The entire population will be on a self-destruction rampage."

The demon hunters looked at the teens present in the conversation, who all had frightened looks on their faces. "You can't let this happen!" Jaime exclaimed, feeling a new wave of fear deep down in her stomach.

"We won't," Grace said, trying to convince not only her newfound friend, but also herself.

"Another thing," John said. "In this battle, you have to banish an ascended demon while being careful not to kill Ankrnot. If you kill Sean's vessel, you lose his soul forever."

Elizabeth passed her hands through her blonde hair as she looked at her demon hunters. She had faced Ankrnot, and the demon was not to be trifled with. But letting her demon hunters face UrthaMal was exposing them to another level of threat.

"If you manage to vanquish UrthaMal without destroying Ankrnot," John continued as he turned toward Grace, "That is the moment you must perform the ritual to restore Sean. But you have limited time to do it."

"How much time?" Izzy asked, dreading the answer.

"Less than a minute," John said.

Grace gulped, taking in the responsibility. "I got it," she said.

"Where is Sabine in all this?" Solas asked. "I can't imagine her freeing a demon of UrthaMal's caliber so that she can become a puppet. What's her endgame?"

"We'll cross that line when we get to it," Elizabeth said, not shaking off the disturbing sensation she had with the ancient vampire. "We tackle the horde first," the Guardian said. "Once we take care of them, we take down UrthaMal. If Ankrnot decides to intervene, leave him to me."

"I can help with Dad," Izzy said.

"No!" Elizabeth snapped. "You need to stand together as a united front against UrthaMal. Ankrnot is not, nor will he ever be, your concern. He's my responsibility."

"Why are you shutting me out of this?" Izzy asked, not backing down.

"You've read what this demon has done," Elizabeth hissed at her daughter. "He'll be focused on me."

Izzy looked around and shut up. She knew she couldn't change her mother's mind right then and there.

"Sounds like sort of a plan," Nikki said. "Any ideas where they took Sean, or where UrthaMal is?"

John pulled out his tablet and opened the town's main map. "It's not the main entrance of the hell spot," John said. "We sealed the cave after the twins died."

"It's gotta be the second source of dark energy," Izzy said, remembering that sensation constantly calling out to them. "It's on the opposite side of town."

"That'll be the second gate," Solas said, walking toward John and pointing at the map. "The one Teresa and Anna wanted me to cover. West side of town, where the abandoned vineyards are located. A tall warehouse still stands. A secret entrance through the cave system leads to the lower level of an abandoned wine cellar inside the building." As the dark-skinned demon said this, he pointed to an entrance on the map. "The access to that particular tunnel starts one hundred yards south, near an abandoned wine shop. You can't miss it."

"We haven't explored that area," Nikki said, standing next to Solas. "It's a perfect spot for vampires to nest."

"I'll guide you there," Solas said to the demon hunters. "I know the route perfectly, and you can access the building undetected."

"I advise you to stay away from the demon hunters," John said as he grabbed the tablet, taking two steps back from Solas.

"Are you going to stop me?" Solas asked, standing up and towering over John, which put all the girls on edge. Nikki stepped up, trying to push back Solas while Izzy protected the young Guardian.

"I'm sure you mean well," John stated. "You did help Anna and Teresa, even though one of them didn't trust you. But that is far from the point I'm trying to make. If UrthaMal rises, her powers will let her control all demons and creatures of the night that walk this town. That includes you. You'll become another footsoldier doing her bidding. It's enough with Ankrnot on the field for them to worry about you also."

"You don't know me," Solas replied. "I'm not a lesser

demon that a spawn of hell will manipulate. This is not the first time I'm in the presence of a higher beast. I failed Teresa and Anna. I will not fail. Not this time."

John turned toward Elizabeth. "Solas is a great asset," the young Guardian said. "But if he turns, UrthaMal will use him the best way she can to defend her position."

Elizabeth looked at Solas and her demon hunters. "I can't risk it, Solas. You helped the twins in countless incursions. And you helped my demon hunters tonight. But this battle is beyond you, and I think you know this. The last thing you want is for another burden to carry beyond the death of Anna and Teresa."

Nikki looked at Solas, who was about to say something, but the red-headed demon hunter stopped him. "If you want to honor the demon hunters you lost, build a second front if we fall."

Solas looked into Nikki's deep blue eyes. He then turned toward the rest of the demon hunters. He silently nodded and took a few steps back away from everyone. The redhead turned toward Elizabeth and awaited her Guardian's instructions.

Grace looked at Jaime and Bryan. "You should both go home," the dark-eyed demon hunter said. She then turned toward Bryan. "I'll call you tomorrow. Maybe we can go out for a movie or something."

Bryan smiled sadly and nodded as Jaime pulled him away.

"Grace," John called as he walked to the back of the SUV. "Let me show you how Sean's ritual works. Time is running out."

Grace nodded and walked with John to the back of

the SUV, leaving Izzy and Stephen alone while Elizabeth and Nikki stood a few feet back.

"So," Stephen broke the ice, looking into Izzy's green eyes. "This is your calling."

Izzy nodded as he looked at the boy. "Not as glamorous as yours," she said.

"Yet not less important," Stephen said. "I always imagined there was something material that went with the immaterial."

"That is my field of expertise," Izzy said with a sad smile.

"I hope we have the opportunity to discuss further," Stephen said. "Exclusively for academic purposes, of course."

"Of course," Izzy said, feeling her cheeks warm up a bit.

"I hope to see you tomorrow," Stephen said, walking away.

"I hope there is a tomorrow," Izzy said, turning around to see her mom and Nikki waiting for her. Izzy approached her mom and sister. "Let's do this."

"We'll pull this off," Elizabeth said, refocusing on the task at hand as she walked with both girls to the back of the SUV, joining John and Grace.

"I got the ritual," Grace said. "Glad Dad made it simple enough."

"I think he designed the ritual with you in mind," John said. "Somehow, he must have foreseen how vital your role would be to the Guardians."

Grace nodded, taking in the idea of her father's thoughts on her. She looked at Elizabeth and Izzy. "We'll not lose Sean. I've got this."

"I trust you," Izzy said.

"Okay," John said as he opened the chest on the back of Elizabeth's trunk. It revealed all sorts of swords, knives, and other demon-hunting gear. The Guardian pulled out an automatic white crossbow with three clips that he handed out to Grace. He pulled a second set and passed it on to Izzy, and a final one to Nikki. "These have been blessed. We're not joking around. Stakes and swords will not be enough for a possible horde."

"Make every shot count," Elizabeth instructed.

"What about UrthaMal?" Nikki asked. "What tips can you give us? What will she be like once she takes final form?"

"Hard to say," John said as he pulled out short swords and distributed them among the girls.

"An idea, John," Grace said. "You studied demonology. You showed us how to kill Athena. You've gotta have something."

"There's a wide variety of demons," John stated as he thought for a moment, looking at the girls. "This demon will have all its hellish powers here on Earth. But she's still governed by earthly law. You can hurt this beast with earthly weapons, but you can't kill it. You can only banish it."

"What do you mean we can't kill it?" Nikki asked, looking at Elizabeth.

"UrthaMal is a purebred demon from hell," the blonde Guardian stated. "Purebreds can't be destroyed on this plane. What we can do is remove all earthly elements that bind it to this dimension."

"Correct," John said. "With nothing tying her to the world of the living, the purebred can't manifest itself and has no choice but to go back where it came from."

"Where's a bazooka when you need one?" Izzy said, getting a little worried.

"If this demon is feeding off human souls and gaining strength from them, she must store that energy somewhere," John reasoned. "I assume her heart."

"It's always the heart," Nikki said.

"UrthaMal has the power to control other demons," John said, pausing for a moment. "Biologically, she would need something to transmit her wave signal. Find that, and maybe you can cut her link to her foot soldiers." John then pulled out from the chest small white earpieces and handed them out to the four demon hunters. "Two-wave radio," John said. "Describe the demon to me the moment you see her. I may give you a better idea before her influence reaches me."

Izzy looked at her mother, then at her sisters. She knew they were going in blind, not fully aware of what was in store for them. She tried to shake the nauseating feeling from her stomach as she turned her attention back to John, who had a smile for her. "You got this," John reassured them. "You'll pull it off. I believe in you."

Somehow those words calmed Izzy down. She took a deep breath as she looked at her mother. "Your call, Mom," she said.

Elizabeth nodded and closed the back door of her SUV, signaling the girls to jump in. John took a step back as the demon hunters boarded the vehicle. He held on only to his tablet as the car engine roared to life. The Guardian watched as his demon hunters rode off, heading west.

CHAPTER XVII

Saint Helena Outskirts West Side;
September 06, 9:30 p.m.

ELIZABETH MANEUVERED HER VEHICLE right next to an abandoned wine shop. The place was right where Solas had pointed out.

"You feel that?" Grace asked her sisters from the back seat.

"I can," Nikki replied. "Feels like a welcoming reception a hundred yards out. These enhanced instincts do come in handy. Can they feel our presence?"

"I don't think so," Elizabeth said, shutting down the engine and signaling her girls to get out of the car. "It's our perk to hunt them down. Not theirs."

"I can't feel Sabine," Izzy said as she looked at the abandoned wine shop. "Can she be with the horde?"

"She'll be with your father," Elizabeth said bitterly as she motioned Nikki to take point.

Izzy pressed on her earpiece as she walked with her mother. "John," Izzy said. "We're here."

"Reading you all loud and clear," John replied. "Don't turn off the earpiece. Please shout out what you see."

"Roger that," Nikki said as she took the lead, letting her instincts take over. She looked at the abandoned store. Dust and rotten wooden planks covered the front doors and windows. The teenaged girl noticed one of the boards was loose, covering the main entrance. She moved it with ease, revealing an access point inside the abandoned building. "Solas was right about the entrance," Nikki noted, as she looked at a large wooden plank that seemed to cover an opening in the floor. The demon hunter removed the board and staggered, feeling her nostrils burn as she identified the putrefying smell of rotten corpses. The blue-eyed demon hunter looked up to her sisters, who covered their noses.

"It smells worse than a fresh grave," Grace muttered.

"The corpses in graveyards are processed," Elizabeth said. "This is a vampire nest in an abandoned area of town. Vampires just disposed of the bodies, hoping the rats would take care of them."

Nikki looked down at the tunnel, letting her demon-hunter eyesight penetrate through the darkness. "Nothing seems to be protecting it. It feels as if all the vampires and demons are on the surface, waiting for a direct assault."

Elizabeth, Izzy, and Grace stood behind Nikki and looked around. "Take point," Elizabeth ordered the red-headed demon hunter. "Pay attention to your instincts. They won't betray you."

"Copy," Nikki said as she entered the tunnel. Her vision adjusted as she guided her fellow demon hunters through the hole. She could feel a tug from her insides as if some supernatural force was driving her.

"I can't believe the ancient ones are former Guardians," Izzy said as she processed the news her mother had shared in the car. The green-eyed demon hunter turned toward her mother, who only nodded. "How can they be so vicious?"

"The Guardians have never claimed to be pure in their actions," Elizabeth said. "Established by humans, the organization has changed over time."

"Maybe you can tell me why these former Guardians targeted my parents," Grace hissed.

"I figure that it has to do with The Tome," John said the earpiece. "Your father found it and deduced the identities of the Ancient Ones, as well as their plans. Ian was there to silence him. He arrived too late, though, since your dad had sent the book to California."

"Why California?" Izzy asked. "Why not send it to The Guardian's headquarters in Ireland?"

"I haven't figured out that part just yet," John said. "I believe that it was some warning to Anna and Teresa. Sabine needs this ascended demon from this particular hell spot. I just can't figure out her motive."

Grace gritted her teeth. "I still don't understand the need to kill my parents," the demon hunter said rhetorically. "It's a former Guardian taking the life of another. They were supposed to be on our side."

"A long time ago, maybe," Elizabeth said. "But with them becoming vampires, the demon inside corrupted them. There is no telling what their purpose is now. But based on what your dad wrote about them, it's all about control."

"Is that why Sabine is so good at fighting?" Nikki asked from the front of the line. "It's like she knew all our moves before we made them."

"She can read minds," Elizabeth stated. "That gives her an edge."

"Sharp edge," Nikki muttered, wincing a bit as the memory of the fight flooded her mind. The beast was a blur when she fought—ancient style with deadly force behind every strike. All of a sudden, she could feel her instincts scream at her in her mind. She raised her hand, waving the squad to stop. "Weapons ready," the redhead ordered. "Fifteen more yards."

The demon hunters slowly made their way down the tunnel when they reached what seemed like a dead end. A dark wooden plank blocked their way. Nikki carefully grasped the sides and removed the plank without making any noise. The young demon hunter felt something touch her army boot. She looked down and saw a decomposing body with his face frozen in terror. Nikki looked further and saw more than two dozen bodies neatly piled up, forming a small pyramid of death. "That explains why vampires didn't notice this access point," she whispered. "Their victims were covering it."

Izzy looked closely at some of the bodies, recognizing two of them. The first one was the old priest the police had arrested a few days prior. The second body was the arresting officer. Their faces looked consumed, as if someone had squeezed the life out of them. Their skin was now grayish-black, and dry. "These are not vampire victims," the brown-haired demon hunter concluded. "No vampire marks. These were offerings to UrthaMal."

As they made their way forward, Isabella saw five bodies with varsity jackets on them. She shook her head sadly as she pointed them out to Grace. The bodies were from the vampire raid just a few hours prior.

Nikki continued leading as she noticed light coming from a black door that was ajar. She slowly made her way to it, feeling the intensity of the dark energy increase behind it. As her hand reached the door, a chill ran down her spine as a sweet voice echoed in the darkness.

"Welcome, girls," Sabine chimed.

Nikki looked back at her sisters, who nodded back at her to proceed. Nikki opened the door, sensing a horde of vampires on the surface. She could only feel Sabine and a massive wave of darkness that dwarfed any lower-level demon she had ever faced. She turned to the right, seeing a circular staircase at the end of a dark hall. Sabine was leaning against the wall twirling a katana with her right hand. "You made it just in time," the green-eyed vampire said.

Izzy, Grace, and Elizabeth joined Nikki and looked around the hall. "Where's Sean?" Elizabeth asked.

Sabine stepped away from the wall and put her katana away behind her back. "Funny, I thought you sensed each other. I guess he's gone."

Sabine's words brought a chill down Izzy's spine as she looked at her mother in fear. The demon hunter searched within her instincts, and a third dark essence had joined the ambiance. The brown-haired girl turned to her left, seeing a dark metallic door. She could feel her heart thump away as her father's words echoed in her mind. *It's not your fault.*

"This is not your fight," Elizabeth hissed at her daughter, pulling her away from the door.

"Why not, lover?" a dark, distorted male voice echoed from behind the door. "Don't I have parental rights over our daughter?"

The door shook and crumbled as two hands grasped it from the other side, detaching it from its hinges. The teens gasped as Elizabeth's face went pale. Sean walked out of the room, but his features had changed. His dark brown hair was gone, replaced by white-as-snow strands. The husband and father's loving, caring brown eyes had disappeared, only for two orange fire orbs to dance in the orbital sockets. "It's good to be free," Ankrnot said as he looked at the demon hunters. The monster, in full power now, had drained the blood from Sean's chiseled features. It was as if a corpse spoke to them.

Behind Ankrnot, a tall, blonde six-foot-one woman stood dressed in a long black silk dress. "Thank you," UrthaMal said, kissing Sean's walking corpse on the cheek as she admired her surroundings.

Nikki pulled out her crossbow and fired a single arrow bolt, aimed at UrthaMal's heart. The projectile hit, but it barely penetrated the demon's chest. The tall woman sneered at the attack. "Like ants trying to stand up to a god! Kill them!"

Ankrnot rushed the demon hunters, running fast as lightning toward Izzy, who was frozen in fear at seeing her father in those demon features. She gasped as Elizabeth moved in front of her, grasping Ankrnot's hands, stopping him in his tracks. The demon and the senior demon hunter were clasped together in a test of strength. "Over my dead body!" Elizabeth grunted.

"I can arrange that," Ankrnot replied. He looked down at Izzy and smiled. "I'll be seeing you soon, daughter." The demon twisted Elizabeth's hand, making her wince in pain as he twirled and hurled the blonde demon hunter upward, releasing her.

The female Guardian flew upward, back-first. She screamed in pain as her body crashed through the wooden ceiling, reaching the upper level. Ankrnot jumped and followed Elizabeth through the orifice he had made.

"Mom!" Izzy exclaimed, ready to jump toward her mother's aid when Grace put a hand on her shoulder. Isabella turned toward her sister, and then toward UrthaMal and Sabine, who now stood side by side.

"What are you waiting for?" Sabine asked UrthaMal. "You're free now. Unleash your power."

"With pleasure," UrthaMal said as her body started to glow with orange and red light. Her eyes lit up as fire sprouted out of her mouth. Her body slowly started expanding as her muscular body slowly ripped through the silk fabric that contained it.

"Girls!" John asked through the intercom. "What's happening?"

Nikki pulled on Grace and Izzy, seeing the demon frozen in its place as Sabine strolled back to the stairs. "You better get out of here, girls," the vampire warned. "The confined space will not let you have a clean battle." Saying this, the vampire ran up the stairwell.

Izzy, Grace, and Nikki felt the ground shake, with the epicenter being UrthaMal's body slowly growing. "Move!" Nikki ordered her sisters as she pushed them toward the stairs.

"What about my mom?" Izzy asked, visibly scared.

"She can handle Ankrnot," Grace said. "The rest is in our hands."

"Girls!" John exclaimed through the intercom. "Talk to me! What's going on?"

"UrthaMal took Sean," Nikki said, running up the stairs behind her sisters. "Her body is glowing, and the ground is shaking around her as she is growing out of her skin."

"She's disposing of her terrestrial vessel!" John said. "She will soon be in her final form!"

"What form is that?" Grace asked as she stumbled up the stairs. The entire building seemed to be collapsing under its own weight.

"A demon from hell," John replied. "Describe her to me quickly, with as many details as possible. Maybe I can spot a weakness."

As the demon hunters reached the upper level, a dozen vampires greeted them with a growl of war. Izzy pulled out her crossbow and fired a few bolts, striking three vampires down. They screamed in pain as they turned to dust, just as beams of wood and steel started crumbling down.

"The building is coming down!" Nikki exclaimed as she pushed her sisters forward. The rumbling of the structure caused the vampires inside to scatter and flee to safety.

Izzy reached the wooden entrance of the building, ramming it hard with her shoulder. The door exploded in a thousand pieces as the teenaged girls stepped outside, only to be surrounded by three dozen vampires. The demon hunters saw Sabine standing on the hood of a car with a dark-haired vampire at her side. The demon unleashed his metal coils from his hands as electricity flowed through him.

"This town is mine!" the male vampire yelled at the demon hunters.

A loud crash caught the girl's attention as they saw Ankrnot's body fly from the wooden wall and roll on the pavement for a couple of seconds before coming to a complete stop. Izzy looked back at the opening, seeing her mom pop out. Blood was streaming down the side of her lip, but other than that, she looked unscathed. The blonde demon hunter cleaned her wound with her sleeve as she measured the demon in front of her.

Ankrnot, on the other hand, looked bruised and beat all over. He looked toward Izzy and smiled as he spat out blood. "It seems your mom has been taking her vitamins," the demon scowled. "I have to get serious."

Elizabeth ran toward Ankrnot, only for him to deliver a right hook to her left cheek. The blonde demon hunter flew to the side and rolled on the pavement. She looked up and saw Ankrnot airborne and ready to land knee-first on her chest. She moved to the side just in time as the demon crashed down, breaking the pavement. "You've gotten quicker," Ankrnot said as he fired haymakers at Elizabeth, who barely dodged and blocked.

"And you sloppy," Elizabeth retorted as she kicked the demon hard on the chest, pushing him hard against the wall of the warehouse. The entire structure collapsed on itself, no longer being able to stand upright.

"Kill the demon hunters!" the male vampire ordered.

Izzy, Grace, and Nikki pulled out their crossbows and fired at the undead that approached. The teenaged girls stood back to back, aiming true as vampires started combusting.

Cassius watched in fear as the demon hunters started cutting his clan down to half its size. He turned his attention toward Sabine, who pulled out her katana, her eyes fixed on the warehouse ruins.

Grace fired her last arrow bolt and dropped her crossbow, pulling out her short sword. As one vampire came forward, she swung to the side, decapitating the beast. She looked around and saw that half of the horde was gone, but the rest had closed in on them. The demon hunter closed her eyes and let her instincts take over. She could feel time stand still as the vampires gradually surrounded them. A fresh wave of energy flowed within her as she moved like water across the horde. She sliced her short sword sideways, horizontally, and vertically. There were no screams of pain and agony. Just the sound of vampires exploding to ash and dust.

Nikki moved away from the horde of vampires and watched as her sister flew through them like a skilled dancer . She turned her attention toward Izzy, who had dropped her crossbow and fired a high kick to a tall vampire as she decapitated two with her short sword. The redheaded demon hunter smiled, still feeling a dark essence from the bottom of the warehouse ruins. But she didn't have time to dwell on that. She dropped her crossbow, pulling out her short sword and decapitating a large vampire who charged her. Dust and ash started surrounding her as she moved to the next five vampires.

Izzy saw her sisters battle the vampire horde when she noticed her mom on the ground while Ankrnot punched hard on her. The blonde Guardian blocked the onslaught of the demon, but more blows were penetrating her defenses.

The brown-haired demon hunter felt her heart was going to burst as the anxiety and fear crept up from her gut. She was seeing the distorted figure of her father beat down on her mother. "Stop!" she screamed, running toward them at full speed.

Grace and Nikki turned toward their sister and the fight Elizabeth was having. Both demon hunters put themselves back-to-back and covered Izzy as the teenaged girl separated from the squad. Both girls swung their blades masterfully as the circle of vampires around them shrunk.

Izzy jumped and fired a flying kick, connecting with Ankrnot's chest. The demon staggered back while the young girl got into a fighting position. "You want to go toe-to-toe with your old man?" Ankrnot asked.

"You're not my father!" Izzy hissed.

"Don't do this!" Elizabeth said, trying to get up and fight, gasping for air.

"Listen to Mom," Ankrnot said. "You're out of your depth. You reek of fear."

Izzy screamed and attacked the demon, throwing her best punches and kicks. The young demon hunter was a blur, but Ankrnot just weaved and dodged each attack without even blocking. "You're so predictable," the demon said, firing a backhand slap, connecting with Izzy's cheek.

Izzy gasped in pain as she felt the stinging sensation on her face. She looked at what used to be her father in horror. *I can't do this,* the girl thought to herself.

"Fear is your undoing!" Sabine called out from afar.

Izzy, Grace, and Nikki looked at the female vampire, who simply twirled her katana while the male vampire looked at her with a confused look. "You're weak and pathetic little girls, afraid of what goes bump in the night," the vampire said with a smile. "There is no victory in your future if you're prey to fear."

Izzy looked at Ankrnot, who attacked quickly, throwing punches aimed at her face. Izzy blocked each strike as the demon changed tactics and kicked to the side, but the demon hunter danced away. "Nice moves," Ankrnot taunted. "Did your mommy and daddy teach you that?"

Izzy tried to control her emotions as Sabine's words echoed in her mind and heart. She blocked and dodged as she looked at her mother from the corner of her eye.

He's not your father! Elizabeth screamed at her daughter with her thoughts as she weakly stood up.

Isabella blocked Ankrnot's right-hand punch, retorting with a straight jab into the demon's chest. The beast gasped in pain as he staggered back, looking into Izzy's green eyes. There was rage and fury in her gaze as she jumped and spin-kicked him on the jaw. Ankrnot took a step back, feeling the demon hunter unleash her power on him. The demon hunter fired a right hook to his face, followed by a kick to the chest. She was spinning and back-fisting him on the other side of his sore jaw.

Ankrnot tried to block, but the girl was just too fast in her onslaught. She finished him off with an uppercut right under the chin that brought the demon to his behind.

"She's good," Ankrnot said to Elizabeth, who was now behind Izzy.

"You've got no idea," Elizabeth said as she kicked the demon on the face, pushing him back.

Ankrnot stood back up and took on both mother and daughter head-on, unleashing his rage. Elizabeth and Izzy dodged and blocked the demon's attacks, but his strength and speed had increased. "This will be the first time I take mother and daughter in battle," Ankrnot said. "Makes me feel special." He jumped and split-kicked both Izzy and Elizabeth in the face, making mother and daughter stagger.

Cassius turned toward Sabine as his numbers had diminished considerably. "Please, Schulmeister," he begged. "I need you to intervene."

"This is your battle," Sabine said, still looking at the warehouse. Wood and debris started moving as if the fallen structure was breathing. "You wanted power and glory," Sabine continued as she pointed her katana at Grace and Izzy. "You have to claim it. Start with taking out the demon hunters who killed the master vampires in Europe."

Cassius looked at Nikki and Grace, who had dispatched his entire clan from the face of the earth. Ash and dust covered their clothes and faces. "That was intense," Grace said to her red-headed sister.

Nikki nodded and looked at Sabine, the male vampire at her side, and the white-haired demon. The raven-haired vampire took a step back, focusing on the ruins of the warehouse. The blue-eyed demon hunter noticed the structure moving.

"Girls!" John pleaded on their earpiece. "Talk to me! What's going on?"

"The horde is gone," Nikki replied. "Just two vampires and an electricity demon."

"What about UrthaMal?" John asked.

"Buried under a collapsed warehouse," Grace said as she measured the white-suit-wearing demon.

"She will get out," John warned. "Describe her to me once she emerges."

Grace looked at Nikki, who was measuring Sabine with her sight. "How do you want to do this?"

"Let me choose for you," Sabine said, getting down from the vehicle and looking at Cassius and Hepheenious. "Cassius, this is your chance to prove yourself. Drink of the red-headed demon hunter and your power will increase tenfold." She then turned toward the head of the Karratt Order. "Hepheenious, the other demon hunter is yours. Fulfill your oath."

Hepheenious extended his metal coils as electricity ran through them.

"Recommendations?" Grace asked Nikki.

"Don't get fried," Nikki said as she took a step to the side and squared, waiting for Cassius to approach.

Hepheenious ran toward Grace as he slashed down with his electrical coils. The sound of electricity running and crackling brought a shiver down Grace's spine. As the demon got closer, he whipped horizontally. The demon hunter did a back somersault, dodging his weapons. As the demon slashed down, he took a step closer toward the teenaged girl.

Grace dodged and moved, seeing the white-haired demon approach. She moved to the left and threw her short sword at him. The demon reflectively slashed at the blade, launching it to the side. Grace was already in motion toward him. He whipped horizontally, only for the demon hunter to slide under the coil and reach the monster. The black-haired girl grabbed the demon's arms and smashed her head onto his forehead.

Hepheenious reeled away, trying to regroup, but Grace was not letting him go. Still in control of his arms, she lifted her leg and smashed her foot against the demon's chin.

For a moment, the sound of electricity faded as the demon's eyes rolled back and flashed. Grace immediately grabbed the powered-down coils and wrapped them around the demon's body. She pushed him away and jumped, spin-kicking the monster in the face. The beast screamed, waking up and releasing all its power. Electricity surged from his eyes to his arms and coils, engulfing the demon in a powerful charge. Hepheenious' body vibrated as his electricity consumed him, smoke emanating as his white skin darkened.

Grace covered her face as the demon exploded, flinging burnt flesh to all sides.

"Short-circuited your ass," Grace quipped.

Cassius charged Nikki at full force. The red-headed demon hunter sliced horizontally with her short sword, but was surprised when the vampire dodged and punched her on the chest. Nikki staggered back and attacked once again, trying to decapitate the vampire. The demon moved to the side and struck two blows to her chest. As the demon hunter reeled back, he jumped and kicked the teenaged girl on the side of her skull.

Nikki gasped in pain as her grip loosened, dropping her sword. She turned toward the vampire, who simply adjusted his suit. "You don't realize who I am, little girl," Cassius said. "I am the vampire ward of the East. All vampires kneel to me."

Cassius attacked once again, punching and kicking down on Nikki, who just blocked the onslaught. Each strike pushed the teenaged girl back toward the warehouse ruins. She felt her arms numb up, as if the vampire was hitting her with iron.

The demon kicked low. Nikki reflectively blocked, only for Cassius to jab her on the side of her cheek. The red-head felt as if her face was going to explode, but she didn't back down.

Nikki's resilience only angered Cassius as he punched left and right at the girl. Nikki took the punches, feeling the side of her face start to bruise. The vampire crouched down and jumped, connecting with an uppercut under Nikki's chin. The teenaged girl's legs felt like rubber as she fell back and landed on the wooden debris.

"I expected more from the demon hunters who put down Lucinda and Athena," the vampire said. Cassius smirked as he looked down at his prey, who had a dazed look in her blue eyes. The vampire crept toward the fallen teenager, ready to pierce Nikki's neck when he grunted in pain. He looked down and saw a piece of wood sticking out of his chest.

Nikki smiled at the master vampire. "You are just an appetizer compared to them." The vampire took a step back and looked back at Sabine before he exploded into ash and dust.

Nikki stood up and felt the wood around her start to move. Her feet started giving out, as the wooden debris contracted and expanded as if it was alive. The demon hunter ran toward Grace as they looked at the warehouse ruins.

"Where's UrthaMal?" John asked over the intercom.

"She's about to come out," Nikki replied as she looked at Sabine, who sat patiently on the hood of the car.

Izzy fell flat on her back, grunting in pain. She looked up to see Elizabeth and Ankrnot in a furious battle. For every punch the blonde demon hunter connected, the monster retorted tenfold. It was as if the fiend fed from her mother's strength, making him stronger and faster while rendering the woman weaker. The teenaged girl turned toward her sisters, who had their eyes on the torn-down warehouse. A creature moved underneath, trying to break free from the rubble. Isabella looked toward Sabine, who stood up and started walking toward her sisters with her katana, ready to strike.

Isabella turned her attention back toward Ankrnot and her mother, and it seemed as if though time was moving in slow motion. The beast fired two right hooks into Elizabeth's unprotected belly, then two jabs at her face before spinning and firing a kick at her head. Elizabeth crumpled down, spitting out blood. "You lose," Ankrnot hissed at his defeated foe.

Izzy screamed, feeling a surge of power come from deep within her. She stood up and ran toward Ankrnot, connecting with a superman punch, staggering him hard to the side.

Sabine paused for a second the moment she heard Isabella's scream, as her attention deviated from the warehouse ruins. She could feel the brown-haired demon hunter tap an unknown power inside of her.

Ankrnot recovered from the blow and tried to block the demon hunter's next attack, but Izzy was faster. She punched high and low, going through the demon's defenses, connecting punches and kicks on his face and chest. A crack followed each strike as Ankrnot felt the demon hunter trash his bones.

Isabella side-kicked the demon, punching down on his face, followed by a kick to Ankrnot's temple. As the monster stepped to the side, dazed, Izzy jumped and connected with a brutal knee to the monster's skull. Ankrnot's eyes rolled back, his body collapsing on the ground unconscious.

The demon hunter turned toward Sabine, who now simply nodded in approval. "Very good," the raven-haired vampire said. "You're reaching your demon hunter potential. But you need more."

"We'll show you more," Nikki said as she prepared to face off against the ancient vampire. Grace followed suit, focusing her attention on the dark-haired demon.

Sabine took a step back and raised her hands. "I can give a rematch any day of the week," the vampire said, looking at Elizabeth, who was now crawling toward Ankrnot's unconscious body. The demon hunter started unraveling the silver chain that hung around her chest and proceeded to wrap the corpse of her lover in it.

"Why not now?" Grace asked as she tested her arms, sensing the strength coming back to them.

"Because I'm not your enemy," Sabine replied as she circularly twirled her fingers in the air.

The demon hunters stopped and looked around. More than a dozen demons and vampires began to appear out from the darkness. Izzy looked around and saw two dwarf demons, followed by two black hell hounds. She saw four slave demons next to what seemed like miniature versions of hell gargoyles with tiny wings to the right.

A loud growl caught the demon hunter's attention. The wooden debris from the warehouse shook violently as a large brown clawed hand appeared. Izzy, Grace, and Nikki looked in awe as a thirty-foot tall demon with black curved horns stepped out of the debris. The face had large red orbs of fire for eyes and a large hairy boar-like snout with large fangs sprouting on the sides. Its muscular dark-brown arms were attached to the chest, consisting of just a black rib cage with pieces of falling, rotten flesh that provided enough protection to a pumping black heart. UrthaMal's legs were hairy and in the form of a giant bull's legs with hooves for feet.

The beast roared a battle cry, echoing in the darkness that made the knees of the demon hunters buckle. UrthaMal's horns started to glow with dark purple energy seeping into them from the air. The teenaged girls could see the energy flow from its horns and illuminate the circulatory system that reached the pumping heart.

Izzy picked up her short sword, joining her sisters just as Sabine stood behind them, admiring the ascended demon.

UrthaMal looked down at Elizabeth, and the knocked-out Ankrnot. The beast then focused on Izzy, Grace, Nikki, and Sabine. "Demon Hunters!" the monster hissed. "The age of darkness will have your bones as a foundation!"

UrthaMal bellowed one final battle roar as the purple energy on her horns intensified. The demon brought down her fists where the teenagers and the ancient vampire stood still, mesmerized at the unparalleled power.

CHAPTER XVIII

Saint Helena High School; September,06, 10:00 p.m.

JOHN PACED IN FRONT of the school bleachers when a roar echoed through the air. The young Guardian looked to the west as he placed his right hand on his earpiece. "Girls, talk to me." There was no response. John looked around when a piercing headache struck his skull, bringing him down to one knee as he grimaced in pain. He looked up and saw several parents, teachers, and police officers crumble down as well.

The young Guardian tried to focus and order the bombardment of thoughts in his mind. Images of demons, monsters, and other creatures of the night invaded his brain. John tried to process the information, but it was too much. Deep inside his soul, he desired to know more. The knowledge stored inside was not enough. He needed to fulfill the thirst to know everything, contemplating every variable, angle, and point of view.

John shook his head as Izzy's voice spoke to him through his earpiece. "John!" the demon hunter exclaimed. "Did you get that?"

"Say again," John strained to focus his thoughts as the image of his demon hunters falling and dying invaded his mind.

"Thirty-foot demon is in play!" Izzy exclaimed through the communicator. "Large horns glowing with dark energy! Only a rotten ribcage somewhat protects the heart!"

John grimaced as he tried to stand up, only for the pain in his head to bring him back down on his knees. *THEY WILL DIE*, his mind screamed at him. *YOUR KNOWLEDGE IS NOT ENOUGH!*

The young Guardian tried to focus, shutting his eyes and ordering his thoughts. "Does the heart react to the purple energy from the horns?" John strained to ask.

"Yes!" Izzy exclaimed. "Grace, watch out!"

"The heart binds UrthaMal on this plane," John instructed as the unhealthy desire to be the smartest Guardian pounded on his mind. "Her horns are the source that feeds her. Remove the horns, and the town will be free. Destroy the heart, and you will send that demon back to hell."

"Easier said than done!" Izzy exclaimed.

"We don't have much time," John whispered as the pain overtook his mind. The pale corpses of his demon hunters drowned in a pool of blood flooded his thoughts. He needed to help his demon hunters. He couldn't fail them as he looked at his blood-stained hands.

"John!" Izzy exclaimed. "John! John, talk to me!"

Izzy's voice was but a whisper that faded away. The young Guardian grasped his head and screamed as the thoughts in his mind were out of control. *I can't control them,* he thought to himself, looking toward the commotion of parents and police officers. They were all screaming and arguing. He felt as if he was in a dream, walking toward one of the police SUVs. John saw the officer's shotgun in the passenger seat. He could almost feel the cold, dark steel in his hands. The smell of gunpowder was burning his nostrils. *Silence your thoughts,* his mind suggested.

The young man reached the squad car when he felt a pair of hands grab him by the scruff of the neck and push him against the car's hood. John looked up, seeing Solas grab the shotgun from the passenger's seat and snap it in two across his raised knee. "Don't even think about it," the dark-skinned demon said. "Get in!"

John momentarily snapped back to reality seeing Solas fling a police officer out of the way as he headed for the driver's seat. "The demon hunters need us," Solas said pointing to the passenger seat. "Get in!"

John reluctantly sat down, hearing Izzy, Grace, Nikki, and Elizabeth scream orders through the intercom. John looked at Solas, who started the SUV's engine. The demon looked back at John with his blue eyes lit in blue flame. "I told you I wouldn't be affected by UrthaMal."

"Destroy the heart, and UrthaMal will be banished," John said sensing his mind begin to torture him again. His heart pounded inside his chest as the wave of knowledge replayed itself over and over. He felt alone and strapped to a rocket with no return voyage home unless he managed to count to a million in less than a minute. "I can't take this," the Guardian whispered.

Solas looked at the pale-faced human beside him while putting the vehicle into drive. "The demon hunters won't let you down," the blue-eyed being said. "Let's give them a hand."

Saint Helena Outskirts West Side; September, 06, 10:05 p.m.

Nikki cartwheeled to the right just as a giant right fist crashed down from the side. She sliced with her short sword, only to hear the steel uselessly clank against the demon's skin. She jumped out of the way as UrthaMal tried to grab the redhead with her left hand.

Izzy ran toward her mother, who dragged Ankrnot out of the way just as two vampires attacked. The brown-haired girl sliced to the side with her short sword, decapitating the beasts and turning them to dust. She threw the blade to her mother, who stood up and grabbed it just as the brown demon troll steamrolled toward her. Elizabeth rammed the weapon into its skull while seeing UrthaMal stand up fully, trying to grab her. The blonde demon hunter jumped and flung her sword, aiming at UrthaMal's eyes. The monster flicked the blade away as if it were a toothpick.

Grace ran toward Elizabeth and Izzy. The dark-haired demon hunter saw Sabine step back while more demons started popping out of nowhere. UrthaMal stepped forward, trying to kick Grace, but the demon hunter dodged to the side, avoiding the massive foot.

"Pesky demon hunters," UrthaMal growled at the teenaged girls and their blonde Guardian. A small horde of a dozen vampires and lesser demons had formed at the monster's feet. "You can't avoid my power forever."

UrthaMal was about to attack when she suddenly flinched. She violently turned her head toward Sabine, who had her katana exposed. "You dare betray me?"

"Death is a necessary evil!" Sabine yelled as she ran toward UrthaMal.

The demon hunters looked surprised as UrthaMal focused her attention on the ancient vampire while she sent her horde of minions toward them. Izzy, Grace, Nikki, and Elizabeth received the onslaught head-on.

Izzy sliced a demon's head off while sticking her stake to a female vampire, when she saw UrthaMal crash both her fists down, trying to crush the raven-haired vampire. Sabine's eyes turned bloodshot red as her fangs grew, while the medallion around her neck glowed with a soft blue light. She jumped over the monster's hands and ran up UrthaMal's arms and right up to her shoulders. Sabine sliced down with her katana, connecting with one of UrthaMal's horns.

The monster howled in pain as the blade sliced one of the horns clean off. The extremity landed with a thud on the ground as UrthaMal, in a burst of speed, reared back and smashed her giant fist across Sabine's body. Sabine screamed in pain as her body flew out of control and crashed against the car she'd been standing on, sending it a few feet back. The katana clanked hard on the concrete.

UrthaMal charged toward the vampire, picking up a small sedan from the street. Grace could see Sabine start to get up, only for UrthaMal to squash the vampire with the vehicle. The vampire's hand twitched for a second, then remained motionless.

Izzy turned toward her sisters and mother. "I've got a plan!" the brown-haired exclaimed as she sliced a demon's head off. "Grace, stay here with Mom and guard Ankrnot!" The demon hunter then turned toward her red-headed sister. "Climb that beast!" Izzy ordered.

Elizabeth looked at her daughter, then at UrthaMal, who was pounding down on Sabine's body with her fists. Her eyes widened as she realized her daughter's plan. She crouched down over Ankrnot's body, which was starting to stir awake. "Good evening, lover," Elizabeth purred. She then smashed her fist down across his face, knocking the demon out. She removed the chains that wrapped her husband's possessed body and threw them at Izzy. "You'll need these."

Izzy wrapped the chains and rolled them together. She then nodded at Nikki, who just smiled. "Let's do this," the blue-eyed demon hunter said.

Izzy nodded as both demon hunters sprinted toward the thirty-foot demon. "Get ready!" Izzy called out as she went low while Nikki went high. The brown-haired teenager slid under UrthaMal's giant arms, grabbing Sabine's katana while Nikki scaled the demon's back.

UrthaMal saw Izzy underneath her and growled, sending her mighty fist against the young demon hunter. Izzy stood up and threw the sword toward Nikki just as the fist came crashing down. Isabella extended her arms and caught UrthaMal's hand, sensing the immense weight as her knees buckled. She grunted, feeling the pavement crack under her boots.

UrthaMal looked shocked at the strength of the demon hunter when she screamed in pain as Nikki severed the other horn from the monster's head. The redheaded demon hunter flipped from UrthaMal's back and landed right beside Izzy. She was about to throw the katana toward the demon's heart when the monster struck down with her free hand. Nikki dropped the sword on the ground and caught the beast's hand. Nikki strained, feeling the power of the giant demon.

"You will die here!" UrthaMal growled as she pressed down, trying to squash the demon hunters as they screamed in pain.

Grace stabbed a troll demon in the chest, then removed her sword and decapitated it. She turned toward her Guardian, who took care of two more vampires, when all of a sudden the onslaught of demons stopped. The creatures of the night looked confused as if they didn't know where they were.

Grace then looked at the hornless UrthaMal, who was about to crush Izzy and Nikki. She was about to run to their aid when she felt Elizabeth's hand on her shoulder. The black-eyed demon hunter looked up to her Guardian, ready to receive orders. "Take care of Sean," Elizabeth pleaded as she took Grace's short sword.

Grace nodded, sitting crossed-legged in front of Ankrnot, pulling out her phone and the ingredients Elizabeth had trusted her with. The teenaged demon hunter looked at the spell on her phone once before turning her attention toward her blonde mentor.

Elizabeth sprinted off toward her girls and the giant beast they faced, twirling the two short swords in her hands. She reached UrthaMal's backside and climbed it at top speed before the demon had a chance to notice. The blonde demon hunter got to the monster's head and jumped, plunging both short swords into the beast's eyes.

UrthaMal growled in agony, reaching toward her face just as Elizabeth jumped, landing behind the beast. "Use the chain!" Elizabeth ordered.

Izzy nodded, unrolling the chain and throwing one end upward next to UrthaMal's head. Elizabeth grabbed one end and ran to the right, throwing the chain toward Nikki.

Nicole caught the idea as the chain reached her. She kept running to her right as the chain wrapped around UrthaMal's neck. The red-headed demon hunter threw her end of the chain back to Izzy, who threw it back to Elizabeth right between the monster's legs.

UrthaMal growled, feeling the chains tighten around her neck and body. The beast tried to grab the metal coil when she felt one of her arms becoming tangled.

Elizabeth flung her chain end to Nikki while Izzy stood her ground, holding the other end. Both teenagers grappled with the metal coil in their hands, trying to restrain the beast. But UrthaMal was too strong.

Nikki gave her sister a panicked look as she slowly began to lose her grip. Nikki closed her eyes, trying to focus her strength. She could feel she was reaching the limit of her power when she felt a pair of hands come to her aid. She opened her eyes and saw Elizabeth throw in her strength and effort as she pulled hard on her side.

Izzy could sense Elizabeth's and Nikki's strength. Unfortunately, she could sense the chain slipping from her hands. She tried to hold on, but her arms were burning, trying to contain the monster. "Come on," Izzy pleaded with herself.

Suddenly a pair of bloody hands appeared out of nowhere. Izzy's eyes widened as she saw Sabine's battered and bloodied body pull the chain on her side. With the vampire's added strength, UrthaMal was brought down on her knees.

"She has to go down!" the vampire exclaimed. "Use the katana to pierce her heart!"

Vampire and demon hunters held tight the chain as UrthaMal tried desperately to escape. "You can't defeat me!" UrthaMal managed to growl, trying to stand up but failing.

Izzy turned desperately toward her mom and Nikki, then at Sabine's katana, which was only a few feet away. The demon hunter looked up at UrthaMal's exposed chest. She tried to think of a solution. She looked at Grace, who guarded Ankrnot's body, ready to restore Sean's soul. "We need help," Izzy managed to say as she held on to the chain.

The rumbling of a car engine echoed, along with UrthaMal's growls. Nikki turned her head and saw a police SUV speed toward them.

Inside the police vehicle, John held on tight to this seatbelt. "Are you sure about this?" the Guardian asked the demon behind the wheel.

Solas pressed hard on the accelerator, ready to ram into UrthaMal. "We need to bring the beast down," Solas said. "Don't worry. The car has airbags."

Izzy, Nikki, Elizabeth, and Sabine watched as the SUV rushed past them. The demon hunters and the vampire released the chain just as the vehicle crashed into the beast.

UrthaMal screamed as the metal collapsed part of her chest, causing her to fall back. Nikki and Izzy were already on the move. The brown-haired demon hunter ran toward the katana on the pavement while Nikki jumped hard and stomped on UrthaMal's chest with her army boots.

UrthaMal growled in pain, black blood spurting out from her mouth. Nikki screamed, punching the demon's chest while trying to bust it open. After five blows, the demon hunter exposed the monster's beating heart. The red-headed teenager could feel her sister's energy. She moved to the side just as Izzy plunged the katana down into the vital organ.

UrthaMal howled in agony as purple energy emitted from the punctured heart. The same dark energy came out of the beast's eyes and mouth.

Izzy froze, looking at the gash in UrthaMal's heart when a small red sphere opened in front of her eyes. The demon hunter looked in horror, seeing right through the portal down to hell.

Nikki tackled Izzy to the side as the red doorway expanded. UrthaMal screamed and tried to claw away, but the portal kept her in place as it slowly consumed her. The demon's purple energy dissipated into the air causing UrthaMal to vanish into nothingness.

Elizabeth looked at the energy and turned toward Grace. "Grace! Now!"

Grace was already working. She opened the vial and introduced the Celtic cross inside just as Ankrnot started to stir awake. "*Fiat lux sit dux vester,*" Grace said. "*Sequere lucem in domum suam. Fiat lux tepido sinu pacem et reddere necesse est poni. Qui nati sunt tibi esse bellator est.*" The black-haired demon hunter gasped in pain as she felt a surge of energy pass through her.

Ankrnot sat up and grabbed the demon hunter by her jacket. "Witch!" he growled. "What do you think you're doing?"

"Putting you in your place," Grace gasped, smashing the vial on Ankrnot's chest. Energy filled the demon hunter's body causing her to scream in pain.

Ankrnot howled in agony as the power surged through his body. "I will haunt your dreams, too," the demon said before collapsing on the ground.

Grace crumpled on the pavement with smoke emanating from her body.

Nikki and John were the first to reach the downed demon hunter. The redhead cradled her sister's body in her arms. "Grace! Grace, talk to me!"

"Did it work?" Grace asked, contorting in pain, feeling as if her body had been hit by a truck.

John smiled a bit, admiring the heart and soul of the demon hunters he watched over. "See for yourself," the Guardian said.

Grace turned and saw Elizabeth and Izzy sobbing over Sean's body as the man's chest moved softly with every beat of his pumping heart. Isabella turned toward Grace and mouthed the words *thank you* as she sank her face onto her father's chest.

Nikki turned her head and saw Solas stare down a silhouette that walked away in the distance. The red-headed demon hunter stood up and walked over toward the demon. As she got closer, she managed to see Sabine disappear into the darkness.

Solas turned toward Nikki as she approached. "She got what she wanted," the demon said, looking at the teenaged girl.

"What was that?" Nikki asked

"UrthaMal's horns," Solas replied, looking back to where Sabine had disappeared to. "She always had her motives."

John walked up to them, with Grace hanging on to his shoulders and Izzy right behind them. "Couldn't she just clue us in to what her plan was?" Grace asked. "You know, like a proper villain."

"I don't think she considers herself a villain," Solas said.

"Like all ancient vampires," Grace replied, feeling disgusted. Another ancient one had gotten away, and she was none the wiser on what their purpose was.

Izzy slowly walked toward where UrthaMal had fallen. She crouched down and picked up Sabine's katana, twirling it. "Not as powerful as Apocalypse," the demon hunter noted, "But it packed a punch. Sharp as I've ever seen." The young girl inspected the sword and noticed an engraving on the side of the blade, triggering a passage from an ancient book in her mind. She turned toward the dark road. "It's not the last we've seen of her."

"How do you know?" Nikki asked.

"Call it a professional hunch," the brown-haired girl said as she saw her parents walk up to them. Sean was leaning heavily on Elizabeth's right shoulder. She walked toward them with the sword in hand.

"You showed up just in time," Grace said to Solas. "Sorry for my counterparts, but let me be the first one to thank you."

Nikki blushed as she looked at Solas, who simply nodded. "Just fulfilling a vow," the demon said. He turned toward John, who nodded, knowing full well what had transpired. Solas then turned his attention toward Nikki. "Be seeing you," he said turning around and walking away.

Nikki watched as Solas disappeared in the distance. She turned around to see Grace grinning back at her standing on her own next to John. "You're so infatuated," the black-eyed demon hunter said. "The guy left you speechless."

"Shut up," Nikki said, playfully punching her sister's arm as she walked back to her Guardians.

EPILOGUE

Saint Helena High School, California;
September 17, 5:55 p.m.

"DONE," GRACE SAID AS she finished the last of the ten math exercises. She looked at Bryan and Jaime, who had looks of concentration on their faces before throwing their pencils down. The dark-haired demon hunter smiled as she looked around the deserted school library. Only the librarian was keeping them company, hidden behind an old book.

"How do you do it?" Bryan asked, capturing Grace's attention. "I am barely up to the third exercise."

"I hate math," Jaime scowled. "These are the moments that I wish you'd let that demon destroy the world."

"You sound like Nikki now," Grace chirped as she looked at Bryan's completed work. "But you're doing fine."

"Guess the brilliance rubs off on you," Bryan said.

Jaime just shook her head. "Ask her out already, would you?"

Grace smiled at her friends. "I promise I will say yes," Grace said to Bryan. "Just so don't you feel pressured."

"There is this Harry Potter festival this Friday," Bryan started. "If you're not busy."

"Cool," Grace said. "I'd love to go." Grace's cell phone sounded an alarm. The young demon hunter picked up the phone and looked at the time. "Duty calls."

Jaime looked at the time on her cell phone. "Where does the time go?" She, Bryan, and Grace started picking up their notebooks as they headed outside to the main hall.

"Where are your sisters?" Bryan asked.

"I'm meeting Nikki now," Grace replied. "She's putting some extra soccer practice while I caught up on my math. Izzy is at home prepping something with her violin for music class."

"How are her parents?" Jaime asked as they exited the school.

"They're doing fine," Grace replied. "I think they're taking a holiday together this week. Decompress from the stress. It's not the first time they've gone through what they did. I guess they're used to it and know how to get things on track again."

"I'm really impressed with you," Bryan said.

Grace looked surprised for a second as she looked at her friend.

Bryan smiled a bit. "You lost your parents not long ago," the young boy said. "I think it was awesome that you did what you did to help Izzy keep both her parents a bit longer. Spare her that pain."

"Izzy has gone through enough," Grace said as she saw Nikki walk toward them with a red duffle bag that matched her red soccer uniform. "If we can spare that pain to someone, why wouldn't we do it?"

"But sometimes you can't," Bryan concluded. "No matter how good you are."

"Sometimes we can't," Grace agreed. "But that doesn't deter us from trying."

Nikki reached the teens as she took a bite of a protein bar. "Hey," the redheaded demon hunter said. "Izzy called me. She says we hitch a ride with John. Sean and Elizabeth are leaving in a few hours. So the house will be all to ourselves."

"That's great," Grace said as she saw John wave at them from the parking lot. She turned toward Bryan and Jaime. "Why don't you both crash on Saturday?"

"Sounds like a plan," Jaime said, nodding to Bryan.

"We'll be there," the young man replied.

The teens parted ways as both demon hunters headed toward their Guardian. John waited patiently behind the wheel of the black SUV. "When do you guys start drivers' ed?"

"I think in two weeks?" Nikki said as she put her bag in the back seat while, Grace rode in front.

John started the engine and drove off the school property. "Izzy thinks her theory will be fulfilled tonight."

"She mentioned that," Grace said, looking out the window. "Sean and Elizabeth not being in town. Perfect conditions."

"Will you be there with us?" Nikki asked. "Elizabeth mentioned you helped her in the last meeting you had."

John looked at the rearview mirror into Nikki's blue eyes. "Of course I'll be there," the Guardian replied.

"The problem is that there are no answers for the questions she'll ask."

"It's not the answers she wants," Grace said as the memory of her parents flashed in her mind. "It's the answers I need."

John turned toward the black-haired demon hunter to his right. "I hope so, too," John said. "I am taking you to dinner. Izzy will meet us at the graveyard."

Guardians' Home, Saint Helena, California; September 17, 7:15 p.m.

Izzy's fingers pressed hard on her brown violin at the piano accompaniment from Stephen. The harmony of the melody vibrated in her heart and soul as the tempo intensified. They were reaching the final page of the score when Izzy just felt one of the strings of her violin give away, snapping.

"Damn!" Izzy exclaimed, stopping the mini concerto.

"Couldn't you continue the last sheet with a broken string?" Stephen asked with a smile.

"Haha," Izzy replied. "I'm good, but not that good."

"You could've fooled me," Stephen said, looking into Izzy's green eyes.

Izzy's mind drifted for a moment as she got lost in Stephen's eyes.

"Izzy!" Sean called from the stairs. Izzy turned toward Sean, who had a mischievous smile drawn on his face. "Stephen's mom is here. She's waiting for him. Practice is over."

Stephen picked up his music sheets and looked at Izzy, drawing a sad smile. "This was great," he said. "Same time next week?"

"You bet," Izzy replied as both of them walked up

the stairs, but not before Izzy playfully punched her dad in the arm.

As they reached the kitchen, Izzy saw an older woman with a cup of coffee sitting across from her mom. "Sorry, Ms. Connolly," Izzy apologized. "I lost track of time."

"It's okay, dear," Stephen's mom replied, standing up and walking toward the front door. "Your mom has been a great hostess. You've got to give me a tour of your home. It's simply stunning."

"I will," Elizabeth said. "Next week, if you like."

"Excellent," Stephen's mom said as she turned toward Izzy. "Thank you for helping Stephen with his music. He's been practicing a lot the last couple of weeks."

"Helping where I can," Izzy replied.

"Thank you, Mr. and Mrs. O'Brien," Stephen said as he walked out of the house with his mom.

"You're welcome," Sean said as he walked with them toward their car. "Good night. Drive safely."

Izzy turned toward her parents. "So, you guys are leaving tonight?"

"Do you want to get rid of us?" Elizabeth asked as the three of them walked back into the house. "You know I can access the systems from my phone, right?"

"It's not what I meant," Izzy said, sounding serious. "It's just..."

"Hey," Sean said as he touched his daughter on her shoulder. "Remember what I told you a couple of weeks ago. This is not your fault."

"It's no one's fault, actually," Elizabeth said. "But when these things happen, it's best for your father and me to clear the air."

"I know," Izzy said.

"Ankrnot is my burden to bear," Sean said. "I've agreed to share this burden with your mother. But this is not yours. It will never be yours. That's a vow I promised I would never break."

Izzy nodded as she hugged both her father and mother. "Other kids deal with their parents' alcoholism or working too hard," Izzy joked. "I have to deal with a demon hunter mom and a dad who has to live with a monster inside."

"No family is perfect," Sean said as he stretched. "Let's have some dinner before you meet up with your sisters. I've prepared your favorite."

"Nikki and Grace won't be joining us?" Izzy asked.

"I had John take them out for dinner," Elizabeth said. "We wanted to chat with you before we left."

"I knew that favorite dinner was not for free," Izzy mumbled as she sat on the dinner table and saw a small piece of fillet mignon with a wild mushroom sauce over it and a side of greens.

"Your father and I have been going over your Sabine theory," Elizabeth said. "With some digging from Guardian Central in Ireland, the assembly thinks your theory holds water."

"What did you find out?" Izzy asked as she took a mouthful of steak.

Sean grabbed a brown folder from the kitchen counter and handed it to Izzy. "Validating what John confirmed," Sean said. "Guardians of old are as vicious as they appear to be. And that trickled down to the entire organization. No exception."

"In other words," Izzy said. "No trust. Don't worry. Grace, Nikki, and I've discussed this. But it feels good just knowing."

"John will be with you tonight," Elizabeth said. "Get the information we need."

Izzy nodded. "Understood!"

Holy Cross Catholic Cemetery, Saint Helena, California; September 17, 8:00 p.m.

"I know, Dad," Nikki said as she walked the graveyard with her earphones connected to her cell phone. She looked back and saw Grace and John walking behind her. "Trust me; I'll get my grades up. Yeah. Grace is good in Math, and Izzy is excellent in English. They'll help me."

"I will?" Grace asked John, who simply smiled back.

"You will get constant reports. I have to go to work. Talk to you tomorrow." The redheaded demon hunter hung up the phone and looked back at her sister and Guardian. "You're going to help me, right?"

"What's in it for me?" Grace asked.

"I'll take on the next apocalypse," Nikki replied.

"You'd still owe me," Grace said, smiling at John, who simply shook his head.

All of a sudden, the two demon hunters felt a presence on the hallowed grounds. John's head jerked up and looked all around him.

"It's okay," Nikki said, trying not to laugh. "Izzy is behind us."

John turned around and saw Izzy walking toward them with Sabine's katana in her hand. "Guess there's no surprise for you guys on your birthday parties," the brown-haired demon hunter said.

"Good," Grace said as she continued walking. "I hate surprises."

"Taking note of that," Nikki replied.

"Do you want to pass Math?" Grace asked.

"Okay! Okay! I take it back!" Nikki said.

"How long has this been going on?" Izzy asked John.

"The entire ride here," the Guardian replied.

"Welcome to my life," Izzy said. "Anything interesting you've read lately in The Tome?"

"Actually, there was," John said, walking along side the teenage girl. "Do you know the expression, 'What does not kill you only makes you stronger'?

"Yeah?"

"Well," John continued. "It would seem the Guardians of old coined the phrase more than two thousand years ago. They used it to describe the demon hunter's bodily resilience to damage."

"Is that right?" Izzy said, drawing a smile as another piece of the puzzle fell into place.

John smiled back at the girl. "It seems your theory holds more water than you think. The old Guardians concluded that if a demon or vampire failed to kill a demon hunter, the girl would just come back stronger, faster, and more agile."

"It all makes sense," Izzy said, looking at the tombstones around the cemetery.

The three demon hunters and the Guardian continued walking until they reached the broken sarcophagus tomb. This time it had caution tape around it, with most of the debris outside the perimeter cleared.

"The services in this cemetery suck," Nikki commented. "It's been two weeks, and no one has fixed it."

"Are you sure this where she'll come?" Grace asked Izzy.

"Mom and Dad left town," Izzy said. "What better place to make her presence known if not where she taught us a lesson?"

The demon hunters didn't wait long, as a piercing headache made the teenaged girls grimace in pain. John took note and looked around. The ancient vampire would soon be joining them. "Like clockwork," the Guardian noted.

A few minutes passed, and the headache stopped. The demon hunters felt the vampire's presence in the graveyard. "What took you so long?" Izzy asked defiantly. "Waiting for Mom and Dad to skip town, or were you just too busy licking your wounds?"

"My," Sabine said as she appeared from the shadows. "Look who grew a spine. But since you asked, yes. I didn't expect UrthaMal to do a number on me. I expected her to do a number on you, though."

"You thought wrong," Nikki said as she stood in front of Izzy, alongside Grace. John stood next to Izzy and started thinking of all the possible variables.

"I guess you girls came prepared," Sabine noted. "Nothing makes me prouder than demon hunters learning from their mistakes."

"You came for this?" Izzy asked as she pulled out the katana. "Fantastic blade. Sharpest we've seen. I love the engraving on it."

Sabine nodded as she sat on one of the tombstones. "No," Sabine replied. "I didn't take it from a demon hunter."

"No, you didn't," Grace said. "You're a demon hunter."

Sabine took a bow. “Recognized,” the vampire said.

“Why?” Nikki asked. “No offense, but I can’t see myself hunting demons and vampires all my life. Why become immortal to do it?”

“Too complicated for you children to comprehend,” Sabine replied.

The demon hunters turned toward John, who looked at Sabine. “I read the last part of The Tome,” the young Guardian said. “The prophecy of the nameless evil. The one that can unite all the hell spots.”

Sabine scowled at the Guardian. Izzy, for the first time, felt she had leverage over the ancient vampire. “The Guardians discover the prophecy. Not trusting the demon hunter lineage, some Guardians and demon hunters turn themselves to vampires, using immortality to stop this prophecy from happening. Does that sum it up?”

“You can’t stop what’s to come,” Sabine said. Her eyes hinted at a glimmer of fear. “You’ve got no idea what will happen.”

“You helped summon UrthaMal,” John said. “You need raw matter from an ascended demon from each Hell Spot. Ten in total. With UrthaMal, you got eight.”

“And I’ve got three years to collect the last two,” Sabine said.

“You knew that we were three of the strongest demon hunters,” Izzy said. “That is why you left us alive. You needed us to become stronger and help you stop UrthaMal once you’ve gotten what you needed from her.”

“Smart girl,” Sabine said. “Now, hand over the sword.”

Izzy looked at the blade and threw it at Sabine's feet. "It doesn't matter how many people die?"

"You can't stop death, Izzy," Sabine said as she picked up the sword. "It's something this generation of demon hunters need to learn."

"Like my parents did?" Grace asked. "Why? Why did Neil kill them?"

Sabine sighed as she put the blade away behind her back. "You wouldn't understand," the vampire replied. "And I'm not inclined to share that information with you."

Grace turned around and looked at Izzy. Izzy nodded. "Even if we tell you why you're getting headaches?" Grace asked.

The comment caught Sabine's attention as she looked at the demon hunters and the Guardian.

"How the tables have turned," Nikki said, crossing her arms. "We have something you want."

"Alright," Sabine said. "Your parents are dead because they asked Neil to do it."

Grace looked at Sabine with rage in her eyes. "Liar!" Grace screamed as she was about to jump the vampire, only for Nikki to grab her arm. "She's lying!" Grace screamed at her sister as tears started crawling down her cheek.

"That's what Neil told me," Sabine said plainly. "Your dad lived by our oldest motto. Death is a necessary evil."

Nikki lost grip of Grace as the dark-haired demon hunter launched herself at the vampire, connecting with a single punch across Sabine's face. Sabine took the strike without defending herself, simply taking a step back.

Grace reared back to strike again when Nikki managed to restrain her. "Let me go!" Grace screamed at her sister.

"Neil knows the details," Sabine said. "He watches over you. He's the one who will provide the answers you seek. Your parents trusted him, and in time you'll learn to trust him, too."

"Never!" Grace screamed as she fell to her knees.

"The truth is hard to understand," Sabine said. She then turned toward Izzy, who took a step forward. "Now, Isabella. Tell me what you know."

Izzy opened her mind and thought about Apocalyps. The image of limbo flooded her mind and fed into Sabine. The vampire's eyes widened in horror as she fell to her knees, recognizing the truth. Izzy turned toward John, who took a step forward.

"Demon hunters are not supposed to become vampires," the Guardian said. "When Izzy bound Apocalyps to the demon hunter line, the Sisterhood was no longer bound by darkness, but with light. That affected you. The headaches are symptoms of the vampiric curse fighting against the force of light infused in you because of Apocalyps."

"How long do I have?" Sabine asked.

"Not enough time to fulfill your mission," John said. "The headaches are just the start."

Sabine stood up and looked at the demon hunters. "A riddle for a riddle," Sabine said, looking at Grace. "It seems we're at a stalemate. Grace does not acquire the closure she desires, and I am no closer to finding a solution to my problem."

"Let's help each other," Izzy proposed. "Give the Guardians all you know about this prophecy, and maybe John can come up with a solution."

"I haven't trusted the Guardians in two thousand years," Sabine said as she turned her back toward the demon hunters. "I am not about to start now." Saying that, the vampire started to walk away. "Everything about the prophecy is in The Tome—including how to stop it." The vampire turned back and looked at Grace, who was still on the ground, her eyes bloodshot from sobbing. "I'd forgotten what sorrow looked like," the ancient one said. "I know it means nothing, but I'm sorry."

Nikki knelt next to Grace, trying to console her sister as the ancient vampire walked away. Izzy took a step forward and called out to Sabine, "Schoolmaster."

The name stopped Sabine in her tracks and she turned toward the young sixteen-year-old. The way she said the name was different from any other vampire who had uttered the word in centuries. "Yes?" the vampire asked.

"The blonde girl in my dreams," Izzy stated. "Who is she?"

Sabine looked at the sky, trying to find the words to say. She just shrugged and looked directly into Izzy's green eyes. "She's your sister."

"That's impossible," Izzy whispered.

"Deep down, you've known all along," Sabine said. "But you just didn't have the courage to face the truth. That is, until now."

Izzy turned around and walked back toward Nikki and Grace, as John watched darkness swallow the silhouette of the ancient vampire.

www.ingramcontent.com/pod-product-compliance
Lightning Source LLC
Chambersburg PA
CBHW031107030726
47496CB00002BA/416
9781774000502